NEWTON ✓ W9-DIE-263
330 HOMER ST.
NEWTON, MA 02459

WITHDRAWN
NEWTON FREE LIBRARY

No Rest for the Wicked

A JANE SERRANO MYSTERY

NO REST FOR THE WICKED

ELIZABETH C. MAIN

FIVE STAR
A part of Gale, Cengage Learning

GALE
CENGAGE Learning

Detroit • New York • San Francisco • New Haven, Conn • Waterville, Maine • London

GALE
CENGAGE Learning⁻

Copyright © 2011 by Elizabeth C. Main.
Five Star Publishing, a part of Gale, Cengage Learning.

ALL RIGHTS RESERVED
This novel is a work of fiction. Names, characters, places and incidents are either the product of the author's imagination, or, if real, used fictitiously.

No part of this work covered by the copyright herein may be reproduced, transmitted, stored, or used in any form or by any means graphic, electronic, or mechanical, including but not limited to photocopying, recording, scanning, digitizing, taping, Web distribution, information networks, or information storage and retrieval systems, except as permitted under Section 107 or 108 of the 1976 United States Copyright Act, without the prior written permission of the publisher.

The publisher bears no responsibility for the quality of information provided through author or third-party Web sites and does not have any control over, nor assume any responsibility for, information contained in these sites. Providing these sites should not be construed as an endorsement or approval by the publisher of these organizations or of the positions they may take on various issues.

Set in 11 pt. Plantin.

LIBRARY OF CONGRESS CATALOGING-IN-PUBLICATION DATA

Main, Elizabeth C.
  No rest for the wicked : a Jane Serrano mystery / Elizabeth C. Main. — 1st ed.
    p. cm.
  ISBN-13: 978-1-4328-2504-1 (hardcover)
  ISBN-10: 1-4328-2504-6 (hardcover)
  1. Widows—Fiction. 2. Book clubs (Discussion groups)—Fiction. 3. Oregon—Fiction. I. Title.
PS3613.A34935N6 2011
813'.6—dc22   2011016083

First Edition. First Printing: August 2011.
Published in 2011 in conjunction with Tekno Books and Ed Gorman.

Printed in the United States of America
1 2 3 4 5 6 7 15 14 13 12 11

To Bob
He turns daily life into the road to Toroweap
and knows all the best rock-and-roll songs.

ACKNOWLEDGMENTS

Writing is a solitary enterprise, yet no author has ever collected a more enthusiastic rooting section than I. Patsy Williams, Sally Bee Brown, and Helen Vandervort provided helpful critiques; many others added encouragement as this project wound its tortuous way toward completion.

In particular, I'd like to acknowledge my late mother-in-law, Dorothy Gillmore Main, for her unfailing interest in my novel. She'd have greeted its publication with joy.

Also, while successfully dealing with her own medical challenge, my sister, Susan Nelson, has always taken the time to encourage me in this endeavor. Her courage is inspirational.

Karen, Eric, Mike, and Julie all deserve special praise for their patience with my monomania.

On the professional side, my thanks go to Roz Greenberg, who went the extra mile for this book. Tiffany Schofield has provided help whenever I've needed it. Last, but certainly not least, I salute Jerri Corgiat Gallagher, surely the best editor ever.

"There is no peace, sayeth the Lord, unto the wicked."

—Isaiah 48:22 (King James Bible)

PROLOGUE

Deputy Brady Newman yawned and fiddled with the scanner as the Russell County cruiser rolled slowly down the back road. Nothing going on, as usual. Just him and the crows. Wishing he'd sprung for a bigger coffee at the drive-through, he lowered the window. Maybe some fresh air. He yawned again and reached for his Egg McMuffin.

Later, he told friends it was just as well he hadn't seen the tan 2008 Sentra on his first pass. Tucked behind a gnarled juniper, it'd all but disappeared into the neutral tones of the central Oregon scrubland. The delay gave him a chance to enjoy the two apple pies that completed his breakfast.

On his return patrol twenty minutes later, the glare of sunlight reflecting off the Sentra's windshield caught his eye. A couple hunkered down for some summer fun? He pulled to a halt, dust enveloping the cruiser as he did so. After the air settled, he jotted down the car's license. A rental.

The figure in the driver's seat didn't move. After a moment's hesitation over whether to call in the plate, Brady stepped from the cruiser and approached the Sentra cautiously. The sight of the smashed driver's-side window stopped him cold. Not good.

Still no movement from inside the car, just a buzzing sound. The jagged hole allowed flies easy access, and the sun had already driven the inside temperature to one-hundred-and-twenty degrees. As Brady leaned close to peer through the ruined window, the stench hit him. He was through with food for the rest of the day.

CHAPTER 1

Everybody wanted me to be Nancy Drew, or maybe Jessica Fletcher. Trust me, I wasn't cut out for either role. At age forty-three, I was located between the two chronologically, but, unlike them, I possessed not a single adventurous bone in my body. I'd solved my one and only mystery ten months earlier purely by accident. Unfortunately, so far I'd been unable to convince others of this significant difference between the legendary amateur sleuths and myself.

While fleeing a killer last August—and let me emphasize that this was not my activity of choice for the evening—I'd jumped from the second floor of Thornton's Books and landed right in the national news. *USA Today* came up with a headline that rocketed around the Internet and pursued me to this day: "Bookstore Heroine Leaps to Right Conclusion." Since that fateful evening, I'd nursed a broken ankle from the fall, testified in court, and read enough fan mail to convince me that people had way too much time on their hands.

I was tagged the "Bookstore Heroine," and that was that. Fans from all over the country, as well as an amazing number right here in Juniper, Oregon, solicited my help in solving crimes. Now I ask you, how should I know who stole the cooling cherry pie off the Thomasons' windowsill?

Okay, I'm not being quite honest here. I'll admit that at first I was flattered at being thought a super sleuth, but the novelty has long since worn off. So much so that when yesterday's edition of the *Juniper Journal* featured the gruesome story of a man found shot to death near town, my first reaction wasn't distress for the poor victim, but, "Oh, no. The crazies will really be after me now."

I know. Truly an unworthy thought when some poor human being had lost his life, but this celebrity business had proved exhausting, and I'd had more than my share. In my defense, I'll say that I was right about the crazies. Tyler and I had been fielding calls and e-mails at Thornton's all day from people wanting to know whether I'd identified the murderer yet. It was shaping up to be one of those weeks.

"I can't believe it," I muttered, pushing away from the computer and standing up to brace my hands on the polished mahogany counter before me. As I felt its cool perfection under my fingertips, I remembered that this gorgeous piece of wood had started life as a bar years ago when Juniper was still a rough timber town. And now people were salivating over another murder. "What do these people want, a return to the Wild West?"

Marcus T. Konig, a successful saloonkeeper and original occupant of this mansion, had possessed more money than taste, much to the chagrin of his Eastern-bred third wife. Over her objections, he'd crammed a discarded bar into their home as a spectacularly inappropriate sideboard. His dream of buying his way into society, such as it was in those days, came a cropper when he was shot to death during a crooked card game in his own remodeled saloon. His wife commissioned an imposing monument to her late husband, shuttered the mansion, and hustled with the bulk of his money back East.

"You say something?" Tyler Kincaid's head popped up from behind the bookcase where he was restocking the latest bestsellers. Tyler was the sixteen-year-old grandson of Laurence Thornton, the owner of Thornton's Books. A retired University of Virginia Classics professor, Laurence had had a dream, too, only it wasn't to sell whiskey over this bar, but fine books. He'd converted the mansion, combining the parlor, dining room, and front hall in the process. The massive bar continued to provide the focal point, dominating the center of the newly created space. It was flanked by a graceful staircase on one side and a perfectly proportioned room featuring floor-to-ceiling solid oak bookshelves and a comfortable bay window on the other. I patted the bar. "Just thinking. Maybe Juniper hasn't changed all that much since Marcus T.'s day."

"You mean like that guy getting shot?" Tyler asked. "Good idea. Put yesterday's front page in the window or something, make a display out of it."

"That's downright obscene. Making money off some poor guy's death. You can't be serious."

The June sun streamed through the oversized windows behind Tyler, shadowing his face and making a halo of his shaggy blond hair, so I couldn't tell whether he was smiling. "It'd be great for business. And you know Minnie and Bianca and Alix will say the same thing. I'll ask Grandpa."

"You'll do no such thing. What are you, a ghoul or something?"

Tyler nodded and lowered his voice. "Okay. Gonna tell me who killed him then?"

I squinted in the sunshine. "You know, with the sun coming from behind you like that, you look like an angel. How could anyone look like that and be so, so—"

He sauntered to the counter and smiled down at me. "Haven't solved the case yet or just keeping the murderer's identity under wraps? You can tell me." He raised his hands in a mock defensive gesture. "Don't blame me for asking. Everybody wants to know. Price of fame. It's not my fault you jumped out that window."

When had Tyler become so tall? A year ago, he'd been a

skinny fifteen-year-old kid about my height of five feet five inches. Now I had to tilt my head up to talk to him. His shoulders had broadened considerably, too, though he was still lean. No wonder more high school girls had been giggling their way through the bookstore lately.

"It was a door, not a window," I replied absently, "and that's old news now anyway."

"Not with a murder on the front page of the paper. Get real. It's already on everyone's mind. Why, a window display would probably qualify as a public service right now. What's wrong with that? And we still have some of the T-shirts and postcards from last year. All the calls we've had today? We could clear 'em out quick. Face it, Jane, your public needs you. They're crying out for your help in solving this heinous crime. That poor man, lying dead . . . and you're just gonna turn your back? The Bookstore Heroine?"

"I wondered how long it'd take you to get to that. You're shameless. I have half a mind to walk upstairs and jump out that door again."

"Too bad it's boarded over." Tyler considered the matter. "It'd make a nice follow-up—"

The ringing of the phone saved me from the rest of his latest brainstorm, but I narrowed my eyes and faked a glare at him as I answered. Hard to reconcile this self-assured young man with the sullen, withdrawn kid who'd landed in Juniper a year ago for what was supposed to be a temporary stay with his grandfather, whom he hardly knew. I'd dragged Tyler into our mystery book club as a favor to Laurence, and the rest, as they say, is history.

Alix didn't bother with a greeting. "I'm still with a client, but Bianca just left."

"Well, hello to you, too. You'll be here later?" No answer. The silence lasted just a beat too long. "Everything all right?"

"What? It's just that . . . well, of course I'll come."

Was it strain I heard in my friend's voice, or just divided attention? I kept my tone light. "You'd better hurry if you want to save me from our young marketing genius. Tyler here is waving that ghastly front page of yesterday's *Journal* around, threatening to make it into a window display."

Tyler leaned across the counter and chimed in loud enough for Alix to hear. "It'd work. Whip up interest again in Murder of the Month."

"See what I mean?" I turned my back to the counter. "I need reinforcements. Minnie has her heart set on reading another true-crime about a homicidal plumber, and I can hardly wait to hear what Bianca wants." I pressed. "Come on, friend. Give me something to work with. Didn't you want Julia Spencer-Fleming? An ex-Army Episcopal woman priest ought to be weird enough for you."

"Start without me." For the first time ever, Alix didn't rise to the bait. Her voice flat, she said, "You choose."

What was going on? "Are you sure there's nothing wrong?"

Another pause. I could practically hear the gears grinding in Alix's normally agile brain. She cleared her throat and finally said with unaccustomed formality, "Would you be willing to stay after the meeting? I'd like to talk to you, alone."

Anticipation of my date with Nick warred with my inclination to say yes. Alix rarely asked for anything. If only I hadn't already put Nick off several times, I'd have agreed in an instant. As it was, I hesitated.

"Never mind," Alix said with sudden energy. "It'll keep."

"Are you sure?" But I was talking to an empty line.

"What was that all about?" Tyler asked.

"I have no idea," I said slowly, "and I've never known Alix to pass up a chance to make a wisecrack about Minnie's book selection."

"She was probably bowled over by my brilliant idea about the window display."

"Sure, she was." I wanted to shrug off Alix's manner, but something from yesterday had just flashed into my mind. I'd been running late for our regular lunch at Corey's Bistro, but when I'd finally slid into the comfortable booth, I'd found Alix staring into space, holding her fork in a death grip.

"Afraid that Caesar is going to attack you?" I'd asked.

"What? Oh, no." She'd looked at the fork and the salad as though she'd never seen either of them before. "I went ahead and ordered. Can't stay long." Her voice trailed off.

"Sorry. The UPS delivery came just as I was locking up. Go ahead, eat."

"Okay." But instead of digging into her salad, Alix dropped her fork and started crumbling her sourdough bread instead.

Before I could say anything else, a shadow fell over the table. I looked up to see a flushed middle-aged woman in a wrinkled muumuu hovering over me. "Excuse me, but aren't you the Bookstore Heroine?"

Judging from the camera dangling from her neck, I surmised that she and her equally bedecked and eager friend were yet another set of tourists, mystery fans who'd identified me from the framed *USA Today* picture that Corey Simmons proudly displayed behind the cash register. Corey's Caesar salad was the best east of the Cascades, so Alix and I took the risk of running into fans there once a week. Though we both knew Thornton's could use all the publicity my celebrity status could generate, I usually skulked into the booth, hoping no one would notice me.

On the other hand, Alix was a businesswoman first, a loyal friend second, so I knew she'd sell me out. "Why, yes, she is. How clever of you to recognize her."

Last year Alix had put her own business on hold and stepped in to run Thornton's while I chased a murderer and Laurence lay helpless in the hospital. She'd determined in an instant that Laurence needed some tough love to make the store profitable. Ever since, she had joined Tyler and Bianca to take every opportunity to set me up with my adoring public.

By the time I finished autographing menus and answering questions for the wide-eyed tourists, Alix appeared to have shaken off her earlier lethargy.

She smiled her shark's smile at me, and I knew she was mentally calculating book sales when she spoke again. "I'll bet Jane will even show you the scene of the crime firsthand, if you'd like."

"But your lunch . . . ?" protested the hopeful fans.

Alix was already signaling Corey to box up her salad. "I have another appointment, and Jane's trying to lose weight."

The latter part of the statement was news to me, but these ladies were carrying tote bags that they'd probably be happy to fill with books, so I stood up, hungry, but resigned to my fate.

With special emphasis, I'd said to the retreating Alix, "I'll talk to you tomorrow night."

Alix had waved over her shoulder as she'd sauntered away, throwing me to the muu-muued wolves. I'd given them my best Bookstore Heroine smile. "On to Thornton's?"

I hadn't thought about our exchange since then, but after Alix's phone call tonight, I'd make sure we finished our interrupted conversation later. Maybe Tyler knew something.

"Is Alix having any trouble at the store? She said she had a customer—"

With practiced ease, Tyler reached into a ceramic jar on the counter, a book-shaped gift from a potter in New Mexico. "Ah, the shortbread nooses." He gobbled the flaky cookie in one bite and reached for another, a blissful smile on his crumb-covered lips. "My favorites," he mumbled through a mouthful, "but we're almost out."

"What a surprise." I slid the jar out of his reach. "Minnie's bringing gingerbread guns tonight."

"They're bigger, but the nooses are way better."

"She'd better make something you don't like, if we hope to have any left to sell."

"Oh, I like the guns all right, just not as much." His eyes lighted with a new thought. "Knives! That'd be great. Make 'em with less dough, but sell for the same as the others. Presto! More profit. I'll bet Minnie loves the idea."

"Don't be too sure. She's already worried that she can't keep up with demand."

The cooking prowess of Minnie Salter, our fellow book club member and friend, was exceeded only by her eagerness to help. No scent of lemon oil and beeswax hung in the air today, so I knew she hadn't stopped by to discharge her self-imposed task of periodically polishing the mahogany counter. She'd probably arrive for tonight's book club meeting clutching cleaning supplies in one hand and gingerbread guns in the other. Fine with me, so long as I could keep her mind off her other passion, her desire to solve another real-life murder.

Tyler shook his head. "Hard to believe she'd run short, the way she churns 'em out."

"In spite of you? Well, genius, why don't you and the rest of your marketing crew get to work on that little problem. Now, what about the Wedding Belle?"

"Oh, yeah. I got distracted. Hadn't eaten in a couple of hours." Tyler had been inching his way along the counter toward the new location of the cookie jar. His long arm snaked out. Grinning, he popped a third cookie into his mouth. "If Alix's customer's that lady from the other day, she's sure not having any trouble with business. You heard about Wendell's big score?"

"You lost me. How does Wendell go with weddings?"

"Shows how much you know about marketing." Temporarily

distracted from his quest for food, Tyler launched into his story.

Bianca's nondescript one-eyed dog had provided the first of many problems when I attempted to establish the Murder of the Month Book Club last year. Wendell's presence at meetings sparked immediate friction between my dog-loving daughter Bianca and the fastidious, sophisticated Alix Boudreau, owner of the Wedding Belle Bridal Shop. Only after Wendell actually proved useful in solving a murder had Bianca and Alix's relationship improved. In fact, things changed so much that Alix offered Bianca a job and, much to my surprise, the free-spirited Bianca took it. The two seemingly incompatible personalities had harmonized beautifully. New responsibility had brought a maturity and focus to Bianca, while Bianca's *joie de vivre* had in turn caused Alix's business to flourish.

"You don't mean Wendell was actually allowed inside the Wedding Belle." No matter how friendly the relationship between employer and employee, I couldn't imagine Alix letting Bianca's scruffy black dog into her posh lavender and lace bower, which featured champagne carpeting.

"You know about Bianca's campaign to let Wendell lie on a special mat just inside the door."

I nodded, knowing from personal experience that Bianca was well practiced in using water torture to wear down an opponent over time.

"Alix finally gave in on that really hot day last week, but she insisted that it was just for that one time. Anyway, Alix was grousing around, saying Wendell'd soon be bald, the way his black fur was migrating to the white rug . . . typical cranky Alix . . . and in walks this lady who takes one look at Wendell and falls in love, saying he looks just like some dog named Bonjo. I s'pose old Bonjo had both his eyes, but that didn't matter. Anyway, right there on the spot she wants to hire Wendell to be ring bearer at her wedding. Funniest thing I ever saw. Before Alix could open her mouth, Bianca begins quoting Wendell's rates."

"Wendell has rates?"

"Yep. Five hundred to appear in a wedding, and six-fifty if he stays for the reception."

"You're kidding." My dreamy daughter, who once scorned material things, apparently had learned to negotiate the capitalist system rather well.

"That lady didn't bat an eye. 'Perfect, as long as it includes pictures after the ceremony.' There was sort of a pause and I figured the joke had gone far enough. Then Alix said, smooth as silk, 'I'm afraid that's extra.' And then Wendell got up from his assigned mat and walked straight across Alix's pristine carpet to the lady and sat at her feet adoringly. It was like they'd rehearsed it."

"Dog biscuit in her pocket?" Wendell was no slouch at finding food.

"You got it. The lady was hooked. 'Let's do it,' she said. 'You're sure he's available on that date?' Alix and Bianca looked at each other—I was just trying not to crack up—and Alix handed something to Bianca. Could've been a book of poetry, for all I know, but she rummaged around for a few pages before she looked up. 'You're in luck. He has no other appointments that day.'"

"I can't believe anyone would—"

"The lady left a big deposit."

"No complaints from Alix about Wendell's black fur on that white rug after that?"

"Nope. Alix was way too busy reassessing Wendell as a rising star. He's taking Bianca with him to the top, too. Alix even suggested that Bianca and Wendell work up some less traditional ideas for a new brochure. You know, wedding with people wearing cowboy boots, standing on a rock in the Deschutes with trees overhead, that kind of sappy thing."

"And using Wendell as best man? Things have certainly changed since I got married."

"Since the Dark Ages, you mean? Big surprise."

"Thanks a lot. It was only . . . well, a few years ago." Twenty-five, to be exact, since I'd given up college for marriage and three children. Put another way—a quarter of a century—it really did sound like the Dark Ages. "You think business at the Wedding Belle's all right, then."

"Better than Thornton's. Alix's one tough lady with the bottom line. If you and Grandpa'd get onboard with our marketing plan, we'd do a lot better here, too. How much did those two women drop yesterday?"

"Plenty, but—"

"But what? You wouldn't have gotten a dime if Alix hadn't roped you into doing the tour. You should do them on a regular basis."

"Why don't you do them? I didn't even get lunch yesterday! Where's the sympathy?"

"Sales first."

"Sales don't come before your lunch, I notice."

"I'm a growing boy."

"I know. That's why we're running low on cookies again." I slid the cookie jar further away. "If you're done emptying that box of books, how about giving it to me so I can dump all this mail."

"Will do." Tyler fetched the box and returned to the counter. "You'll answer the letters, won't you?"

"So long as you keep up the blog."

"I'm on it. No problem, 'specially now that I'm getting English credit. How cool is that?" He hesitated before saying, "Speaking of marketing, the online club is—"

"What online club?" Recognizing that suspiciously casual

tone, I folded my arms and waited.

"Oh, didn't Bianca tell you?" He shoveled mail into the box, head down.

"Tell me what? Whose idea . . . ?"

With a look of relief, Tyler turned toward the sound of running feet outside. "She can tell you herself."

Energy personified, my daughter flew into the store, all tanned arms and legs and flying corn silk hair. As usual, she was flanked by Wendell, running circles around her in hopes of scoring a dog treat. I couldn't help smiling at the sight. My twenty-year-old daughter had always charmed the socks off everyone, including me. The youngest of my three children, she skipped through life trailing creative ideas and fervent causes in her floral-scented wake.

"I was just telling your mom about the new online book club."

"Doesn't it sound great?" Without pausing to close the door, Bianca fed the ecstatic Wendell two treats. "Price break for members. Free shipping, too. You'll write the reading group questions, of course, and host the monthly web chats. Minnie's offered to send new subscribers a dozen cookies as a thank-you gift. This could be huge."

"Uh huh. What I really want is a combination publishing and baking empire at Thornton's. Isn't there already enough going on?"

Tyler gestured toward the paperback mysteries stacked on the chair behind the counter. "But I was hoping to pick the first books tonight."

"Eliot Pattison. That Chinese policeman in Tibet," Bianca offered. "Nonviolence as a path to solving murders."

I raised my eyebrows. My, my. Quite a change from last year, when Bianca's choice for protagonists had been the dog detectives, Bipsy and Mr. Potts. "I know you mean well, but no more projects right now."

"If that's the way you feel, then we'll have to get more punch from what we have." Bianca flourished a copy of yesterday's front page. "Terrific window display?"

"What'd I tell you, Jane?" Tyler held up his page in support.

"You, too, Bianca? You can't use that poor man's murder to sell books."

Bianca waved her hand. "You gotta go with what works, Mom, if you want Ty's grandpa to succeed in the market."

"The T-shirts and postcards are still selling, thanks to the website and the blog," Tyler added. "Cutting-edge stuff. Thornton's has made it to the twenty-first century, in spite of Grandpa and you pushing Plato and Shakespeare. Good luck with that. Look, we're sorry that guy's dead, but that shouldn't stop us from getting a publicity bump. We'll make it tasteful. Right, Bianca?"

"Sure. Think of Hamlet, Mom. You wouldn't object to using him in a window display."

When I opened my mouth to protest, Tyler neatly cut me off. "Or maybe you're too classy to sell books now, fancy new degree and all."

Low blow. Tyler knew how long I'd pecked away at classes at the U of O for years just to finish college, let alone my M.A. I'd recently begun taking courses toward a Ph.D. in English Literature. I hoped it wouldn't take another twenty-five years.

"Hamlet was a character in a play."

Tyler was relentless. "Face it, you and Grandpa weren't making a profit before we took over the marketing. Think of it this way. We sell a bunch of cra . . . crummy books, you're in a better position to sell more classics. It's just using marketing expertise to spread culture."

"And a window display containing pictures of a murdered man is spreading culture? No way. That's final."

My two young entrepreneurs raised their hands in simultaneous, well-orchestrated gestures of surrender. "Fine," said Bianca, "but what about the online club?"

"Gotta keep our ideas fresh," Tyler chipped in.

I knew when I'd been outflanked. "Okay. We'll give it a try. But no window displays using that picture."

The triumphant smiles Tyler and Bianca exchanged told me they'd already achieved their primary aim by securing my agreement about the online club.

"You're the boss," Bianca said. Now that I was on board, Bianca was all business. She dropped the newspaper on the counter and held out her hand for a list Tyler instantly produced. "The books for the first subscription series. I say Eliot Pattison and Ty wants G. M. Ford. He's violent. Makes a nice contrast."

"He's also funny and a Northwest writer. Maybe he'd come here to do a signing. Jane could contact him." Tyler was ready to go, and even more ready to hand off tasks to me. "That Buddhist stuff sounds boring, but some people might like it."

"We could all stand to learn more about Buddhism." Apparently my daughter hadn't become so immersed in capitalism that she'd abandoned her long-standing interest in Eastern culture. "More educational than Minnie's true crime. She still wants the killer plumber."

Tyler pantomimed a gagging reflex, but nodded. "Whatever Minnie reads, her church friends read, too. She's sort of like a . . . what do you call those counties that always vote on the winning side in an election?"

"Bellwether?" I asked.

"Yeah. That's it. Minnie gives us a whole different demographic." My budding young marketing whiz was on a roll. Demographics, yet. I tried not to smile as he explained his logic. "Expand the fan base. Thinking pure thoughts all the time at church must get old. Minnie and her friends sure like the gory stuff."

Bianca agreed. "We can try it, see how it goes. Who do you want, Mom?"

"Donna Leon. Quality writing, Venetian setting, strong family interactions, not much violence."

"Sounds boring as the Buddhist," Tyler said, "but we want balance. How about a six-month rotation: lots of blood, then exotic setting, then tough cop, philosophical detective, maybe a quaint English village . . . and, of course," Tyler shot a look at Bianca, "adorable animal detectives. How about a parakeet that sings clues?"

"Is there one?" Bianca asked.

"He's putting you on," I said. "Bianca, how about Alix? She mentioned reading Julia Spencer-Fleming."

Bianca wrinkled her brow. "The helicopter pilot priest? Doesn't grab me. Too far-fetched."

"As opposed to Bipsy and Mr. Potts?" I chided.

Bianca crouched by Wendell and cupped his silky black ears with her hands. "Don't let them make fun of doggy detectives. You did a great job for us." She pulled another treat from her pocket to soothe his presumably wounded feelings, though he didn't look all that distressed to me. She popped back up. "Say, did Ty tell you about Wendell?"

"Yes, that's great, but what about Alix? And where is she?" I jumped in quickly. Once Bianca got started on Wendell's exploits, it would dominate the conversation for some time to come.

Bianca looked thoughtful. "I thought she'd be here by now. She's been preoccupied this week, probably with the new wedding ideas. Let me tell you about Wendell."

Recognizing an unstoppable force, I leaned against the wall and allowed myself to be treated to a second, even more enthusiastic recitation of Wendell's spectacular entrance into the wedding biz. Maybe Wendell could also be hired to give guided tours of the bookstore so I could return to selling books and taking classes. Ah, the good old days of obscurity.

"Hey, you listening?" Tyler waved a hand in front of my eyes. "If all this marketing stuff is too low-brow for you, maybe you'd rather hide out on the third floor and write your dissertation. Hey, how about using some famous fictional killer, like Lady Macbeth?"

Bianca picked up on his enthusiasm. "Classy, Ty, and not so obviously commercial. I like it. If you could use a bunch of four-syllable words to compare Lady Macbeth's motives to that of a real-life regular guy killer, we might even get a publishable book out of it. We could sell it right here at Thornton's, along with our regular mysteries. Boy, 'Murder of the Month' was a stroke of genius as a name for the book club."

She and Tyler exchanged high fives.

"I'm not sure if you're smart or nuts. The jury's still out on that."

"Know what, Bianca?" Tyler spoke in a stage whisper. "I think your mom's just bent outta shape 'cuz she hasn't figured out yet who killed that guy. That headline brought in a ton of customers, and look at the mail piling up. I gotta tell you, we're going national again, with or without the window display."

"Forget it. This murder investigation has nothing to do with us, especially when it comes to window displays."

"But your fans—" Bianca's protests were drowned out by a shout from outside.

"Help! It's Alix!" Minnie Salter came huffing her way up the sidewalk, clearly agitated and calling out before she reached the store.

We all converged on the doorway, but the expanse of lawn outside was empty and quiet. Minnie leaned gasping against the door frame.

"What is it, Minnie? Should we call 911?" Bianca asked, brow furrowed with concern.

"Not me. Alix," Minnie snapped. "We were on our way here when that idiotic sheriff of ours pulled up in his patrol car. Arnie said . . . he said . . ."

"Where's Alix?"

Minnie poked the air angrily, causing multiple bracelets to jangle and bright neck scarves to flutter like captive birds. "I told you. He wasn't a bit nice about it either. You know, I don't think Arnie learned a thing from us last year. Wasn't our fault we solved the murder and made a fool out of him. He never would've figured it out."

"Where's Alix?" I repeated.

"Aren't you listening?" Minnie paused in mid-rant to wave her arms even more erratically. "I just told you."

"No, you didn't." I grasped her plump hands. "Please concentrate."

"That impossible Arnie Kraft took her to the station . . . about that man's murder."

"What?" The sprinklers clicked to life on the lawn, injecting some normalcy into the bizarre scene. "Why?"

Minnie shrugged her ample shoulders. Bianca and Tyler looked bewildered.

I was completely at a loss, too, crazy thoughts whirling in the silence until my gaze encountered the front-page picture from yesterday's *Journal*, still lying on the counter. I dropped Minnie's hands and stepped back. "Ha ha. Nice try. The new marketing plan, right? You know, you almost got me this time."

Tyler and Bianca looked blank, but they were better at jokes than Minnie, so I rounded on her, expecting a telltale glimmer of humor in her blue eyes. Nothing. Minnie's flushed face merely reflected outrage at Arnie's attitude. This was no joke.

"Get her some water. Here, Minnie, sit down before you have

a stroke." As I eased Minnie onto the floor, her back against the door frame, the sprinklers continued to whir in orderly circles. How soothing to sit there and listen, while the tranquility of my life evaporated faster than the droplets falling on the lawn.

Minnie, Tyler, and Bianca watched for my response. Even Wendell stared at me. The tick, tick, tick of the sprinklers almost obscured Tyler's whispered comment.

"Here we go again."

CHAPTER 2

Minnie's words came firmly. "You'll straighten it out, Jane." No question.

It'd been a long day, and Minnie's attitude hit me exactly wrong. I aimed for patience and lost. "Well, Minnie, why don't you just run down to the station, and solve things yourself?"

Minnie leaned back, a look of bewilderment on her usually smiling face. "Why I . . . I just thought that once I told you . . ." I knew for the first time how it must feel to kick a puppy. Minnie's full lower lip quivered. "You're her best friend, and, besides, you always know what to do."

My impatience melted. I put my arms around her and patted her broad back. "Sorry I snapped at you. You just . . . just took me by surprise."

Minnie accepted my inane apology on the spot, straightening up to fumble in her voluminous straw bag for a handkerchief. She blew her nose vigorously, happy again now that the natural order had been restored to the world. "That's okay, Jane. I understand. It was my fault for not explaining the situation better." Clarity of thought was not Minnie's forte, but at least she looked hopeful again, which was about all I could ask for. "Well, it's a good thing we settled that. We have work to do. Remember, 'If the trumpet give an uncertain sound, who shall prepare himself to the battle?' "

"Another Bible verse." Tyler rolled his eyes.

Minnie sprinkled conversation with random, often incompre-

31

hensible, Bible verses as plentiful as raisins in her oatmeal cookies. Sometimes she even mixed in lines from Shakespeare that
she felt ought to have been in the Bible. The sly smile on her
face now invited me to challenge this one, tipping me to the
likelihood she was on firm ecclesiastical ground today. I didn't
rise to the bait, but Bianca did.

"What does it mean?"

"Why bless you, child. It's First Corinthians 14:8," Minnie
said, with a nod in my direction. "And it means we need to pull
together to get Alix out of the clink."

"Coulda fooled me," Tyler said.

"There's no rest for the wicked, you know," Minnie said.
"I'm paraphrasing now, Jane, so don't expect another citation.
It's somewhere in Isaiah. Anyway, here we are. The Murder of
the Month Book Club is ready to ride to the rescue, almost
exactly like last year, only it was Bianca in jail that time instead
of Alix. Same miscarriage of justice though." Minnie's eyes
sparkled. "Let's saddle up."

"Whoa!" I had to stop the stampede now. I'd been down this
trail before with Minnie and the John Wayne dialogue was an
ominous sign. "What miscarriage of justice? Alix is simply being
questioned. Probably some mistake. And you remember what
happened last year. Arnie won't appreciate another scene like
that at the clink, as you call it."

"Oh." Minnie frowned at the memory, caught between her
zest for action and her knowledge that I was the acknowledged
super sleuth. For once, discretion won the day. "But you'll
straighten things out." Again, not a question.

"Don't get your hopes too high. I got lucky."

"Mom, you caught a murderer!" Bianca chimed in. "You
jumped out a—"

"Different situation," I reminded them, though without much
hope. They had long since dismissed my disclaimer as modesty,

so they merely smiled patiently and waited for me to fix things. "Okay, I'm going. But first, did anything unusual happen at the Wedding Belle today?"

"The cash register balanced," Bianca said promptly.

"Excellent," I said encouragingly. With Bianca, the handling of money was often a challenge. "Anything else? Maybe late in the afternoon?"

"Well, let's see. Alix and I were talking about how many flowers have to die each time there's a wedding. She thinks I'm silly to worry about that, of course, but it bothers me to cut them off in their prime. On the other hand, silk flowers are so expensive."

"Bianca?" I interrupted as gently as possible. "I meant something that might have had a bearing on why Arnie might want to question Alix."

"I can't think of anything. Mrs. Starrett was going over samples for Amy's bridesmaids' dresses, but she does that about three times a week, so it wasn't unusual. I don't think she's ever going to make a decision, but she studies every sample each time, so Alix told me I might as well come along to the meeting." She shrugged. "Alix had to wait for Minnie anyway."

Minnie took over. "Jeannette Starrett had left, and Alix was locking up by the time I arrived. I don't know whether she settled on a sample this time, either, but she was gone. Arnie pulled his cruiser up to the curb right behind me. Didn't say hello or anything. Just told Alix she needed to come to the station so he could talk to her. Brady Newman was with him, and he was being very official, too, calling him Sheriff Kraft instead of Arnie, and he didn't even look at me. I've known him since he was five years old, and it's the first time that ever happened."

"Arnie just wanted to talk to Alix." Brady's reaction to his old Sunday school teacher did sound odd, but I stuck to the main point. "That's not so bad."

"That's exactly what Alix said, though she seemed a little

pale to me. Maybe it was just the light though. She made a joke out of it—you know how she does—and asked whether Brady just wanted an excuse to get her into his patrol car, and he blushed—you know how he does—but he went all formal, saying this was official business. And then I guess Arnie didn't think Alix was taking them seriously enough because he got mad and sort of grabbed Alix by the arm. 'You think a murder investigation's funny?' Alix pulled away and said, 'No, but the idea of you running one sure is.' That did it. Arnie got real red and then Brady stepped between them and asked, real nice, like his regular self again, if Alix would please get in the car. She smiled and went all friendly, 'Well, of course I will, Brady,' and they left. I came straight here."

I made more reassuring noises, but privately I wondered what was going on. Whatever it was, I knew better than to feed Minnie's fascination with the dramatic.

Bianca looked stricken. "You know, maybe Alix has been worried about something. She actually forgot about a client appointment yesterday, and that wasn't like her at all. And she's smoking more again."

Not a good omen, since Alix had been proud she'd cut down. And forgetting an appointment? Completely out of character. "But she hasn't said anything?"

"No. You don't suppose she's sick or something? Wouldn't she have told you if something was wrong?"

"Maybe, but you work with her every day."

"She doesn't ever talk about personal stuff, you know, like confiding about guys or anything. We just work together. You're her friend."

Bianca apparently knew even less about Alix than I did. Now that I thought about it, how much did I know about Alix? She typically stuck to mundane topics and rarely volunteered information about herself. Beyond making a few caustic remarks, she hadn't ever discussed the irony of owning a bridal shop when her multiple marriages had been, by her own admission, total disasters. Reluctant to pry into an obviously sensitive subject, I had always put her reticence down to a general disappointment with life. She had been a staunch friend to all of us over the past year, and great fun to have in the book club, but I realized how little I really knew her. I certainly didn't know much about her innermost thoughts. But of one thing I was certain. Alix was no more lethal than I was, except perhaps with stinging quips. What kind of craziness was it to question her about a murder? I gave myself a mental shake. Far better to check this out myself than to leave everyone stirred up. "You're right. I'll just run down to the station. Shouldn't take long to straighten this out."

Minnie clapped her hands, all smiles again. "Everything's going to be fine now. Shall we start the meeting later, after Jane gets Alix, or just wait until tomorrow?"

"I'm supposed to meet Nick later," I said. "So if we're running late, maybe tomorrow would be better."

"Oh ho. Then by all means, let's meet tomorrow." Minnie was all for romance. "Tyler, could you help me carry the gingerbread guns I have in the car?"

Watching Minnie and Tyler amble down the sidewalk, I wondered how many of the guns would make it from the car to the cookie jar.

"I knew we could count on you, Mom. And now that the meeting's off, I can run back to the Wedding Belle to see a lady who wanted to meet with Wendell tonight."

Amazing, the ease with which order had been restored for everyone. I flashed back to the days when a kiss on my daughter's skinned knee could make everything all better. Bianca apparently still had perfect faith in my ability to work magic, right up to and including getting a friend out of jail. I wish I had the same optimism. Dread lurked in the corners of my mind, whispering that something wasn't right. "Sure. Wendell has an appointment?"

"To test colors. You know, for a special collar to match some bridesmaids' dresses. No, not the Starrett wedding."

I looked at the all-black dog. Should be easy to accessorize, no matter what the bridal color palette. Maybe if I concentrated on Wendell, the fact that my friend was being questioned about a murder wouldn't seem so surreal. Bending down to pat Wendell's sleek head, I murmured, "Fame isn't all it's cracked up to be. You even have to work nights." My hand encountered a folded paper attached to his collar. "What's this?"

Bianca clapped her hand to her mouth. "Nick told me to deliver it the minute I got here. Sorry, in all the excitement . . ."

"No problem. You've delivered it now."

"And I didn't read it either, in case you wondered."

I smiled at the old family joke. Respecting the privacy of others had been a big deal when the girls were growing up.

Bianca went on, "I mean, if you have anything special to tell me, you will, right?"

My face warmed at the studiously casual look on her sweet face, and I knew phone calls would be beaming in short order to her sisters, Susannah and Emily. All three girls were hoping Nick would soon be joining our family. They figured that two years of widowhood was long enough.

"You'll be the first to know. Thanks, Wendell." Talking to the patient dog before me beat worrying about Alix. Just one more peaceful moment and I'd take up reality again.

I unfastened the rubber band holding the paper to his collar. He stood and wagged his tail, eager for the expected treat. I dug around under the counter for the biscuits I kept on hand for his visits. Since they smelled of mint to keep Wendell's breath kissing fresh, they were easy to locate. Bianca made them from natural ingredients and cut them into interesting shapes, in another of her creative business ventures. Today's biscuit formed a question mark, in case the dog consuming it wished to contemplate the deeper meaning of life while he snacked. Wendell had never shown much interest in philosophy, but he was an excellent eater.

Only after Bianca and Wendell had exited the bookstore did I unroll the parchment and read the fancy lettering. Where on earth had Nick Constantine, attorney by trade and rumpled fisherman by inclination, come up with this wording, not to mention the ornate font?

Milady, please to cast aside care, don fine raiment, and lower the drawbridge at eight o' the clock this very even to sup with me on wheaten bread and guinea fowl, accompanied by copious sweet mead? Ah, Madame, far, far too long has't been since our lips last met, our hearts entwined. We have matters of great import to discuss.

Translation: Nick planned to bring over chicken sandwiches and wine after he got back from fishing and I finished the book club meeting. For a moment, Alix's situation faded. His playful words made me smile, briefly, before thoughts of Alix's situation resurfaced. No matter how tempting it was to think about seeing Nick, it would have to wait. First things first. Unfortunately, I'd already rescheduled this date twice. Alix's predicament was yet another in an unfortunate series of obligations to others that I couldn't ignore.

Should I call now to tell him I was on my way to the sheriff's department? No, not until I knew more. It was only six-thirty. Only two days ago, after the latest rescheduling of our date, Nick had asked me to think seriously about my tendency to let other people dictate much of my time. He'd been patient for a long time, and I owed him an answer.

Tyler returned from the car, carrying a plate of cookies and chewing energetically. "These are great. Want one?"

"Later. And there'd better be some left when I get back."

"You know," he said, "these cookies would be much safer if I locked up and went with you."

"No way."

"Hey, it was Alix who insulted that jerk of a deputy last year, not me."

"Yes, but you were part of the group outside chanting, 'Free Bianca.' I'm hoping to achieve a slightly lower profile this time around."

"Okay." Tyler shrugged his shoulders, my logic getting through to him in spite of his disappointment. "I'll work on the blog. You'll be back soon?"

I went with the confident approach, but whether for myself or him, I wasn't sure. "Sure. This is some kind of mistake. You know Arnie."

The look on Tyler's face mirrored Bianca's and Minnie's earlier relief. My super sleuth credentials remained supreme with everyone but me. Now, if only I could convince myself of my invincibility. A voice in the back of my head told me that surely any sheriff, even one as inept as Arnie Kraft, would have established some connection between Alix and the murdered man to justify taking her in for questioning. I'd better find out what it was.

CHAPTER 3

I pulled my Volvo into the nearly deserted parking lot of the Russell County Courthouse. The expanse of empty asphalt appeared well suited to a pickup basketball game or the swooping of skateboards, anything to make the place less forbidding. Before stepping from the car, I took some of the deep, cleansing breaths Bianca recommended from her yoga practice. Couldn't hurt.

The gray building cast a shadow over the entrance as I approached. Was the resulting chill in the air just my imagination working overtime? Taking one more deep breath, I pushed through the heavy doors and smiled at the bored guard, whom I caught in mid-yawn. He ditched a fistful of Cheetos behind the counter before hiding his orange hands in disposable gloves and rummaging, red-faced, through every inch of my voluminous bag. Too bad I hadn't stuck in one of Minnie's gingerbread guns along with my lipstick. That'd wake him up.

"Ouch!" He snatched his hand out. "What the . . . ?"

"Oh, the can opener. For our book club meeting," I explained as he held up the can of pineapple tidbits. He didn't appear impressed at my attempt to provide a healthful snack, but what could I expect from someone who ate Cheetos?

"Oh, yeah. You're that Murder of the Month woman." His tone didn't suggest an immediate interest in getting my autograph. "The can opener stays here 'til you come out."

"Afraid I'll use it—metaphorically speaking—to get someone

39

out of the 'can'? You can keep the pineapple, too, if you want."
No response, so I lowered my voice. "You know, that can's
heavy. Make a good weapon." His look caused me to abandon
further attempt at conversation.

During the extended screening, I surveyed the room beyond
the metal detector. The deputy at the desk wasn't familiar,
thank goodness. I relaxed a fraction. Anyone we'd met here last
year would view me with all the enthusiasm they'd show an
escaped ferret. Cheeto-hands finally motioned me on.

At the desk, the deputy smiled. "Good evening, ma'am. I'm
Deputy Swenson. How may I assist you?" He was not only
polite, but he had beautiful teeth.

I wondered whether Deputy Grumpy at the door knew that
smiling wasn't against departmental policy. "Is Brady Newman
on duty tonight?"

"Let me check." He tapped out a few strokes on his keyboard.
"You're in luck. He's in the building. If you'll wait over there,
I'll get him for you . . . ?"

"Jane Serrano. Yes, thank you."

I moved toward the bank of chairs he indicated. I never could
decide whether the domed circular reception hall of the new
courthouse reminded me of a space ship or a train station.
Whatever, this monstrosity had been built with expansion in
mind. Why such a grandiose building for out-of-the-way Russell
County? Too many vacationers and developers had already
found us, with more on the way as the building boom in
neighboring Deschutes County spilled over.

I sank into a chair. Last summer I'd been so focused on getting Bianca out of here that I hadn't looked around before. The
elevated ceiling swallowed sound, almost as though humans
didn't really belong here. That was fine with me. I'd be on my
way as soon as possible.

Attempts had been made to make the place inviting, with

magazines scattered on the low tables and scenic photographs of the high desert on the walls. Nice photos, though their magazine selection could use some work: *Field & Stream, Woman's Day,* and, inexplicably, *Arizona Highways.* Perhaps Thornton's could donate copies of *Crime and Punishment,* or possibly *The Trial* to remind people that breaking the law wasn't a good idea.

"Ms. Serrano?"

From the concerned look on Brady Newman's face, I suspected that he'd been standing there for some time. His uniform was pressed, his shoes shined, but his round young face—surely he wasn't old enough for this job—made me wonder why the county gave babies badges and guns.

"Oh, Brady, I didn't hear you." I rose to greet him and found myself still looking up a considerable distance. Minnie's former Sunday school pupil had put on a few years, and more than a few pounds, since Minnie had taught him his Bible verses. "I'm so glad you're here tonight. You know how much we appreciated your help last year with that horrible mix-up." I paused to let him remember that bond on his own, trying to indicate without words that surely people who wanted to do the right thing, people who were not intimidated by bureaucratic rules and regulations, people who'd learned their Sunday school lessons well, should stick together.

Brady's eyes didn't quite meet mine. "It's nice to see you again, too."

The fact that he looked somewhere over my left shoulder as he spoke told me that he remembered, all right. This bland facade, so different from Brady's natural friendliness, chilled any hope that Alix's detention had a simple explanation.

I tried for an offhand tone. "There's been some misunderstanding about Alix. I understand she's here, and I'd hoped I could see her, or you could tell me—"

"Sorry." Brady's voice was low. Without moving a step, he retreated further into himself. Now he was looking over my other shoulder. "I can't do that."

"Which part?" I smiled as best I could while my stomach muscles knotted. "I can't see her, or you can't tell me what's happened?"

"I'm really sorry, Ms. Serrano."

"Ms. Serrano! What happened to 'Jane'?"

"Sorry, ma'am. I'm on duty." Brady's reddening cheeks made him look younger by the minute, even as he concentrated on presenting himself professionally.

We faced each other in silence. As I tried to think what to do or say next, he settled the matter by looking directly at me for the first time. The despair in his eyes made me gasp. This young deputy had experienced something that haunted him. He didn't need further problems from me.

"I understand. Thank you for seeing me."

He looked so relieved at my sudden about-face that I was ashamed of myself for having tried to play on his friendship. This was serious stuff, whatever it was. "Would it be all right if I waited here for Alix? She'll need a ride home."

"It might be a long wait."

I thought of Nick, gave an internal sigh. No choice but to cancel again. I pictured his wry smile as he'd composed his silly note earlier, anticipating our plans for the evening. This wasn't the way either of us had envisioned it. "That's okay. I've got time."

Brady strode ramrod-straight to the opposite side of the lobby and disappeared into the back rooms. I picked up the nearest magazine and stared at the cover for some minutes without seeing it. The June day had been warm enough for my short-sleeved top and sandals, but now goose bumps rose on my arms. Leaving the magazine open in my lap, I rubbed them and wondered how long I'd have to wait. No sign of Alix yet. I'd call Nick. I longed to hear his voice, though he wouldn't like what I had to say.

A warm hand landed on my shoulder just as I flipped open the phone. I turned to find Nick easing onto the seat beside me.

"*Field & Stream*? I had no idea you were such a fan." His intense scrutiny belied the bantering tone as his warm brown eyes searched my face for clues about the situation.

"I'm so sorry." The hours of strain broke through my control. I dropped the phone, and my words tumbled out. "I was just about to call. How could this have happened again?"

He waved away the apology and set the phone on the table beside me. "Hey. Take a deep breath." Enfolding my icy hands in his large warm grasp, he continued. "Tyler told me. Of course you had to be here." He looked around at the quiet lobby. "What have you learned?"

"Just that the security guard needs a personality transplant."

"Ah, now you're sounding more like yourself. Things can't be all that bad then. Have you spoken to Alix?"

"Not yet. Brady told me I could wait. Said it might be a long time." I pressed my lips together and suppressed the memory of the grim look on Brady's face when he talked about Alix. Better to concentrate on annoyance at the security guard's attitude until or unless I learned for sure there was something bigger to worry about. "But what are you doing here?"

"You've got problems. Where else would I be?"

Nick's simple reply sabotaged my attempt to maintain emotional control and tears sprang to my eyes. "But after you said—"

He noticed; he gathered me into his arms and stroked my hair. "Yeah, I know, but this is something else. We'll talk later. You can't get rid of me that easily."

"But this keeps happening." I leaned back to look up at him.

Nothing but concern written on his face. Why was I so lucky? "I thought you'd be mad."

"Come on. Give me some credit. You didn't plan for this to happen, or did you? It does seem to keep happening. Hmmm." As I opened my mouth to protest, he gave my shoulders a gentle shake. "I'm kidding, Jane. This has to be some kind of mistake. This is our friend Alix we're talking about, not some serial killer. On the other hand, if you're really sweating it, I can present myself as her attorney. Might speed things up."

"I've probably been sitting here too long, thinking up scary stories. But an attorney? I don't know. Somehow seems like—"

"—we think maybe there's a reason she'll need one?" I nodded, prompting him to continue in a low, reassuring voice. "Look, if Brady told you to wait, that's a good sign. I'll stay out of it for now, if that's what you want, but I'll leave the cell on, just in case. Here." He dug in his shirt pocket and pulled out a Snickers bar. "I don't want you complaining that I did you out of dinner. Sorry, but that's the best I can do. I ate both our chicken sandwiches on the way over here."

"I've got a can of pineapple, but Mr. Sunshine wouldn't let me through security with the can opener."

At his questioning look, I elaborated, becoming more relaxed every minute as I looked into his comforting face. When I'd finished the story, Nick looked at the clock over the reception desk. "If they're going to let Alix out tonight, it shouldn't be too much longer, so maybe you'll get that pineapple yet. Nice chaser for the Snickers. You call it. Shall I stay or go?"

The normalcy Nick had brought to the moment as he'd smiled at my silly recitation was just what I'd needed to ground me in reality again. Things would be fine.

I smiled at him. "Much as I like having you around, maybe Alix will feel more inclined to talk if I'm alone. She might tell me—I don't know—something, if it's just me. You know how private she is."

Nick stood. "You got it. How about we talk tomorrow, unless something unexpected comes up tonight? Meanwhile, I'll go home and read an article on the Metolius River I somehow missed in that October issue." He gestured toward the discarded *Field & Stream.*

"You were looking at headlines of a fishing magazine while I was pouring out my heart to you?"

"Guilty as charged. What can I say? They really do have good articles. You ought to read this one while you're waiting."

"You're hopeless. I think you just came down here to look at the magazines."

"Hey! I saved the wine. Does that count as a point in my favor?"

"Okay. One point. But if you want more, you'll have to do better for dinner than a Snickers bar to go with it."

"And we'll have to meet somewhere other than the lobby of the Russell County Courthouse," Nick said, smiling.

"You're on." Funny how a few simple words immediately caused the room temperature to rise.

CHAPTER 4

The joys of fishing the Metolius hadn't exactly taken hold of my imagination by the time Brady returned to tell me Alix was on her way out another exit, and I should meet her outside. I thanked him warmly and wasted no time in gathering my quarantined can opener on my way out the door. That can of pineapple was sounding better by the minute.

Alix's usual confident swing was missing from her stride, so at first I didn't recognize her as the woman making her slow way, head lowered, toward my car.

I doubled my pace and caught her just as she arrived at the Volvo. "Are you all right? We were so worried."

Alix tossed back her hair and straightened. "No need for that, really, but it was good of you to come. They offered me a lift home, but I've talked to enough deputies for one day."

"I'll bet." I unlocked the car from her side and went around. "You're probably starved, too. Didn't you miss dinner?"

Alix dropped into the passenger seat. "Yeah, I guess."

She lapsed into silence, so I followed her lead and drove without comment back to the Wedding Belle. From time to time I glanced over at her, but she just gazed passively out the side window, like a tourist who'd never seen the town before. When I eased to the curb in front of the Wedding Belle, she looked up, apparently startled that we had already arrived. Moving in slow motion, like a swimmer underwater, she opened the door.

"Thanks for the ride." She fished in her bag for her keys and walked away, leaving me with only the sound of the motor running.

Astonishment kept me rooted behind the wheel for a moment. I'd missed my date with Nick and perched on the world's most uncomfortable chair for hours reading magazines I didn't like and worried myself silly. Oh no. This wasn't all I was going to get. Maybe Alix was just in shock.

I jumped from the car and spoke the first words that came to mind. "I'll fix you some soup."

"No, thanks." Alix fumbled with her keys.

"Let me do that." I grabbed them from her cold fingers and pushed open the door.

After flipping on the inside lights, I turned to face her where she still stood on the step, immobile as the proverbial deer in the headlights. Dark shadows under her eyes highlighted her exhaustion.

"Aren't you coming in?"

"Yes." She spoke and moved like a wind-up doll with a low battery as she moved past me. She dropped her bag on a floral loveseat and leaned against its back. "I'm going to bed."

Compassion for my weary friend warred with annoyance at her summary dismissal. Annoyance won. I was hungry, tired, and I'd missed an evening with Nick over worry for her. I bit back what I wanted to say and perched on the sofa arm near her. "Come on, Alix. I know you like your privacy, but you need to let me in. I want to help. We're friends. That's what friends do."

"Friends? We have lunch together and discuss books and kid around. But you don't really know me."

"I know you didn't kill that man. Is that what's worrying you? After all we've gone through, you can't possibly think I'd consider you capable of murder. Neither would any of your other friends, who, by the way, I had to forcibly restrain from coming with me tonight. They're waiting to hear what happened, not because they want to gossip about you, but because they care."

"Fine. I'll tell you. Then we'll see how much you—any of you—want to be my friends." A fire ignited in Alix's eyes and she pushed away from the loveseat.

I took a step backward, startled by the abrupt change from the withdrawn woman I'd driven home.

She forced her next words through a throat so constricted with emotion or pain that I could imagine hands squeezing her windpipe. "Arnie had a high old time asking me questions about Hunter Blackburn." Alix motioned quotation marks around the name and nodded with a bitter smile.

"Hunter Blackburn? Is that the man who was killed?"

"That's right. He was a con man, a crook who changed his name for whatever current scam he was running. He was a real peach, even stole money from little old ladies. Whatever he wanted, he took. And now, it appears that somebody finally got fed up with that mean, disgusting, sorry excuse for a human being."

"You knew him." I mouthed the words, astounded.

She knew Hunter Blackburn. I didn't say anything out loud, but she must have caught the dawning awareness in my expression. She sagged back against the loveseat, the fight leaving her. "Oh, yeah," she said quietly. "You could say I knew him." She looked up at me. "And when I finish what I have to say, you may wish you'd never known me."

I kept my tone matter-of-fact. "I'd never wish that."

She put an arm over her face, hiding her eyes as she spoke. "You know all those ex-husbands I don't talk about? He was the first." I could barely make out her next words. "And the worst."

Images from the past year crowded my mind. Alix driving the badly injured Wendell to the vet's office in her immaculate convertible, Alix standing up to the deputies when Bianca was in jail, Alix unobtrusively managing Thornton's while Laurence was in the hospital.

She had wisecracked her way through every crisis, mocked any hint of sentiment, but she'd repeatedly come through in the clutch for me. For all of us. She'd even manufactured a creative job for Bianca at the Wedding Belle, an opportunity that had allowed Bianca to flourish. Alix was prickly and aloof, but she was no murderer.

I knelt in front of her, speaking softly. "I can't pretend to understand how you got mixed up with someone like that, but we all make mistakes."

Alix abruptly leaned forward, resting elbows on knees so that her hair covered her face once again. "Not quite like that."

"Maybe not, but if it's true that you're known by the company you keep . . . well, let's just say you've come up quite a few notches. We'll work things out. That's what friends are for."

I watched as a single tear dripped onto the back of Alix's slender hand.

"Oh, you think so?" Alix whispered.

"Sorry, your cover's blown."

She looked up, reading in my face the support she'd been afraid wouldn't be there.

I smiled and made a circling motion with my hand to indicate haste. "So, let's get on with it. Finish the story so we can both get some sleep."

"Okay." Alix nodded slowly and swallowed a few times, then continued. "When they found his body, he had my telephone number in his pocket."

CHAPTER 5

I stared at Alix, startled by her revelation. My attempt to imagine this wonderful, sophisticated friend married to a common criminal absolutely failed, like the struggle to jam the pieces together of two separate puzzles. And why was he carrying her phone number years later?

The salsa rhythm of my cell's ring tone jolted me back to the present. I raised my eyebrows at Alix as I flipped it open.

"Mom, where are you? Is Alix okay? We've been waiting at the store for hours." Bianca's barrage of words allowed me to collect my scattered thoughts while I watched Alix grimace and shrug her shoulders.

"I was just about to call you." I stalled for time until my brain could shift from neutral to drive. "You went back to the store? And Tyler's still there? It's almost eleven o'clock."

"Well, duh! Minnie, too. You didn't think we'd just go home tonight!" No one could do indignation better than my daughter. "I mean, we knew you'd take care of everything, but were you going to leave us hanging all night? What's the story?"

I watched as Alix stretched out on the loveseat, one arm over her face again as though to shut out the world, at least for a while. The vision of Bianca, Tyler, and Minnie, quivering with pent-up energy and ready to charge over here to help, gave me all the impetus I needed to do what had to be done. I lied.

With forced gaiety I said, "No story. Sorry. Didn't mean to worry you."

"So . . . a misunderstanding?"

"More or less." My conscience was poking me, but I didn't want to get into the truth now.

"I knew it. What was it?" Bianca wasn't going to let go that easily. I lowered my voice to a near whisper before answering.

"Call it a weird coincidence. Look, it's late, and Alix is trying to go to sleep. I'll explain tomorrow."

"Well, okay, but before the meeting, right?" Bianca asked.

"Sure." What meeting was she talking about? I'd agree to anything to get me off the phone without spilling the beans.

"You still want me to introduce Dr. McCutcheon?" Bianca's clue gave me my bearings. The Save Our Seniors meeting.

"Of course. He was really impressed that someone of your age cared about elder abuse. You don't have to say much, but it'd be a help."

"Well, if you think so." I heard Minnie's voice in the background before Bianca spoke again. "Minnie's going home now to make lemon scones for the meeting." Minnie was famous for baking at all hours of the day and night, especially when she was upset. Better to have her in the kitchen than here.

"Great. Guess we'd all better finish up the day. It's been a long one." With a sigh of relief, I signed off and turned to Alix, surprised to discover that she'd fallen asleep while I'd been on the phone. She must have been exhausted. Her arm had dropped away from her face to expose her expression, now beautiful and serene. What a far cry from the anguished look I'd glimpsed only a few minutes earlier.

Who was this person? I knew Alix as a loyal friend and excellent businesswoman, but when I searched my memory for information about her marital background, I came up only with the snide remarks she often made about the general worthlessness of men. The same facade that had allowed her to run a successful bridal shop in spite of three failed marriages also allowed her to keep her friends in the dark about the existence of ex-husbands who were liable to get themselves murdered.

Her breath came gently, regularly. Fair enough. I wasn't going to disturb my friend now, but tomorrow . . . that was another story. I pulled a soft pink throw over her and let myself out, locking the door behind me.

Once outside in the cool night air, I hesitated only an instant before pulling out my phone.

I'd guessed right. Nick answered on the first ring. "How'd it go?"

"I didn't wake you? We didn't set anything up, so I was afraid—"

"Figured you'd call tonight, one way or the other." His voice was warm, reassuring. "So, everything okay?"

"I think so. Alix is home, but—"

"Complication?"

"Well, sort of. They let her go and I brought her home. I'm just leaving her place now."

"No charges?"

"No, nothing like that," I said slowly. "Alix told me something personal . . ."

"Let me guess. She didn't give you permission to tell anyone, and now you're wrestling that famous conscience of yours."

"How'd you know?"

Nick chuckled. "Been observing your conscience at work for quite a while now, Ms. Straight and Narrow, and, believe me, I don't want to put that baby into overdrive. It gets enough exercise on its own."

"Well, thanks a lot. You make me sound like a real prude."

"Oh, I wouldn't go that far." His deepened voice and the way he drew out his words reassured me that he was teasing as he continued. "Let's just say nobody doubts that you most definitely have your principles."

"That's better than being 'Ms. Straight and Narrow,' anyway. It's just that Alix explained why they picked her up, and I want to tell you about it, but I'm not sure I should." I sighed in frustration. "Guess you're right about me."

"Relax. Like Mr. Rogers said on that kids' show, 'I like you just the way you are.' Truth be told, can't be too serious if they let her go home."

"I'll tell you everything soon as I can."

"Great. If you think things are okay, let's just call it good for now, okay?"

"Thanks for understanding. Should've known I could count on you."

"For this and whatever else you need. I'm on your side, remember? Now, do you think you can get some sleep?"

"Yes, at least I think so. I'll be mulling things over, but, yes. Alix is already asleep, so that must mean she's not worried." My voice was gaining conviction as I thought it through. "I guess I just wanted to talk to you."

"That's a plus. And I have something else I want to talk to you about, too, but not until you think Alix is all squared away."

"Alix and I aren't done talking yet. That's for darned sure, but now you have me curious. What do you have in mind?"

"Meet me at Fourth and Main at nine tomorrow morning?"

"There's an SOS meeting at ten-thirty." I suddenly remembered my promise to explain Alix's situation to Bianca before the meeting, but I couldn't tell Bianca anything until I'd received clearance from Alix anyway.

"We'll be done by then."

"I don't even know whether Alix will be up that early so, sure, I can meet you. Give me a hint."

"It's something good. At least I think you'll like it."

"C'mon. A better hint than that."

"Nope. This'll give you something to ponder other than Alix

when your head hits the pillow tonight."

"It's already so late that I'm not sure how much pillow time I'll put in pondering anything. Animal, vegetable, or mineral?"

"Oh, animal. Most definitely animal."

Chapter 6

Once home around midnight, I turned off my cell phone to discourage Bianca from last-minute questions and stumbled into bed. Sleep dropped over me like a blanket. I'd expected to pound my pillow for hours, seeking answers to the day's questions, but without consulting me, my brain called a much needed time-out. I knew nothing more until a shaft of morning sunlight warmed my face. Jumping up in confusion, I realized I'd failed to close the bedroom curtains. It was already past eight, barely enough time to shower and meet Nick. Coffee later.

I grabbed today's *Journal* on my way out the door. The puffy face of Sheriff Kraft stared out at me from the front page. His expression was no doubt designed to convey steely-eyed competence, but I knew him too well to fall for that. The headline over his picture screamed, "Sheriff promises quick resolution to murder investigation." I skimmed the accompanying article for any reference to Alix, but, to my relief, found none. The paper must have gone to press too early to report her relationship with Hunter Blackburn. A few more hours of grace before the hounds detected the scent. My second reading of the article revealed that it consisted entirely of generalities, indicating only that the local murder investigation was well under way, with "promising leads."

I couldn't resist a detour past Alix's house, slowing as I rolled by. Her newspaper was still out front, so I continued the short distance to Juniper's six-block downtown business area. Nick's blue Jeep was nowhere in sight as I parked near the corner of Fourth and Main as instructed. Only five minutes late. Not bad. By nine-fifteen, I began to wonder where Nick was since he was chronically punctual. Only then did I remember that I'd turned off my cell.

Sure enough. When I powered up, several messages popped up on the screen. The two from Bianca I ignored for the moment, scrolling to Nick's first.

"Turn-about's fair play, right? How many times have you cancelled on me? Never mind. Guess your cell's off. You won't believe this, but remember my parents' friends in Marion County, Joe and Nellie Arganno? The ones with timber theft problems? Anyway, they need me over there right away, and I'm driving west now. Sorry, but maybe this is better anyway. You should be able to go straight into Wanderers Travel and talk to your old pal Cheryl. She knows all about this, and so would you, if we ever had time to talk. I won't be back until late tomorrow or the next day. No cell phone coverage at Joe's cabin, so I'll call when I can, or you can leave a message, let me know what you think." A short pause before Nick cleared his throat and concluded, "Or don't, if the whole idea stinks."

What on earth? Cheryl Younger and I went clear back to middle school, when her name was Phillips and she sported braces. As an adult, she'd planned every trip I'd ever taken. I studied the inviting tropical posters in the Wanderers Travel office down the block. Before following Nick's instructions, I listened to Bianca's messages. The first asked where I was, and the second caused me to snap the phone closed. She and Minnie were on their way to Alix's house, unable to tolerate any further delay in hearing about what had happened last night. Well, Alix was a big girl. She could tell them whatever she wanted. I had something else to do at the moment.

The exotic young woman ensconced at the front desk at Wanderers Travel provided a more inviting entrée to the agency than any of the glossy brochures on display. Her almond eyes welcomed me, but she was on the phone, so I merely smiled as I made my way past her to Cheryl Younger's desk further back in the room. Cheryl waved me to a seat and continued clacking away on her computer while talking into the headset that connected to a wire in her ear. The stack of memos obscuring the desktop was testament to her popularity as a travel planner. Whenever she and her husband could find a babysitter for their four lively children, they also did some adventure travel of their own.

Cheryl finished her transaction, pulled off the wire, and checked an entry in her tattered looseleaf binder with competent hands that didn't appear to waste time on manicures. "Hi, Jane. Glad to see you again so soon. How's the new grandson?"

"Just as cute as the other one, and a lot more cuddly at this stage. How do you keep track?" I waved my hand at the general mess.

Cheryl laughed and removed her reading glasses, letting them fall by their cord to her chest in a practiced move she likely repeated all day long. "You get used to it. Besides, compared to keeping up with our brood, this is simple."

"I barely managed my three."

"You did all right. You must have had something to do with all those awards they collected at school banquets over the years. And apparently you haven't lost a step since they were small. So . . . too bad Nick got waylaid." Cheryl's eyes were bright. "You apparently left him with the impression I can do anything with a computer."

"You've certainly proved that over the years. Some of the deals you've found me? I was bragging on you just last week when Nick was looking at fly fishing books for Belize, but I didn't know he'd been to see you."

"That's what he told me this morning. Apparently, he didn't get a chance to talk to you. This really is a surprise then?"

"You could definitely say that. So, how about letting me in on it?"

"Glad to. He was trying to plan a weekend trip that would appeal to you, but the whole idea seems to have flustered him. Kept rubbing the back of his neck, saying it was time for a haircut. A long time since Tim got that flustered planning something for me." Cheryl watched me the way a cat watches a mouse. "Anyway, sounded like it was important to pick something you'd like, but he wanted me to tell him what I thought. Said he didn't understand women."

"I can hardly wait to hear what you suggested." I tried for humor to disguise the sudden thumping of my heart. "If Nick's involved, fishing probably came up."

"Well, it involved water anyway. Knowing you, I said a weekend at the beach. Nice dinner somewhere, and maybe a play. Was I close?"

"What did he say to that?"

Cheryl burst out laughing. "Nothing about fishing, I assure you. His face looked just about as red as yours is right now. He said, 'Well, if you think she'd like it.' I gave him some brochures and he said he'd talk to you, but—"

"Something unexpected came up."

"That's what he said. Anyway, what do you think? Want to see the brochures?" Cheryl handed me a rubber-banded stack and lowered her voice. "Look, I don't mean to embarrass you, but—to be blunt—he was asking about two rooms, so I don't think you have to worry. I mean, if that's what you're wonder-ing."

"I've got to go." I scrambled to my feet.

Cheryl stood, too. "Hope I didn't overstep, but I thought you might want to know."

"Of course. Thanks. I'll look at these."

I smiled and waved the brochures to back up my words, nodded blindly to the young woman at the front desk, and pushed my way out the door. Though the sunshine outside was warm, it still felt cooler than my face. I took a couple of brisk steps away from the plate glass windows before sagging against the building. Putting hands to my overheated cheeks in an agony of embarrassment, I waited for my breathing to steady. Through my embarrassment came a warm glow of excitement, tinged with amusement. I'd known he had a determined streak, but imagining practical, down-to-earth Nick trying to plan a romantic weekend told me that he was even more determined than I'd realized. Our relationship was about to take a turn one way or the other. He'd just upped the ante considerably by guaranteeing that we'd finally get some time alone. Was I ready for that?

A glance at my watch reminded me that, once again, I'd have to put off thinking about Nick until later. The Save Our Seniors meeting would start any minute at Thornton's, and Bianca shouldn't be left on her own to introduce the speaker.

I had my hand on the car's door handle when, out of the corner of my eye, I registered a blur of movement down the block. Was that Tyler's blond head peeking out of the alley? Impossible. He was scheduled to open the store ten minutes ago. I swung into the driver's seat, keeping watch ahead of me as I buckled my seat belt. Sure enough, a head emerged again from between two brick buildings like a turtle venturing out of its shell. The face was turned away, but I recognized the mop of hair. I was right. It was Tyler. Sighing, I got out of the car.

CHAPTER 7

I didn't have time for this nonsense. Reaching the alley with a few quick strides, I said, "Dr. Livingston, I presume."

Tyler did a comic crow hop before whirling to face me. "What are you doing here?"

I shook my head. "That's not the question. What are you doing here? You're supposed to open Thornton's. What about the SOS meeting?" The stench from a nearby dumpster hit me. "Phew. Remind me not to eat at the Thai Treasure again. Taken up dumpster-diving, have you?"

"Quick! He'll see." Tyler grabbed my arm and pulled me into the alley. Gasping for breath, he leaned back against the warm bricks. "Ran all the way from the store, after the phone call. Look, Grandpa'll be along any minute. This time I'm gonna catch him."

"Catch him doing what? What phone call?"

"I'll explain later. Peek out carefully. Is he at Liberty Bank yet?"

I took a cautious step forward, happy to move away from the dumpster, and scanned the deserted sidewalk down the block to the right. Then I looked left, almost bumping into a young woman propelling a double stroller as I did so.

"Sorry." I tried to sound harmless, but apparently didn't succeed. The woman gave the alley a wide berth and watched to make sure I wasn't following. I resisted a sudden urge to chase her. Ducking back into the alley, I said, "Your grandfather isn't out there, but I scared some young woman. That what you had in mind?"

"Not exactly. Maybe this'll work better." I watched in amazement as Tyler crouched close to the alley entrance and positioned a mirror to view the sidewalk. "If that lady comes back, she'll really freak at this."

I could see his point. The mirror he was holding formed the top half of a hot pink compact that I usually stashed along with some lipstick at Thornton's for quick touchups during the day.

"Have you been reading private eye novels when you're supposed to be working?" I asked. "Speaking of which—"

"There he is. Look."

I rolled my eyes at the mirror Tyler offered and poked my head carefully around the corner. Sure enough, Laurence had arrived in front of the bank. He leaned heavily on the cane he usually insisted he didn't need, looking up and down the street.

I pulled back fast, bumping into Tyler crowded up behind me, his gaze pinned on his grandfather. His eyes widened and he dropped into a crouch, ostensibly to retie the laces of his running shoes. They looked fine to me.

The overpowering odor of cheap cologne stung my nostrils. Someone swept by on the sidewalk, heading in Laurence's direction. The lingering smell was a step up from the odor of rotting shrimp emanating from the dumpster, but not much of one.

Tyler edged the mirror into position again. "Okay, they're talking. See? They're talking."

"Isn't that wonderful? Let's try that ourselves, on the way to the store. No one can get in until one of us opens the door." It was beyond me why Laurence's errand to the bank, or his encounter with someone he knew, was in any way alarming.

"I can't leave Grandpa now. Honest, I'll explain everything later." The sweat pouring down Tyler's cheeks wasn't from heat or exertion. He was seriously agitated. "Please, Jane," he breathed. "I'll work every Saturday. I'll never ask for another favor. I'll—"

"Are you in some kind of trouble? Do we need the police?"

"No!"

The genuine shock in his voice convinced me to forget the police.

"Can you trust me on this?" Tyler's frantic plea, his uncharacteristic display of emotion, won the day. Trust was an element that had been sadly lacking in his young life before his arrival in Juniper. He needed me to be a friend.

"Okay, okay. I'll go to Thornton's and you finish . . . whatever it is you're doing. But you owe me a major explanation."

"You'll get it, I promise."

Shaking my head, I raced back to the car and made straight for Thornton's. First Alix's bombshell, then Nick's surprise trip, and now Tyler's mystery. Everyone I knew seemed to have something to explain to me when things stopped whirling by so fast. They might have to take numbers, like in a shoe store. I was afraid to even think about Bianca and Minnie on the loose this morning, presumably hunting down Alix. Meanwhile, I had to deal with the people waiting at the store for the SOS meeting, though I felt like sending an SOS myself.

Phil and Eileen Hedstrom were peering in Thornton's window when I finally arrived. As usual, they wore matching blue jogging outfits, their bowling pin shapes suggesting that they did more sitting than jogging, and confined most exercise to strolls between couch and refrigerator. Beside them stood the omnipresent Velda Kubek, who never missed an occasion involving Minnie, whose zest for detective work Velda greatly admired. Even though this meeting was about elder abuse and had nothing to do with Minnie's highly debatable skills as a detective, Velda would be here. Hard to feature Minnie attracting a groupie, but Velda's role as caretaker to her invalid aunt, Eleanor McKay, wasn't exactly a thrill a minute, so Minnie's somewhat spotty record as a detective no doubt sounded glamorous by comparison. Even before coming to Juniper a year ago, Velda had kept house for her elderly father in Key West, Florida, so she probably hadn't had this much fun in years.

I glanced at my watch. Twenty-five minutes past ten. "Sorry I'm late."

Phil and Eileen turned in unison, their round faces breaking into broad smiles as they tripped over each other's words.

"We thought we had . . ."

". . . the wrong date or time, but of course . . ."

". . . it wasn't likely we'd both written it down wrong and . . ."

". . . Velda thought the store opened at ten, but we all agreed that the meeting wasn't until ten-thirty."

Velda spoke for the first time, her voice sounding even softer than usual in contrast to Phil and Eileen's energetic duet. "I've been looking forward to this meeting, so I was especially careful to write down the time." Her brow creased. "Minnie will be coming, won't she?"

"Yes, I'm sure she'll be here soon. She's bringing some treats and . . ." I trailed off, not wanting to mention whatever else Minnie might be doing this morning, like grilling Alix about her murdered ex-husband. I rooted in my bag for the keys. Naturally, they had gone to the bottom. Bianca kept telling me to carry a slim wallet on a chain, but I couldn't seem to manage without the half dozen extra items I always seemed to need.

"Can I help?" Velda held out her arms to take this week's armload of bedside reading. A bestselling thriller, a new biography of Frank Lloyd Wright, and a slender volume by a hopeful local poet who called herself Swaying Willow.

"Thanks." I handed over the books and dived into the bag again. In addition to lipstick, wallet, and checkbook, I dug past the troublesome can opener, an address book Bianca had left at my house, and a Mickey Mouse puzzle that I had picked up for Kevin, my three-year-old grandson. Good thing Bianca was probably helping Minnie cross-examine Alix right now instead of witnessing this performance. She wasn't shy about suggesting improvements to my way of organizing my life.

At last, I held the store keys aloft in triumph. Phil and Eileen, busy gathering up various parcels, weren't watching. Velda had observed the awkward search, but she was smiling, as always. I smiled back. It was nice someone approved of me.

No sign of Minnie and Bianca yet, or Tyler or Laurence, of course, so it was up to me to get the meeting started. The Murder of the Month Book Club had been the first group to meet at Thornton's regularly, as it featured an intrinsic connection to the store, but somehow Thornton's Books had become a mecca for other local groups, hosting meetings for organizations as diverse as the Women's Empowerment Group, the Class of Eighty-Four Reunion Committee, and today's group, the Save Our Seniors (SOS) organization. Minnie and Bianca had formed this group recently after their volunteer work at the local senior center had made them aware of numerous frauds that had been perpetrated on the vulnerable elderly population of Russell County over the past two years. Their tender hearts had led them to spearhead this effort to educate local elders about the predators who often targeted them.

I was glad to see that Tyler had found time to arrange chairs in a semi-circle in the bay window before he'd taken off to spy on his grandfather.

Velda set my books on the counter and spoke in her usual hesitant manner. "If it would be helpful, I can heat the water for tea while you get settled."

The door opened to admit Mr. Jorgenson, who pushed his wife's wheelchair over the threshold with difficulty. Serena Wannick clumped in behind them with her walker. Most groups met upstairs, but this group stayed on the main floor, for obvious reasons.

"You're a lifesaver, Velda. Come on in, everybody. Take a seat." I moved toward the door to help those entering. "The tea bags are—"

"I'll find them." Clearly delighted to help, Velda scurried as fast as her aching back would allow her toward the office. I watched her go, thinking as usual how unfair it was that someone so young had to contend with a chronic limp.

Tyler burst in the door, almost crashing into Serena. "Oops. Sorry, Mrs. Wannick."

He flushed and started toward me just as Desmond Mc-Cutcheon, the guest speaker, swept into the store. The original idea had been for our speaker to arrive a few minutes after the general meeting had begun, but people were still milling around. Things weren't exactly going according to plan this morning.

I greeted him. "Dr. McCutcheon, we're so glad you could join us. We're running a bit late."

"So I see." After taking a particularly long look at the enormous bar-turned-counter, he pronounced judgment. "Quaint."

I kept the smile on my face. Dr. Desmond McCutcheon had been teaching three miles up the road in the Sociology Department at Russell County Community College for twenty years, but he rarely mingled with the common folk of Juniper. Only the fact that Bianca had asked him to speak today had pried him loose from his classroom, or, more realistically, his mirror.

Unfortunately, Desmond McCutcheon reminded me of a popular drama professor I'd had in college long ago. He'd wowed the young women on campus with his wit and wisdom, especially those who hadn't been away from home long enough to recognize clichés. Young enough at the time to sit entranced through his lectures, I hadn't realized until years later that he had lifted most of his mannerisms straight out of old Cary Grant movies. His "original" ideas were anything but.

"If Bianca will be so kind as to introduce me, I'm ready to commence." He arranged a pair of half glasses and took pages from his briefcase. "I gave her some introductory remarks, you know."

"Apparently, Bianca's been detained. If you could wait just a minute, she spoke last night of her planned introduction."

Another end run around the truth. I was getting good at this. I just hoped that Bianca had conjured up something to say, if and when she actually arrived.

"She did seem most eager." He gave a tiny smile. The promise of Bianca's presence had definitely been the right carrot to lead this middle-aged horse to Thornton's today. Dr. McCutcheon dismissed his aged and ailing audience with a cursory glance. "Hmm. Let's wait for Bianca then. I require a glass of water nearby for my presentations."

Velda materialized at my side carrying the requested water. Having her here was better than hiring a personal assistant.

She turned to me anxiously. "Alice Durand said she'd come, but she's not here either. And where's Minnie? She was bringing lemon scones."

Eileen spoke up from her perch in the front row. "Minnie promised me poppy seed pound cake."

"She'll be here soon." I hoped Minnie had somehow found time to bake pound cake in addition to last night's scones. She slept little and baked whenever the urge struck. Probably just as well Fred was in Washington this week helping his sister move. Minnie's husband could stand to drop a few pounds, as could the Hedstroms. Was visiting Alix this morning a legitimate reason to renege on a promised pound cake? Anything short of a death in the family likely wouldn't constitute a legitimate excuse for Phil and Eileen.

I took momentary heart as the front door banged into the wall, assuming Minnie and Bianca had arrived with their usual panache. But it was only Laurence stomping in, followed by Alice Durand. They wore identical scowls. This whole group could use a quick double shot of Bianca's sunny disposition and Minnie's refreshments. To be fair, a recent feature in the *Juniper Journal* highlighting the prevalence of elder fraud in rural Oregon had made them understandably nervous and focused on Dr. McCutcheon's topic.

Of course, Laurence was always cranky when people cluttered up his bookstore. He liked books better than people, and he wasn't about to change at this late date. It always worked best when someone other than Laurence waited on his customers. Still, he seemed even more agitated than usual today. Maybe there was something to Tyler's concern.

I didn't bother urging Laurence to stay for the meeting. His oft-stated position was that the Save Our Seniors group was for old people, not him. "Bah! Old fools deserve whatever happens to 'em when they lose their money. Should spend their time reading, not watching TV." He made his way straight through the room and up the broad staircase. Most likely he'd hole up in the history section and read about the glories of ancient Rome until the meeting was over.

Alice Durand took a seat in front and folded her skinny arms over her chest. Perpetually tired and resentful, her scowl was nothing new, but I couldn't really blame her for her sour attitude. Her widowed father had socked away money over the years, but last year, a con man had threatened him with legal action about some imaginary debts. The old man, confused and terrified that he'd be locked up, had withdrawn savings from his bank account and handed the money over without a word to Alice, who'd discovered the problem the next month. The con man had disappeared. Now Alice cleaned houses six days a week, after which she went home to tend to her aging father's needs. Her one pleasure in life was to plot revenge on that con man and others like him. This group provided her with a focus for her anger.

Essentially the same scam had been tried on Velda's Aunt Eleanor, but Eleanor had become suspicious before losing much money. Outraged at being defrauded, she'd alerted the authorities immediately. Unfortunately, in the two years since, her health had deteriorated, making it impossible for her to leave her home. Now Velda worked through the SOS group on her aunt's behalf to educate seniors about such predators. Other SOS members had either experienced something similar in their own lives, or feared that they might. I felt a twinge of pity for Dr. McCutcheon, who had come hoping only to impress a lovely young woman.

As Bianca flung open the door, scattering apologies and sunshine, I sighed in relief. She not only let in the warmth of the June day, but she bore a large tray of scones. Minnie pattered along in her wake, hoisting what looked like the highly anticipated pound cake. The mood of the room immediately brightened, as I had expected. Now, if only Bianca had prepared appropriate remarks to introduce our speaker.

After setting down the tray, Bianca turned to Dr. McCutcheon and, with her first words, made his day. "Dr. McCutcheon, we're thrilled and honored that you're here today. Everyone already knows you're an expert on the subject of elder abuse, but even you don't know how especially appropriate it is that you're here this morning. We just found out something really, really important. That man who was murdered was a criminal, a con man."

She turned to face the audience before finishing with a flourish. "He was actually one of those people like the ones Dr. Mc-

Cutcheon will tell us about today. Someone here could even have been one of his targets. Just think what could have happened—to any of us—if he was still out running around. Dr. McCutcheon, you can help us understand just how close we all came to such a dangerous man."

Bianca impulsively grasped both of Dr. McCutcheon's hands. "Thank you for being here."

If I'd had any doubts that Bianca's introduction would lack punch, she'd just laid them to rest. I only hoped that she hadn't breached Alix's privacy by sharing more information with us than Alix had given the sheriff. Short of stripping to her underwear, she could hardly have focused the attention of the audience with more skill. Dr. McCutcheon's entire demeanor had changed to that of a man who had just won the lottery, though he did his best to appear suitably grave.

I took care of intermittent store business while he outlined scams ranging from home improvement rip-offs to telephone fraud, touching on problems often arising from an obsession with sweepstakes entries. His audience listened, spellbound. He might be a pompous windbag, but he was a knowledgeable one. Old Mr. Jorgenson valiantly took notes with his arthritic hands, while Serena Wannick had her pocket tape recorder running.

By prior arrangement, Velda was asked to repeat her aunt's history as an object lesson in the problems that could occur when a swindler came to town. She bravely spoke up, in spite of her chronic shyness about addressing a group.

It was only when Mr. Jorgenson offered Velda sympathy that she became reluctant to continue. "Young thing like you ought to be jetting off to Tahiti, not stuck at home with your aunt all the time."

"I'm fine, really," she murmured. "And Aunt Eleanor needs me."

"When was your last day off?" he pressed. When she didn't

answer, he said, "Thought so."

At this, Dr. McCutcheon urged Velda to obtain some respite care for her aunt, citing statistics that showed the toll taken on caretakers' health when they didn't get regular relief from their duties.

Alice snorted at the very notion. "Sure, if you have money to throw around."

From Velda's downcast eyes, I surmised that was not the case in her situation. Minnie had said recently that Velda had hired someone to do occasional housekeeping now that Velda's back problems were getting worse. With that added expense, and Eleanor's lengthy illness, there probably wasn't much money left over for discretionary spending, either in Oregon or Tahiti.

At the close of Dr. McCutcheon's presentation, he was besieged. Alice demanded to know why the governor let this stuff go on, and launched into yet another description of how her father had been cheated of his life savings.

He cut her off with a brusque, "Unfortunate, but common."

"Easy for you to say. It wasn't your life savings," Alice said. "How'd you—"

"Thank you once again for coming, Dr. McCutcheon." Though I felt sorry for Alice's hard life, our speaker wasn't in a position to help her. I hurried to close the meeting with a round of applause. "You've given us a lot to think about. Now, would you care for some refreshments?"

Dr. McCutcheon backed away from Alice's determined advance. "Sorry, but I, er, must return to campus. Immediately."

"In that case, Bianca, could you see our guest out? And Minnie, I'm sure you have some takers for your refreshments. Oh, thank you, Velda." Velda was limping toward me with the platter. "Here's Minnie's pound cake. She put the lemon scones on the counter over there."

"Never too late for either one." Phil and Eileen Hedstrom

70

rose and hesitated, unable to decide which snack to sample first. They looked at each other in understanding and then separated, each to stake out a claim on several of the treats to share.

I snagged a piece of pound cake and offered it to Alice as a peace offering. "Would you like some? You could take a piece to your father, as well."

Alice was having none of it. "I come for information, and I'm already behind on my work. Expected more outta the meeting, too. Stuffed shirt's what he is."

I risked a look behind me. Bianca had successfully shepherded Dr. McCutcheon off the premises and out of earshot of Alice's continuing vitriol.

"Never worked a day in his life. Did you see those fingernails? Manicured, sure as anything. What's he know?"

I was working on a diplomatic response when Velda slid up beside me. "Excuse me, Alice, but Minnie needs to talk to Jane."

I breathed another silent thank you to Velda for her help as I murmured an apology to Alice. I wove my way through the crowd toward Minnie. She held up the now-empty platter in front of me like a stop sign. Subtlety was not Minnie's strong suit.

Minnie darted a look around to make sure no one was close enough to hear and then spoke out of the side of her mouth like some demented gangster. "We talked to you-know-who."

"I got Bianca's message. Upsetting, but things will be fine."

"Oh, really?" Minnie raised her eyebrows. Sighing at my naiveté, she continued her ludicrous James Cagney impression. "She was told not to leave town."

"They let her go. It was just circumst—"

"But, she's not to leave town." Minnie emphasized each word. "You've read the same mysteries I have."

In truth, I avoided the bloodthirsty true crime that Minnie

loved, so this was something of a misstatement, but I sensed the volcano building. For Minnie, reading mysteries had become a pale substitute for solving them. Minnie intended to play detective again, even if it meant turning a circumstantial molehill into a sinister mountain on the verge of eruption. From the flush on her plump cheeks, I surmised that the Murder of the Month Book Club was preparing to use its deductive powers to save the world, or, at least, Alix.

"But there's nothing to do." Damage control was a nonstarter, now that Minnie was on the track. I might as well have told Nick everything last night. The cat was so far out of the bag that it was probably in the next county by now.

"Yet. Be grateful for that. It gives us time to plot strategy." Minnie looked past me and smiled at the sight of Bianca in conference with Velda. "Good. Bianca's filling Velda in. I'll stay to bring Tyler up to speed, but you go see Alix, before the press gets there."

"Has something new happened?" Dread built in the pit of my stomach.

"I saw Brady this morning. He looked absolutely stricken. He found the body, you know."

Before I could ask again, Velda limped up to us. "How can I help?" Minnie turned to her. I seized my chance to intercept Bianca.

"Everything's okay." I propelled her into the office, closing the door behind us.

"You don't understand. There's something you don't know."

"Then she told you about . . . ?"

"The marriage. Yes, and she was acting so weird."

"Probably embarrassed. Look, honey, everyone makes mistakes."

Velda stuck her head into the room. "Sorry to interrupt."

I snatched a tissue and thrust it toward Bianca. "What is it?"

"Sorry, but Tyler and Laurence have both disappeared and people want to buy books. Should I tell everyone the store is closed, or what?" Velda twisted her hands in indecision, her plain face still blotchy with the strain of trying to work up the nerve to speak in public.

I exhaled in frustration. Couldn't anyone manage anything without consulting me? "I'll be there in a minute. Thanks."

Velda let her hands drop to her sides, almost like a soldier coming to attention. "I can do it." She started to close the door, but stuck her head back inside. "Would it be helpful if Minnie and I cleaned up the refreshments?"

I couldn't believe the indecision Velda brought to the simplest task. How did she decide which clothes to put on each day? "That'd be great."

Velda made her painful way toward the front of the store. Now that she had a clear notion of what was expected of her, she was on firm ground. I only hoped I could work similar magic with my daughter.

"Look, Arnie knows Alix had nothing to do with the murder. Otherwise he wouldn't have let her go home last night." I smoothed Bianca's silky hair and spoke in my most soothing voice. "Everything's fine."

"But Arnie knows Alix saw Hunter Blackburn the day he was murdered. You think he's going to forget that information when he can't find the real killer?"

"Alix told Arnie that?" Alarm raised my voice about an octave.

Bianca nodded, her long hair bouncing with the intensity of her movement.

I flashed back to my interrupted talk with Alix last night. Asleep, she'd looked so peaceful that I hadn't awakened her to finish the conversation. Seems I should have.

"Get Tyler behind that counter. Now. We're going to see Alix."

CHAPTER 8

Alix was scrubbing the sink when Bianca and I burst into her kitchen. After one startled glance at us, she returned to her task. "Coffee if you want." She gestured toward the sleek black Cuisinart coffeemaker.

Fleeting thoughts of Lady Macbeth washing away imaginary blood rushed through my mind before reason could reassert itself. This was my friend Alix, not some evil monster, but I was off-balance and frustrated. "Why didn't you tell me last night that you'd seen him?"

Mechanically, Alix polished the already-gleaming chrome faucet before turning around at last. "I'm sorry. I should have told you—would have—but it felt so good to get out of that place last night that I . . . just let go. That make any sense? You were gone when I woke up."

"And Arnie knows?"

A rueful nod. "Figured he'd find out soon enough. Better to come from me. And Bianca and Minnie double-teamed me this morning. You know how that is."

Her wan smile coaxed a reluctant one in return from me. Bianca and Minnie acting in concert constituted determination personified and doubled. I reached for a kitchen chair and dropped into it. "Okay, let's hear it."

"Yes, please explain it to her, Alix." Bianca danced from foot to foot, hardly able to contain herself.

I looked at her, but my normally loquacious daughter didn't

seem to have anything to add. Were we playing "Twenty Questions"? If so, I needed a few more clues.

Alix snapped off her yellow rubber gloves and flung them into the now pristine sink. "I just told the police that one thing. They let me come home, so maybe it didn't matter all that much."

Bianca looked helplessly at me. I was too amazed at Alix's attitude to answer.

I found my voice at last. "You're right. Why should something as simple as learning that you saw your ex-husband, a man who was murdered later the same day, be of any interest to the sheriff?" Concern for my friend gave my question a calculated sharpness as I struggled to break through Alix's defense. I could barely hear her low response.

"It's not something I want to think about."

I continued to press her. "You can avoid the topic with us, but how do you plan to avoid it with Arnie? Unless the murderer strolls into his office and confesses, I guarantee you'll meet Arnie again in his official capacity rather soon. Alix, we're on your side, but you have to think this through. Probably reporters are setting up their cameras outside right now."

Alix still didn't seem to get it. "But I didn't know Hunter was going to get himself murdered."

"That's certainly good news," I said. "And I hope Arnie appreciates that when you discuss the matter again, as I have every expectation that you will."

"Please don't be mad at her, Mom," Bianca said. If I hadn't been so focused on getting Alix to take an interest in her potential peril, I'd have been amused at Bianca. My daughter had no trouble finding fault with me for being too conventional, but she skipped right over any possible flaws in Alix, who apparently shed husbands the way an umbrella sheds raindrops. "Alix is just in shock. She wants your help. Don't you, Alix?"

An uncomfortable silence hung in the air until Alix put out a hand to me. Without actually looking up, she whispered, "Please."

Embarrassment at witnessing her humiliation washed over me. Some friend I was. My attempt to force her to talk only caused her more pain. I reached out my hand to join hers. We might have remained locked in a tableau of mutual discomfort for some time if Bianca hadn't piped up.

"Should I get some paper, Mom? You know, to take notes?"

Now Alix and I cast sidelong looks at each other, smiles tugging at our mouths in spite of the tension between us. Bianca had many fine qualities, but secretarial ability wasn't among them. The idea of her taking notes was ludicrous.

"Thanks for the offer." Alix flicked a glance at Bianca before she squared her shoulders and looked at me. "But what we really need right now is—"

"Tea. I have some nice green tea in my bag," Bianca said. "We could sit and—"

"I was thinking more along the lines of an apology," Alix said.

"That's okay." A big smile broke out on Bianca's face. "We didn't mind."

Alix tossed her hair impatiently. "No, it's not okay, Bianca."

"You were upset. We knew that. When I was a kid and rude to Mom, she knew I'd just had a fight with a friend or something. She never took it personally."

Yeah, right, I thought. Superwoman that I was, I never took it personally when my daughter was rude to me. I absorbed those situations like a blotter. Couldn't get enough of them.

Alix gave Bianca a long, level look that indicated she was reading my mind. When she spoke out loud, she confirmed it. "Thanks for trying, Bianca. Go ahead and make tea, get paper and pencils for notes, do whatever you want, but please let me get through this apology. I'm out of practice." She paused. "Who am I kidding? I'm not sure I've ever tried before . . . to apologize, I mean."

"Or ask for help," I said slowly.

"That either."

"Apology accepted," I said. "Also, the offer of tea." Alix sat down across the table from me and we watched in silence as Bianca poured water into the tea kettle and rescued several packets of Tazo tea from her fashionably slender wallet on a chain.

"You have room for tea in that tiny thing?" I deliberately made idle conversation to give Alix time to collect her thoughts.

"Always room for tea."

Bianca moved around the room with swift, sure motions, setting out three oversized white mugs decorated with abstract patterns, pouring soy milk into a squat pottery jug. I couldn't imagine Alix buying soy milk, so Bianca probably had contributed that to the kitchen supplies. Bianca didn't offer sugar, of course, as she was on a permanent campaign to wean me from its non-nutritional grasp.

"A matter of priorities. You drag that suitcase of yours around to make sure you have a can opener, while I stick to essentials like green tea." The kettle whistled and she poured steaming water into our cups. "Okay, ready."

Alix sat silently at first, turning her cup around and around. Without looking up, she said, "I don't know where to begin."

"His real name," Bianca said. "What was it?"

"That's your first question?" Alix and I asked in unison.

"Well, I have a bunch of them, but that seemed sorta basic."

"Martin Selway."

Bianca made a face. "No wonder he changed it."

Alix nodded. "Yeah, later, after we split."

"Then you were actually Mrs. Martin Selway?" Bianca's tone

left no doubt as to how she felt about that concept.

"Yep, briefly. I was eighteen." Alix went silent, perhaps searching her memory for clues to an earlier self. "I bailed, once I got the stars out of my eyes and found out what he was really like, crooked as they come."

"And that was what . . . fifteen years ago?" I prompted. "So why'd he have your phone number?"

Alix crossed her arms over her stomach, almost as though in pain. "Look, I didn't kill him."

"We know that."

Alix looked everywhere but at us before she shrugged, seeing no way out. "He was hoping to shake me down again."

"Again? This happened before?" Bianca was incredulous. "You actually paid him?"

"Just a couple of times." Wincing at the disappointment on Bianca's face, Alix turned to me, as though maybe I'd understand better. "I knew he'd be back—the proverbial bad penny—but it was a short-term fix."

"Why pay him at all?" Bianca asked. She was getting a crash course in a world she knew nothing about. "He sounds like a creep."

"He was, but he could have made life embarrassing for me."

"That's just wrong." Bianca was red with youthful outrage. "You should have stood up to him, not let him get away with that."

"I was hoping he'd just go away. Didn't work out that way."

"So you saw him the day he was killed, and Arnie knows it," I said.

Alix nodded. "I assumed someone would have seen us talking. Thought it would be better if I admitted it up front. That was hours before he died anyway, according to the paper."

"It's good that you told Arnie yourself. Shows good faith," I said. I hoped Arnie would look at it the same way. Talk about taking lemons and making lemonade.

"I was hoping . . . I don't know . . . for a miracle or something. Maybe they'd find the killer right away and no one but Arnie would have to know I'd seen him. I thought maybe if I had time to think, I'd be able to come up with something to help. I'm sure Arnie'll keep me in mind if he doesn't find the killer."

"And then he'll come right back to you," Bianca said. So much for putting a positive spin on things.

"The fact that I'm innocent ought to slow him down at least a little bit."

"You don't have an alibi," I stated. She would have mentioned it before this if she did.

"That would clear everything up." Bianca brightened at the thought. "He was killed the night before he was found, or maybe early that evening? And you saw him at . . . ?"

"About three, give or take. From what I read, he died about six or seven that night." Alix spread her hands wide, palms up, in a helpless gesture. "I was at the Wedding Belle. No appointments, no phone calls, not even Wendell. I was upset after seeing him, so I wasn't looking for company. Bad choice."

"If you knew this creep was prowling around Juniper, why didn't you warn anyone?" Bianca voiced the question I'd been about to ask. "You actually could identify someone you knew was a criminal, maybe save someone from losing his life savings, so—"

"Why didn't I?" Alix flushed and spoke harshly. "Don't you think I thought of it? Sure, I thought of it a lot, but . . ." She covered her face with her hands.

Bianca's voice was thick with scorn. "But what? You chickened out because you were embarrassed. You didn't want to ruin your image. That's . . . that's—"

"—human," I finished.

Bianca was still young enough to be judgmental, certain that she would always do the brave thing, the right thing. I'd been around long enough to know that as people age, they sometimes blur what were once bright lines in order to make it through tricky situations. Suddenly, I remembered a recent conversation at the book club the night we discussed Sue Grafton's *T is for Trespass*, which centered on elder abuse. The usually cool Alix had been uncharacteristically vehement in her comments about it.

"It was you who suggested the SOS group. In fact, you practically insisted on it, but you stepped back from organizing it. Now I see why."

"Well, I don't." Bianca stood with arms crossed, still disgusted.

"You're right, Bianca." Alix intertwined her long fingers in front of her on the table like a penitent schoolgirl, her embarrassment emblazoned across her cheeks. "I knew it all along. I should've told someone, but I just . . . just couldn't face having that man investigated here, where I live. I hoped to learn where he was headed and contact the police in the next town he targeted, but, obviously, I never got the chance."

"So starting the SOS group was your way of warning the people around Juniper without exposing yourself," I interjected. "Pretty smart."

"With Bianca and Minnie's activist track record, I knew that once they got fired up about elder abuse, it'd generate a ton of local attention, which it has. I had him outfoxed temporarily. Thought the publicity would move him out of here fast."

Bianca was softening fast, her naturally tender heart overtaking her initial shock. "Well, I guess that makes sense. Too bad somebody killed him before he left though."

"Sure is," Alix said. "Could have saved everyone a lot of trouble. I don't know who killed him, but late last night I had one idea. You won't believe it when I describe a game he used to play, but it's the best lead I can come up with."

CHAPTER 9

The more Alix told us about her ex-husband, the less I wondered at her sour attitude toward men. Bianca and I listened, incredulous, as Alix described Hunter's game. He'd make an appointment with a female real estate agent to look at an expensive house and then seduce her during the tour. To make the contest interesting, he looked for agents who were attractive, married, and under the age of forty.

"How did you find out about this . . . this game?" Bianca wanted to know.

"He couldn't wait to tell me about it when he saw I was really going to leave him. Wanted me to know what a big hit he was with other women. Told you he was a creep."

"You think he might have tried that here?" I might be a generation older than Bianca, but I was just as naive about the existence of such a cruel personality. "I can't believe anyone went for something so ridiculous."

"Oh, believe it. He kept score. He was handsome as they come, and smooth. Took me a while to get past all that." At my obvious skepticism, Alix gave a short laugh. "You've led a sheltered life. Anyway, I told you this was a long shot."

"Mom, we have to do something, even if it sounds stupid. Besides, Minnie's already on her way over here to help." Bianca was back on board, her excitement building. "It'll be like old times. The Murder of the Month Book Club rides again."

No point in dashing cold water on Bianca's enthusiasm, but

I'd do everything in my power to keep the whole gang from saddling up again. They had a tendency to ride off in all directions when they did. Still, Bianca's words reminded me that Alix was in no immediate danger at the moment. Perhaps she would appreciate a show of support from her friends right now, even if that was all it amounted to.

Besides, people didn't get murdered every day in our little town, so how long could it possibly take before the sheriff, even one as inept as Arnie Kraft, stumbled over a better suspect than Alix? Far better to keep Minnie occupied chasing a long shot with me than causing even more trouble by striking out on her own.

The list of real estate agents who fit Hunter's bizarre criteria was mercifully short. I thanked my lucky stars that Bianca was needed here to help Alix with the details of an imminent wedding. The frantic woman I passed on my way out of the Wedding Belle nearly ran me down. I'm not sure she even saw me.

"The color of the programs doesn't match the bridesmaids' hair ribbons," she wailed.

Armed with the list and promising a report as soon as I knew anything, I left Alix and Bianca to their task. Better them than me. It shouldn't take me long to check out the whereabouts of the several possible real estate agents on the day of the murder, and then I could honestly report that I'd done what I'd promised.

Minnie didn't even bother coming inside when she arrived. She just stood on the front steps and announced, "Sorry that Velda couldn't come, too. She needed to get home to her aunt." She turned and made straight for the passenger seat of my car without even waiting to be sure that I was ready to leave.

She leaned forward like a racer in the starting blocks. "Keith Strand first, of course. I've never liked the way his hair waves so perfectly in front. He must do it with a hair dryer, and you know what they say about men who blow-dry their hair."

"How did you know I was on my way to see Keith?" I didn't ask what they said about men who blow-dry their hair. Making sense of Minnie's conversation was hard enough without adding extra topics.

"Bianca called. Caught me just as I pulled up." Minnie brandished her tiny new cell phone like a flag. "Handy. I should've had one years ago. Still haven't figured out how to get rid of that new-fangled message feature. What are you waiting for? Let's go."

"I wanted to talk about keeping a low profile."

"That's why I didn't bring Tyler. Velda was disappointed that she couldn't come, either. I thought of bringing Wendell along, too, but I didn't see how he'd help our cover story."

Neither did I, but, again, I chose not to muddy the waters by asking why she'd entertain the notion that a dog's presence would add anything to the expedition. I'd stick to the point, assuming that Minnie had one. "You already have a cover story?"

"Why, bless your heart. I'm good at this detective stuff. I'll fill you in as we drive. Meadowbrook Realty."

I turned the key in the ignition, thinking just two words: damage control.

Minnie flipped open a red notebook, but she didn't glance at her notes. "You've probably seen Rita Strand's picture in the Meadowbrook ads. They always use her for publicity. Keith's attractive too, if you like the type, but he doesn't sell as much as she does. I hear she's in a whole different category."

"Where do you hear that?" I wasn't looking for clues with the question. I was just curious. No one ever gossiped to me about real estate agents.

"Here and there. Mostly church, I guess."

"Any hint of trouble?"

"People say she's better at her job, and you know how touchy men can be about that sort of thing."

"What I meant was, have you ever heard anything about Rita running around?"

"She wouldn't be that stupid. It'd hurt her sales." Minnie spoke emphatically. "She and Keith have three of the cutest little boys you've ever seen. Keith dotes on them."

"What about Rita?"

"Rita's busy selling houses."

"Now I see why you wanted to start with them." I wasn't about to bet money on the Keith and Rita Strand saga leading to anything other than a possibly frayed marriage, but if checking this out helped to calm Alix's nerves, it was as good a way as any to kill time until the sheriff turned up the real killer. Since Arnie Kraft was barely capable of writing speeding tickets, let alone running a murder investigation, it wasn't a particularly reassuring line of thought.

Also, having Minnie come along had complicated things. Given Minnie's flair for the dramatic, I was afraid to ask myself just how much harm she could do. Best to roll with whatever cover story Minnie had concocted and hope for the best. It would all be over soon.

Meadowbrook Realty claimed the high ground in the middle of the Meadowbrook Golf Club and Country Estates complex. Handy if you wanted to knock off a game of golf, stop by the clubhouse for a drink, and buy a mansion on the way home.

I'll give her credit. Minnie did her best to be unobtrusive, but with her trademark floppy black hat and colorful scarves, she was difficult to ignore. I could only hope that the chic receptionist would take her for an eccentric movie star in need of an extra villa.

"Mrs. Salter!" The receptionist sprinted around an acre of

desk to hug Minnie. "I haven't seen you since, well, it's been years."

"Tina. How wonderful to see you. Jane, this is Tina Wendover. She was one of my star Sunday school students."

Tina laughed, delighted to be recognized. "You're being tactful. I haven't seen you in years, but I know you're remembering the day at church when I forgot my Bible verse and cried." She hugged Minnie again. "I was mortified, but you were so nice. You know what? I can still recite that verse: Psalms 30:5. 'Weeping may endure for a night, but joy cometh in the morning.' Too bad I couldn't come up with it that day."

"I'm sure nobody noticed," Minnie said kindly.

"Are you kidding? Bobby Varnette came next, and no one could hear a word he said over my sobbing. Boy, was he mad!" Tina turned to me and continued as though we were old friends. "I hid behind the stage until Mrs. Salter found me. She gave me a special sugar cookie that had my name frosted on it and said my posture had been the best of anyone in the program."

"Impressive. Minnie doesn't frost sugar cookies for just anyone."

"Well, you do have wonderful posture," Minnie said.

Belatedly, Tina recollected her professional obligations. "I haven't even asked why you're here."

I hoped Tina couldn't hear the rusty sleuthing gears in Minnie's head grinding into action. "Oh, that's right. Jane's sister is in the market for a new home, but she's very particular. She needs a real estate agent who really knows what he or she is doing, maybe even a team of them so she could get both the male and female perspective. You don't happen to have any married couples on staff, do you?" She peered over Tina's shoulder as though expecting the required experts to pop out of the filing cabinet behind the desk.

"As it happens, we do." Tina didn't seem at all put off by the ridiculous request, but since Tina had known Minnie from church, she probably wouldn't expect her to be devious. "Keith and Rita Strand. Either or both of them would do a fine job."

"But do they work well together?" Minnie asked. "Are they happily married?"

Tina looked puzzled. "Happily married?"

As a soother of bruised feelings, Minnie was a pro, but she was still feeling her way as a private eye. "Well, you see . . . Jane's sister and her husband are having a bit of trouble, and—"

"Well, remember: 'Weeping may endure for a night, but joy cometh in the morning.' " Tina's eyes widened as she realized her little joke might offend me during this time of supposed family trauma. "Oh, I'm sorry."

I didn't have any frosted sugar cookies on me, but I did what I could to let Tina off the hook. "Don't worry. They're not having that much trouble."

"Thank goodness. I just meant . . . I'm sure everything will work out."

"Of course it will," Minnie said, "but they need to be surrounded by calmness. Yes, that's right. Calmness is the key."

"We'll have my sister get back to them," I said, taking the business cards Tina offered. "Wouldn't that be a good idea, Minnie?"

"What? Oh, yes, yes. By all means." Minnie's gaze was focused on the cards. I knew that she was already plotting our next move, which—unless I could prevent it—would probably involve staking out the Strands' house, crawling through their shrubbery, and hoping to catch at least one of them in the garage wiping off a bloody hatchet. I took Minnie by the arm and said a pleasant good-bye to the helpful Tina.

"I really hope your sister and brother-in-law work things out," she said.

"Thank you. I'm sure they will." Since they were both

imaginary people, I knew I'd be able to manage them much better than I could manage Minnie.

As we wound our way out of the lush grounds of Meadow-brook, Minnie's phone suddenly gave out with a spirited version of "Onward, Christian Soldiers."

"Sorry." Minnie located the phone after the second ring. In hysterical tones, audible to me, a woman's voice reminded Minnie that ten apron-clad parishioners and one hundred pounds of donated hamburger awaited her at the New Community Church for instructions on the assembly of meatloaf suppers for the needy. "Just a minute." Minnie covered the receiver and turned to me. "Serve, Save, and Sanctify Committee. I forgot all about it. What should I do?"

"You're the chairman, right?" I was guessing about that, but the stricken look on Minnie's face told me I'd scored a bull's-eye. "Then you'd better go. They need you."

Still, she wavered for a couple of minutes—detective work beat hamburger and foil pans any day—but finally duty won out.

"Drop me off at church. I'll get a ride back to Alix's later and catch up with you. Where's some paper?" She scribbled her cell phone number on the back of a grocery list from her bag. "Call me right away if you uncover anything suspicious. Don't do anything dangerous."

From the wistful expression on her face, I knew she really meant that I shouldn't do anything dangerous without calling her first so that she could be in on it. "I won't."

As it turned out, I might as well have spent the afternoon making meatloaf. Instead, I'd driven to Keith and Rita's house without a real plan. No cars in their driveway, but I spotted a neighbor planting purple petunias across the street, so I pretended to be an old school friend looking for Keith and Rita. The nice lady said what a shame it was that they weren't home, but they were visiting Keith's family in Missouri. Keith, Rita, and the kids had left Juniper the day before the murder.

Even as I fumed about the time and trouble it would have saved if Tina had simply mentioned their trip, I knew that judgment wasn't fair. She hadn't known what we were after. Besides, whenever Minnie was involved, conversations rarely proceeded in a straight line.

My subsequent inquiries about the alibis of other real estate agents proved equally fruitless. As I turned at last toward the Wedding Belle to report in, I consoled myself by acknowledging we'd known that this "romantic realtor" notion was a long shot. Maybe the murderer was Colonel Mustard in the ballroom with the candlestick. Alix and Bianca's hopeful looks turned to disappointment the minute they saw my face.

"You said yourself it was a long shot," I said.

"Yeah, I know."

"I should have gone with you," Bianca grumbled.

"So you could have done what?"

"I don't know. Something."

Striving for a pleasant tone of voice, I answered her. "Well I did do something, Bianca. I found out that Rita and Keith Strand have been out of town this week. Stanley Wirth was involved in an all-day trial and Paul Moffitt just had knee surgery. Neither of them could have been the hypothetical jealous husband."

Bianca wasn't yet willing to give up. "What about the agents themselves? A woman could have done this. Maybe he tried to rape one of them."

Alix shook her head. "Not his style."

"Cindi Wirth was showing a ranch property clear over in Deschutes County that day and Tanya Moffitt was shepherding a bunch of agents from the Portland office around Juniper."

"Maybe Tanya ditched them for a couple of hours," Bianca

said, "or Cindi got back to Juniper early. We could make Arnie fingerprint them or—"

"That idea's just not going to fly," I said.

"You're going to give up just like that? I can't believe you'd leave Alix to—"

"Your mother's right. There's nothing to go on," Alix said.

"Well, okay." Bianca flopped into a nearby armchair. Apparently, my assessment of the situation didn't count, but if Alix said something, it must be right.

After a moment's silence, Bianca spoke again. "So, Mom, what do we do next?"

I felt sudden heat creep up my neck and across my face. Bianca had begged me to help, insulted me for not finding a murderer in two hours, and now was asking for my help again. "If you have a bright idea," I began, "feel free . . ."

My daughter's cavalier dismissal of my afternoon's efforts stung. I reminded myself that she was young, and she was worried about our friend, but for once my pep talk didn't help. Sometimes being a mother wasn't all it was cracked up to be.

Alix read my stiffness better than Bianca did. "You know what? Let's take a break, give Arnie a crack at solving this thing. Stranger things have happened. Look, I appreciate your efforts, Jane, but it was a long shot, at best. Besides, Tyler's called a couple of times, wondering whether you're coming back to the store today."

Tyler. That poor kid. I'd completely forgotten about his distress over his grandfather. Had that been only this morning? Things were moving way too fast. "Well, if you're sure." Alix didn't need my help right now, but I had another friend who did. "You know where to find me."

CHAPTER 10

I flipped open my cell phone before reaching the car. No message from Nick, but I hadn't expected one. He was either busy with his client or, more likely, waiting to hear my response to his weekend plan. Momentarily forgetting my annoyance with Bianca, I savored the wording of my answer. However, after making my way through four messages from Tyler, my guilty conscience shoved Nick into second place. How could I put aside Tyler's evident distress from this morning any longer? I'd be at the bookstore in five minutes. After I helped Tyler with his grandfather, I'd have plenty of time to think about Nick.

Expecting a distraught and downcast Tyler to rush me at the door of Thornton's, I was pleasantly surprised to find him in animated conversation with three girls outfitted all in black when I walked in. I'd forgotten that students from the Juniper High School drama class would be here this week filming a re-enactment upstairs of my heroic exploits from last year. They seemed to be doing wonders for Tyler's mood. No anxiety or ruffled feathers in evidence now. If anything, he was preening those same feathers at the feminine attention he was getting. He attempted a nonchalant, "Hi, Jane," but his blush gave him away.

"Done with the filming?" I asked.

When I received three identical nods from girls with heavily made-up eyes, I disappeared tactfully into the office in an attempt to give Tyler the maximum scope to operate. Apparently, my presence had broken the spell though because I soon heard the front door open and close. In a couple of minutes, Tyler appeared at the office door.

I looked up from today's invoices. "Sorry if I cramped your style. No wonder you liked the idea of the class coming to film at the store. They were cute."

"Oh, get off it. It's good publicity." Tyler looked at the floor and cracked his knuckles, instantly reverting from teen heartthrob to nervous boy.

Sometimes I forgot he was only sixteen and subject to the insecurities that went with the age. Looking at the top of his blond head, I felt a sudden pang, Over the past year, he'd become like a member of my family. Would one of those cute girls break his heart? I decided against embarrassing him further.

"So, how'd things go this afternoon? Sorry to leave you in the lurch, but I didn't get your messages until just now." I gave him the opportunity to bring up this morning's scene downtown in his own good time.

"Fine. Minnie and Velda helped me clean up, we got four boxes of books . . . you know, the usual. I think maybe the screams from the filming upstairs kept some customers from browsing, even when I told 'em about the filming, but it was a little noisy. Bianca called a couple of times later to update me about everything. She sounded steamed that you're dropping the investigation."

"Did she mention that Alix asked me to do just that?"

"She thought you could've put up more of a fight."

I pushed some bills around on the desk without seeing them. "Alix couldn't think of a plan, but I was supposed to?"

He put up his hands in a defensive gesture. "I'm just telling you—"

"I know. Not your problem." If that wasn't a clear invitation to tell me what his problem actually was, I'd never given one.

Nothing but silence. Fine. I could wait. "I'd better get caught up." I made my way to the front of the store.

Tyler trailed me and handed over the bank deposit bag. "It's just that Bianca and Minnie . . . well, all of us really . . . depend on you. And Alix, of course. We're not trying to dump problems on you, but it's like . . . we always know you can help."

No wonder I liked this kid. "That's a comforting way of looking at it. Maybe you can help Bianca not to get 'steamed' when I don't instantly fix everything."

"Well, you know Bianca. She's your daughter. It's her job to give you a hard time, keep your brain from getting rusty."

"Great. She's got a talent for it. I'll give her that." I smiled at him. "Speaking of talent, did you ever consider a career in diplomacy?"

"I might, if my deal with the Red Sox doesn't work out." He shuffled his feet and looked inquiringly at me. "So Alix was really married to that guy?"

"Hard to believe, I know, but it was a long time ago."

"But she's in the clear, with the sheriff and everything."

"Yes. And that's just about all we know."

"But we could investigate . . ."

"That's what Minnie wants, and probably Bianca. If the book club gets into it, it'd be great publicity for Thornton's, but," I paused, unsure just how to say the next part, "well, Alix is pretty embarrassed about ever having been associated with him and she's hoping . . ."

". . . that everybody in town doesn't have to know about it, too." Tyler finished my sentence and gave me a wry look. He knew all about trying to keep embarrassing family history private, given his mother's continuing trouble with drugs and alcohol. "I'm cool with that."

"Good. So let's hope that, for once, Arnie can actually do his job."

"What are the odds?"

"I know, but for now, Alix wants us to let it rest. Okay?" I motioned for him to join me in the cushioned chairs in the bay window. "It's been a long day."

"It sure has," he agreed. "You up for one more problem?"

"As long as you don't pull a Bianca and snap if I can't solve it instantly." I was relieved to see that my mild joke provoked at least the ghost of a smile.

"Check. No snapping." He leaned forward and hesitated. At length his mouth settled into a grim line and he began. "There's one thing. You have to promise you won't tell my parents."

Uh-oh. Not a good start. I answered carefully. "I'd like to say okay, but it depends. Are you in trouble? If it's something they need to be aware of . . ."

"I knew you'd say that."

"Well, then . . ." The silence stretched for several minutes while he made his decision.

When Tyler finally spoke, his words caught me flat-footed. "I don't want to go back."

"To Nevada? I thought it'd been settled you'd stay here through high school."

"It's Mom. Now she's been clean a couple of months, she wants me back."

"I see." My heart ached for this nice kid. How he'd turned out so well after spending the first fifteen years of his life with his screwy parents was beyond me. I was just grateful that he'd found a good home here in Juniper.

"No, you don't. You're a parent. You probably think my parents should decide, but Dad's halfway around the world and Mom's . . . well, she's still Mom. I'm not going back."

"I can't believe . . . why, your grandfather loves having you here." My words came faster as I thought through the situation. "Is that what's worrying you? Laurence won't let you go, not if you don't want to. Besides, you're old enough to have a voice in this."

"You still don't understand. I think there's something wrong with Grandpa. He's getting senile, or he's got Alzheimer's or something."

"Laurence?" I felt like laughing at the very idea, but there was no mistaking the genuine fear etched on Tyler's face. "He's one of the sharpest eighty-year-old men you'll ever find."

"That's what I thought, but you don't know what he's been doing lately. If Mom gets even a hint that he's losing it . . ."

"You're getting way ahead of yourself. Let's back up and go through this one step at a time." I stood up, relieved that the problem appeared to be a simple matter of reassurance. "Know what? There's some Coke in the office fridge and I could use some tea while you tell me why you think your grandfather is 'losing it.' " As I casually made my way back to the office, Tyler dogged my steps, his words coming fast now that he had decided to talk.

"Grandpa's started acting weird over the last few weeks. Maybe he had a little stroke or something, I don't know. All of a sudden, he's different. He grabs the phone before I can get to it, acts all sneaky and stuff, like today. And he's starting to fill a drawer with those dumb sweepstakes entries. He never did that before, and he's trying to keep me from seeing them."

"Lots of people like entering those sweepstakes. It can be harmless." Even as I said it, I remembered Dr. McCutcheon's warning that a senior's sudden preoccupation with sweepstakes entries sometimes masked a larger problem. "Sure you're not letting your imagination run away with you after hearing that talk? You know, blowing things out of proportion."

"I didn't imagine a phone call he got at home this morning. He closed the door and talked real low, but I could hear part of it, something about a meeting at ten. I didn't want him to think

I'd noticed anything, so I left real early to open the store. Soon's I got here, I called him about Mrs. Phillips's special order. *The Illustrated History of Wood Ducks* is out-of-print, but we can get it from the publisher for forty-nine-ninety-five. He told me to order it and not to bother him at home with any more fool questions."

"What's the problem?"

"Don't you see? By calling from the store, I let him know the coast was clear for his secret meeting. While we were talking, I set out the chairs for the SOS group. Then I locked up again, sneaked home, and followed him downtown. That's when you saw me."

"Ah, yes, for your mirror trick. Forget the career as a diplomat and go straight to the CIA. So he met someone downtown. I still don't see—"

"After you left, that man seemed to be threatening Grandpa, poking him in the chest even. That's when I got scared and came out of the alley." Tyler clenched his fists as he recounted his movements, but then his shoulders slumped. "The guy saw me coming and all of a sudden he made tracks down the sidewalk the other way. Grandpa turned toward me before I could jump back into the alley. He wanted to know what I was doing downtown when I was supposed to be opening the bookstore. Told me he wasn't paying me to be irresponsible, stuff like that." Tyler chucked the empty Coke can with unnecessary force into the recycle box. "I couldn't tell him what I was really doing, so I just let him think I was goofing off."

"That must have hurt, not to be able to set him straight."

"It didn't feel great, but that wasn't what was so bad. When I asked him why he was downtown, know what he said? That he needed cough drops. Then he patted his pocket, but I knew he hadn't gone anywhere near a store. He looked—I don't know how to describe it . . ."

"Guilty?"

"Yeah, that's it. Reminded me of the way he acted when he was hiding cigarettes from us last year."

"And it took a heart attack to get him to quit them." Uneasy, I remembered that strokes were also linked with long-term smoking. Could that be what had happened to Laurence?

Tyler nodded and went on. "Anyway, since he'd already lied to me once, I went ahead and asked who he'd been talking to on the street, just to see what he'd say." The look on Tyler's face telegraphed his message before he got the words out. "He told me I must be seeing things, said that he hadn't talked to anyone. Now do you see why I'm worried?"

"Oh, Tyler, I'm so sorry." If Tyler was imagining that meeting, then so was I.

CHAPTER 11

Following our talk, Tyler seemed to relax a bit. In fact, he was so much more comfortable that I risked a joke about his harem returning to Thornton's tomorrow for more filming. His half-smothered chuckle told me that his spirits were well on their way to recovery. He'd watch his grandfather carefully, looking for more clues that might help us figure out what the old man was up to, while I'd go home and surf the 'Net for articles on Alzheimer's and senility. We'd talk again tomorrow at Thornton's. Though voicing his fears had calmed Tyler, I now had a knot in the pit of my stomach. I couldn't imagine what Laurence was doing. Cantankerous, yes, but he'd never shown a hint of mental trouble.

First Alix, and now Laurence. I needed help, and not the fanciful kind the Murder of the Month group offered. I needed Nick, solid, dependable . . . and totally out of range until he finished up with his inconvenient client. After months of dithering, why did Joe Arganno choose this particular week to show such an interest in settling his case? His family had owned that mountain for years. It wasn't as though the timber on it would walk away.

On impulse I pulled into the crowded parking lot of Donnelly's Country Market, choosing the smaller, more expensive store because it carried Nick's favorite asiago bread. After threading my way through the narrow aisles, I found only one loaf in the wicker bin. Probably Nick wouldn't be back tonight, but I snatched it up anyway. It would hold until tomorrow. Surely Nick would be back by then. I moved on to select New York steaks and portabella mushrooms. Into the cart went three kinds of lettuce, a perfectly ripe Bosc pear, and Danish bleu cheese to top the salad. After the merest hesitation, I also snagged a bottle of Brunello di Montalcino. In for a penny, out for thirty bucks. Imagining Nick's raised eyebrows when he saw the wine, I smiled. Something as uncomplicated as shopping for dinner was just what I needed. I rolled my shoulders a few times and felt the tension ease as I waited in the checkout line.

Once at home, I dumped the sacks on the counter and saw the message light blinking on my answering machine.

Nick's disappointed voice came in bits and pieces. "I climbed a damned mountain . . . get signal, but you're . . . and reception's . . . Got to . . ."

The line went dead. The call had come in only ten minutes earlier. Why hadn't he called my cell instead? I dug in my bag. No phone. It was only then I remembered leaving it on the passenger seat while I'd been shopping. Rushing back to the car, I grabbed the cell, but all that showed was one missed call. With sinking hope, I tried the number as I returned to the kitchen. The caller was now unavailable.

I stuffed the groceries haphazardly into the refrigerator, all interest in dinner gone. Leaning wearily against the adjacent counter, I reviewed the situation. If I'd been in a better mood, I might have found it amusing that, for once, it was Nick breaking a date, but the truth was that I'd come to depend on him more than I realized. If he felt the same way about me, as it appeared he did, no wonder he'd been upset when I'd broken several dates, the most recent last week.

That evening hadn't started well. Instead of showing up at Nick's for dinner, as planned, I'd been on the road between Juniper and Prineville after Bianca's bicycle chain had snapped.

Not wanting to make my daughter ride all those miles in the dark, I jumped in the car to pick her up. Besides, Wendell's black fur wouldn't have shown up at night. No, it simply had been too dangerous to leave them to find their own way home. I'd still have arrived at Nick's house on time if a hay truck hadn't overturned and closed the highway on our return trip.

While Bianca, Wendell, and I had waited for the road to be cleared, I determined to get a cell phone the next day, as Nick had been urging me to do. I simply hadn't gotten around to it. Bianca refused to carry one because she worried about throwaway electronics polluting the environment. Wendell didn't express an opinion, but I was sure he agreed with me that anyone who didn't carry a cell might consider carrying a spare bicycle chain.

When I'd finally rushed in Nick's door at nine that night, a single glance illuminated the magnitude of my *faux pas*. A crisp white tablecloth, its creases fresh from the package, graced what I assumed was Nick's battered relic of a card table. It usually sported fishing lures, half-eaten bowls of Grape-Nuts, and copies of *Northwest Fly Fishing* magazine, but never before a tablecloth. Wax from two half-consumed crimson tapers threatened the snowy cloth while giving mute evidence of my tardiness. Nick hadn't bothered turning from his position at the sink at my arrival. He continued washing dishes, his stiff posture making my apology all the more awkward.

"I'm so sorry. You didn't tell me you were making a special meal. I thought we were grabbing burgers."

Nick finally turned around. "Which of your friends needed you this time?" When I couldn't conceal a flash of annoyance, Nick turned back to the sink. "Thought so."

"It wasn't like that. Well, yes, Bianca's bicycle chain broke and I went to pick her up, but I'd have been back if a hay truck hadn't overturned." I came up behind him and wound my arms around his waist. "They closed the highway for two hours. I'm really sorry," I said into the back of his shirt, "and very hungry."

"You should've called."

"I'm getting a cell phone first thing tomorrow."

He turned around and gathered me into his arms. "Excellent idea."

"Is there any food left?"

He laughed. "Okay, but only because you're finally getting that cell phone."

The trout almandine was dried out, the rice lumpy, and the salad had that funny smell that told me he'd dumped it straight from the package, but the evening had turned out fine.

Now I glared at my new, and currently useless, cell phone. "Okay, Nick, I got the cell phone as promised, but you have to stay within range if it's going to do us any good."

Meanwhile, with Nick stuck somewhere on a mountain helping a client, I'd better keep my promise to do some research for Tyler.

Was he right about his grandfather? I didn't know much about senility, but I had my computer and an empty evening to educate myself. A bowl of Quaker Oatmeal Squares would do for dinner.

Again, my thoughts strayed to Nick, who liked both Laurence and Tyler. He'd have been as upset at the potential problem Tyler had outlined as I was. No doubt about it, I liked having him around, and not just because of the way his presence heated my blood. His steady good sense also made him a comforting presence at all times, whether or not there were problems to be solved.

Surely he'd be back tomorrow. Tomorrow night would be soon enough to make good use of the food and wine I'd purchased. This time, he'd been the one answering a call for help. Though I wanted him here with me, I was glad he was someone who went out of his way for others. My turn would come soon enough.

As I googled for information to help Tyler, my thoughts kept straying to Nick. I frowned when it occurred to me that he might not get back tomorrow. His garbled message hadn't been clear. I paused in my research to make a cup of Tazo chamomile tea. As I waited for the water to boil, I considered the question. The answer came to me just as the kettle whistled. Tomorrow I was scheduled to work at Thornton's. If I hadn't heard from Nick by tomorrow night, I'd try another idea.

Nick loved fly fishing more than anything. I'd leave a note on his door and a message on his answering machine suggesting that everything was all right here, but that I'd be very busy the next day. With that kind of encouragement to make other plans, I knew he'd make a beeline for the nearest stream if he returned to Juniper late. I'd show up unannounced at his house with a picnic lunch and an offer to go with him.

I returned with renewed energy to my computer research. If he came home tomorrow, we'd have the fancy dinner here. If not, I'd go to the backup plan. As I sipped my tea, I almost hoped he wouldn't come back tomorrow. It was more fun to anticipate his surprise at seeing me at dawn the next day, since I'd never shown any interest in fly fishing. First thing in the morning, I'd have to find out where to buy a fishing license.

CHAPTER 12

Though Laurence and Tyler arrived at Thornton's together the next morning, I heard none of the usual banter between them. At my questioning look, Tyler merely shrugged his shoulders. With Laurence in the room, I couldn't talk to Tyler about my Internet research, so I merely asked him to wash the display windows and went on restocking the shelves containing nature literature. It seemed that Juniper's tourists this month wanted to read about cougar attacks, though most people didn't stray more than fifty feet from the nearest restaurant when they visited.

Hunter Blackburn's murder again dominated the front page of today's *Journal*. As expected, today's lead featured the unwelcome information that the murdered man had "once been married to local wedding consultant Alix Boudreau, who was cooperating with authorities." I'd known Arnie would leak that tidbit to the press. Somehow, it was worse seeing it in print. I could only imagine how it would deflate Alix to read this very public statement of something she'd spent years hiding.

From past experience, I knew that the hordes would soon descend on Thornton's in search of true-crime fiction so they could scare themselves vicariously about something other than cougars for a while. Predictably, a couple of letters to the editor had already voiced requests for the Murder of the Month Book Club to step up and find the killer, since the Russell County Sheriff's Department hadn't yet done the job. For once I felt a flash of sympathy for Arnie. It had only been a couple of days. I recognized one of the letter-writers as a woman who had been crushed that we hadn't opened up membership to the book club, in spite of her entreaties. We'd imposed a blanket hold on adding new members, keeping it to the original five of us in self-defense after having been deluged with bizarre membership requests from all kinds of lunatics after we solved last year's murder. People just refused to believe that we gathered simply for the pleasure of reading mysteries, not to solve actual crimes. Well, Alix and I did, anyway. Minnie, Tyler, and Bianca were a different story. The woman who'd driven all the way from Burns swathed in black netting and carrying a caged bat had made the decision to close membership easy.

Most of the disappointed locals had contented themselves with coming to Thornton's, asking me to retell the story, and then leaving with an armload of books. I hoped Tyler's website might deflect a few more from directly pleading to be admitted to the club, but this latest murder was certain to stir things up again. My call to Alix this morning had confirmed that she'd heard nothing further from Arnie, which was reassuring. The fact that he hadn't returned to harass her further suggested that he somehow had stumbled upon another lead. Hard to believe, but I wished him success in following it up.

Laurence stood in the center of the room and studied the wall clock behind the counter. Its ticking provided the only sound other than the thumps as Tyler removed the bestsellers from the window shelves. Normally, I didn't even notice the sound of the clock, but now it started to get on my nerves.

After I'd emptied the last box and straightened, Laurence was still rooted in place, staring at the clock.

I frowned. "Are you waiting for something?"

"What makes you think that? Can't a man stand still for a minute without someone jumping at him?"

"Sorry." No point in antagonizing him at this point. "Say, do you feel up to working for me tomorrow? I'd like to—"

"Fine, fine." Laurence looked at Tyler on a ladder washing the bay windows and raised his voice. "I ran this place on my own before you came, and, by God, I can run it for one day without you now."

"Of course you can. I just didn't want to inconvenience—"

"About time I worked more, anyway. Can't sit around counting boards in the floor all the time, that's for sure."

A massive woman swathed in a maroon tent dress swept into the store and fixed a stern gaze on Laurence. "Antique bottles?"

He recoiled.

"How should I know? Ask her." He waved a bony arm in my direction and stomped off toward the office.

The woman advanced on me. "What a rude man. I thought he worked here."

"Mmm," I said. "Let me check the inventory. Tyler, you don't happen to . . . ?"

"Try hobbies."

An unearthly screech came from the back of the store, startling the customer. "What was that?"

"Back door needs oiling." I looked at Tyler as I spoke.

He jumped off the ladder and sprinted out the front door in an attempt to follow Laurence unobtrusively. No wonder Laurence had been staring at the clock. He was probably counting the minutes before another rendezvous.

The customer stared after him. "What a strange store. Do you have a book on antique bottles, or don't you?"

"I'm checking." I returned my attention to the computer screen.

"Oh, never mind. I don't have all day." As grandly as she had entered, the woman swept back out the door without a backward glance. So much for that sale.

Another screech from the back door. Maybe Laurence hadn't been sneaking off, after all. I scrawled "WD-40" on a Post-It note and waited for him to appear. He didn't. I called out, "Laurence?" No answer.

The office appeared empty, but I checked behind the door anyway. Nothing there but an umbrella missing a couple of spokes. As I moved to toss it into the garbage, a whisper from the far side of the desk froze me in place.

"Are we alone?"

I lifted the useless umbrella in a defensive gesture before peering around the desk.

Velda Kubek crouched there. "Are we alone?" she repeated in the same urgent whisper. At my nod, she stood up and leaned toward me. "I need to talk to you." Her breathing was rapid, as though she'd been running. "About Alice Durand."

"Alice? Is she all right?"

"Far's I know," she whispered, "but—"

"You can speak up. No one else is here."

"Oh, sorry." Velda bent her head like a schoolgirl being chastised.

"Nothing to be sorry for." I suppressed a flash of annoyance. Velda meant well, but she was so sensitive that it was hard to avoid hurting her feelings. "Please, go on."

Though she continued to look uncertain, she finally spoke up. "Alice has been acting very odd. You must have noticed yesterday."

I thought back to Alice's tart exchange with our guest speaker at the SOS meeting. Abrupt, discourteous perhaps, but that was Alice. "Well, she's—"

"So I knew you'd want me to follow her."

"I'd want you to . . . why would I want that?"

"Because she was acting strange," Velda said patiently. "And then you left, so it was clear that you couldn't follow Alice

106

yourself." Her voice returned to a whisper, but gained in intensity as, once more, she leaned close. "Your book club? The murder? I can put two and two together." She folded her hands before her as though in prayer and waited for my response, her eyes bright behind oversized glasses. I was still trying to make sense of her logic when she burst out, "I know you aren't adding new members, but I thought if I could find out what Alice was up to . . ."

Oh, no. Another Minnie Salter in the making. Velda was twenty years younger and a few pounds lighter than Minnie, but they both might as well have the words "Please, Let Me Help" tattooed on their earnestly furrowed foreheads. Unfortunately, taking care of Velda's Aunt Eleanor or providing refreshments at an SOS meeting required slightly different skills than those needed for catching a murderer.

I cleared my throat and tried to let her down easily. "Our book club isn't actually—"

"With another murderer on the loose? With the sheriff actually consulting Alix, one of your charter club members, for help?"

I opened my mouth to set her straight, but closed it immediately. If she didn't quite understand why the sheriff had "consulted" Alix, I saw no reason to enlighten her. Velda continued. "Minnie hinted that the book club is an integral part of this investigation . . . and you're not just reading about murder."

At my startled look, she nodded. Velda Kubek, Private Eye, was on the case, and now that she had started, she could hardly wait to tell me about her prime suspect: poor, overworked Alice Durand.

"Did you notice how Alice got all red in the face when Dr. McCutcheon described confidence men? She was mad!"

Velda's cheeks were pink, her expression more animated than

I'd ever seen it. No doubt about it. This was a confirmed Minnie clone.

I tried to slow her avalanche of words. "Well, of course she was angry. Her father lost all his money to—"

"To a con man. Exactly! But what if it was the same man who just got himself murdered?"

A short laugh erupted before I could stop it. "Oh, Velda. How likely is that? He lost his money several years ago."

Velda bit her lip and blinked hard, crestfallen at my dismissal of her brilliant theory.

Fearing that she was about to cry, I tried to make amends. "Why don't you just tell me what you found?"

That did it. Like a newly watered daisy, she perked up. "After we finished cleaning up, I went looking for Alice downtown. Found her, too, at the First Credit Bank. Stroke of luck, that. Anyway, I hid behind one of those islands where you make out the deposit slips, and what do you think? The cashier counted out a whole bunch of money into Alice's hand, and I mean a whole bunch. She went from the bank to the post office, picked out one of those brown mailing envelopes they have, and mailed something. I couldn't exactly see, but what if it was the money? What if she was paying someone off?"

The sound of voices in the other room saved me from manufacturing a response that wouldn't hurt Velda's feelings further. "Someone's out front."

By the counter, we found Minnie and Bianca deep in conversation.

Minnie put up a hand to silence Bianca when she saw Velda and adopted her version of a poker face. "Hello, Velda. How's Eleanor today?"

"About the same. She does her best, but . . . well, she's getting weaker all the time. In fact, I need to get home to fix her lunch. Just came to town for some chicken broth." She glanced at me, then addressed Minnie again. "Actually, I came to offer my help."

"With what, dear?" Minnie asked. "The next SOS meeting isn't—"

"Not SOS. I want to help solve the murder. I was too embarrassed to ask before, but now I've found a lead."

Minnie squirmed.

Velda continued. "You said the sheriff's already asked for Alix's help."

"That's not the way I'd describe it," Bianca said. "They grilled her. They made a mountain out of a molehill."

"Oh, dear. How awful." Velda's rapt expression belied her words.

Glaring at Bianca, I cut in. "Look, Alix is fine. She's done her, uh, consulting, and now Arnie is following other leads. We all need to calm down."

"Mom, someone killed that man, and it wasn't Alix," Bianca said. "But Arnie doesn't like Alix. Do you honestly think he'll look for another suspect? He's too lazy."

"That's just it," Velda said proudly. "I found one. Another suspect, I mean."

I watched helplessly as Minnie and Bianca looked at each other and nodded. Apparently Velda was in, whether she was a card-carrying member of the Murder of the Month Book Club or not. And, like Bianca and Minnie, apparently she was in with the same mistaken belief that membership suddenly granted her super-sleuth powers.

Velda quivered like a bird dog on point. "Yesterday at the SOS meeting, it occurred to me that various members of this group had previously been victimized by a con man. They might hold a grudge. I started looking around."

"My thoughts exactly," Minnie said.

Birds of a feather, I thought. Or perhaps birdbrains of a feather.

"The nervousness, avoidance of eye contact—"

"It was the anger I spotted," Velda said. "That's why I followed her."

"You mean 'them,' " Minnie corrected.

Velda shook her head. "Alice was alone."

"Why were you following Alice? It was Phil and Eileen Hedstrom who needed to be tailed."

"But Alice mailed cash," Velda insisted.

"Please stop," I said. "We were sitting right here yesterday with a group of nice people, and all of a sudden you're thinking one of them—"

"Or maybe more than one," Bianca interjected.

Et tu, Brute? I thought. "Okay . . . one or more of them murdered some perfect stranger? Do you think everyone in the SOS group is a murderer?"

Silence. I thought for one thrilling moment that logic had prevailed.

Then Minnie gave me a disapproving look, as though I'd belched at the dinner table, before she cranked it up again. "That's just plain silly. Of course they're not all murderers. Just one . . . or two . . . of them."

"What do you have against Phil and Eileen?" I asked. Unlikely though it was that Minnie's answer would make any sense, I might as well try.

"Oh, that's right. You'd left by the time people were looking at the newspaper. No wonder you didn't understand. Phil and Eileen were studying the front page—you know, with the article about the murdered man possibly being involved with elder fraud—when all of a sudden they just up and left. Not a word to anyone. They looked positively grim. How do you explain that?"

"Maybe they had an appointment or indigestion or—"

"Don't be ridiculous. No one ever got indigestion from eating my pound cake," Minnie said stiffly. She narrowed her eyes. "I think when they read that article, they discovered they'd left a clue at the scene. That's what I think."

"But Alice looked so guilty," Velda said.

"You might be right," Minnie said. "Hard to tell at this point. We'll need to spread out and multiply our coverage. I'll take the Hedstroms. Can you follow Alice again, Velda?"

Velda's face glowed. "I need to fix Aunt Eleanor's lunch first, but I'll get Maria to stay with her during her nap."

I half-expected Bianca to chime in with an offer to follow Dr. McCutcheon, but she had something else on her mind. "I'm supposed to meet Ty downtown. He wanted to talk to me about something, but he didn't say what. Maybe he has another suspect. We can all check in with you here, Mom."

"Roger that."

No one picked up on my sarcasm. Judging from the shine in Velda's eyes, she hadn't had this much fun in years. I already knew of the special talent the rest of my fellow Murder of the Month Book Club members showed for getting into trouble.

Since I couldn't order this suddenly expanded group to behave sensibly, it was time for me to step out of their way. Maybe if they shadowed perfectly ordinary people for a while, they'd feel useful but wouldn't interfere with the official investigation, such as it was. This silliness was bound to blow itself out sooner rather than later, but I wouldn't hold my breath until it did.

"Now, about tomorrow . . ." Minnie said.

I stopped her. "Sorry. You'll have to use your new cell phones to rendezvous then. I'm going fishing."

CHAPTER 13

When I hadn't heard from Nick by the end of the day, I left a note on his door and a message on his home phone as I had planned. With an anticipatory smile, I ignored his return message on my machine that night telling me that he was on his way back to Juniper, but he'd arrive too late to call. Then I went to bed, hoping my favorite fish would take the bait.

I timed it perfectly. The pre-dawn darkness hadn't yet begun to lift when I pulled up in front of Nick's house, but his living room lights were on. Several moments later the front door opened, silhouetting Nick briefly against the light. I'd guessed right. He was carrying a backpack, creel, and net.

As the house went dark, I stepped from my darkened car across the street and spoke in a low tone as he approached his Jeep. "Nick."

I could barely make out the oval of his face as he turned. "Jane? What are you doing here? You said you were going to be busy today."

"I was. I am. Going fishing with you . . . I hope."

A dog barked over on the next block as Nick turned this development over in his mind. I held out the fragrant sack still warm from the Do-Nut-Forget-Me Bakery, where I'd been the first customer this morning. I moved closer, letting the aroma of cinnamon fill the air.

Slowly, Nick reached into the bag and brought out his prize. "Apple fritters?"

"First batch of the day."

"Oh."

Without another word he unslung the pack from his shoulder and stowed his gear in back. Only then did he lean against the fender, arms crossed over his chest.

The early morning chill wasn't the only thing giving me goose bumps. I took a deep breath and plunged in. "You were right. I haven't been careful to make time for you, for us, lately. Sometimes I get caught up with other people and their problems and . . . well, I'm sorry. If you'd rather go fishing by yourself . . ."

"Well, a gift of warm apple fritters makes me glad to have company." Nick pushed away from the car and uncrossed his arms. "Let me get this straight. Your idea of fun has suddenly become fishing the Metolius at dawn?"

"Why else would I be here at this beastly hour?" I leaned a half step closer to him, drinking in the fresh smell of his skin. "Fishing is my life."

"And all this time you've hidden your passion for the sport so well." He pulled me into his arms. "Didn't you once say any sport that required getting up before sunrise was barbaric?"

"You must have misunderstood me," I murmured against his chest.

"You don't even have a license," he said.

"I do, too." It was hard to concentrate while he was nuzzling my neck, but I managed to squeeze out the words. "Since yesterday afternoon." Could he feel the pulse hammering in my throat?

"Pretty sure of yourself, weren't you?" Rhetorical question.

He kissed me before I could answer. My arms wound around his neck and the morning chill ceased to be a problem.

Eventually, I broke away to regain my bearings. What had Nick just asked? Oh yes. I dragged air into my lungs and tried for a casual tone of voice. "I wasn't sure of myself at all. That's where the apple fritters came in. Also, I brought lunch."

Apparently I wasn't the only one finding it hard to refocus my attention. It took Nick a minute to adjust to the change of subject. He finally said, "Lunch? So did I. Kipper snacks."

"You might want to take me along. I brought more than that." I held out my new cell phone for inspection. "See this? It's magic. I hit the 'off' button, the screen goes dark, and we have the day to ourselves. Alix is fine, Bianca is fine. No interruptions. Okay?"

Nick's smile left no doubt about his opinion. "More than okay. Even beats apple fritters. Joe and Nellie Arganno should be squared away for now, but I'll need to check in with them this afternoon." He hauled out his own cell phone and turned it off before swinging open the passenger door. Bowing low, he said, "Meanwhile, your carriage awaits, milady."

As we left the dry terrain around Juniper and approached the country flanking the Metolius River, towering ponderosa pines and lush grass replaced the juniper and sagebrush. By mutual consent we agreed to lay aside the problems of others, at least for a few hours, and to enjoy the unexpected gift of the free day together. We dropped back into the easy relationship we'd enjoyed for the past six months, arguing amiably about books, politics, and philosophy as we drove. Underlying the conversation was my unspoken reaction to the trip Nick had suggested, but the emotional currents running between us left little doubt about my answer.

The hour's drive passed quickly, and we were soon carrying our gear along a grassy path by the river's edge. The water spun and danced past us, its surface catching the light of the rising sun in random flashes.

Nick raised his voice over the background song of the river. "Need help rigging up?"

I knew what he thought of women who couldn't manage

their own gear, so I just made a face at him. He moved closer, his intent look suggesting that he had more than trout on his mind.

The minute he came within reach, I smiled sweetly and handed over my fly rod. "Well, sure, since you're offering." I burst out laughing at his grimace. "C'mon, Nick. Get with the program. Lesson number one."

Lesson number one involved fitting the parts of the fly rod together and choosing a fly from Nick's extensive collection. I couldn't imagine that any fish would find these bits of thread and feathers attractive, but he was the expert. Lesson two taught me that casting wasn't nearly as easy as Nick made it seem. Lesson three involved a lot of untangling of my line from rocks in the river, branches overhead, and even from the scarlet foliage of the Indian paintbrush nearby. Eventually, I set down my rod and strolled downstream along the riverbank, perching at last on a lichen-covered boulder for some solitary contemplation. The changing light brought the morning to life as the rising sun revealed an astonishing range of greens and golds in the surrounding meadows. No wonder artists loved to work with river scenes. Easy to see why Nick loved being here, too. I stretched out on the warm rock and dozed in the sunshine, rousing a few minutes later to the harsh sounds of blue jays in heated dispute over some tidbit.

"Haven't you guys heard about peace and tranquility?" They retreated a few feet at the sound of my voice, but resumed their argument there. "You win. It's lunchtime anyway." I dusted off my jeans and returned to the Jeep.

With excellent timing, Nick reappeared from fishing upstream just as I began unpacking the food. He didn't waste any time tucking into the thick roast beef and cheddar sandwich on sourdough bread I'd brought for him. The sandwich was laced with tomato slices and horseradish, just the way I knew he liked it. A chilled bottle of Deschutes Black Butte Porter, crisp dill pickles, Kettle Chips, and shortbread cookies rounded out the meal. He demolished every bite before pronouncing judgment. "Definitely a step up from my kipper snacks."

"Only one step up?"

"Maybe two."

Silence surrounded us. I couldn't remember the last time I'd spent a day this satisfying. Being with Nick felt right.

"Thank you," he said, "for the lunch, for wanting to come today. This is nice. Actually, it's a lot better than nice."

"My sentiments exactly. Thanks for the fishing lesson."

"Anytime." Nick settled back against a log before speaking again. "So, what kicked you into high gear today? Not that I'm complaining."

"It's pretty simple, when you get right down to it." I shrugged my shoulders. "When you broke our date yesterday, I didn't like it. The Argannos needed you and you went. Don't get me wrong. It's great that you rushed off to help them, but it's the first time the shoe's been on the other foot, with me waiting for you."

"So you finally figured out why I didn't like that role? After how many broken dates?"

"Don't remind me. I think maybe I've just fallen into the habit of saying yes whenever anyone asked for my help."

"And fishing today is going to change everything? You're not going to break a date every time Minnie loses her flour sifter?"

I tossed a sandwich wrapper at him. "Well, today's a start. Besides, Minnie probably has an extra flour sifter somewhere. I'll try to remember that."

"Don't beat up on yourself too much. I like the way you care about people who need your help, too, but I have to admit that I don't much favor coming in third or fourth . . . or whatever . . . on your list of priorities." Nick spoke quietly.

The dates I had broken in the past apparently had reminded him of his ex-wife. He and Amanda had divorced eighteen years ago. Their marriage had failed when Amanda's public relations career proved more interesting than Nick and their twin sons, Pete and Theo. Amanda had moved alone to Chicago, leaving Nick to cope with the boys as best he could.

"You're high on my list, Nick. It's just not always that easy to make choices. If your sons lived here instead of Santa Monica, you'd have more of these same conflicts."

"Probably so, but I don't have friends who routinely get tangled up in murder investigations."

"Just twice," I joked.

"In less than a year," he reminded me gently. We both laughed, but then Nick took my hands and turned serious again. "Look, Jane, I'd like some idea of where this relationship is going."

"I thought I'd made that clear . . ." I let my voice trail off, but he didn't pick up the thread, so I finished with a playful question, ". . . or was that someone else in the driveway this morning?"

"I was there, but were you? Every time I think we're getting closer, you pull away." He put up a hand to forestall my denial. "I'm not imagining things. It's happened more than once, and I can't help wondering—"

"What? You think I'm just playing a game? Give me some credit." I couldn't see the problem.

"Sometimes I think I'm competing with a ghost. I understand that you had a happy marriage. I'm glad you did, but Tony died two years ago. Sometimes I wonder whether you think you're still married to him."

I was stunned. "You really wonder that? It's . . . it's absurd."

"Is it? You know I didn't move to Juniper for the fishing. It's been six months and, frankly, I thought we'd have a lot more settled between us by now."

"Well, I'm here today. Doesn't that count for something? I had no idea—"

The rest of my words disappeared into Nick's shirt as he crushed me to him in a fierce embrace. His words came hesitantly. "It's just . . . I don't know what to think and it's driving me crazy. I don't know if it's Tony . . . or if you're using your friends as a shield to keep me at arms' length—"

From my safe haven against his wool shirt, I felt hope stir. "If that's what I'm trying to do, it isn't working very well."

His shaky laugh reassured me. "No, but that's okay with me."

We stood locked together in silence until he abruptly pulled back, dropping his hands to his sides.

He took a deep breath and blew it out. "Sorry, but I can't think very well when you're that close to me."

I smiled. "Good."

"I think we need time together . . . uninterrupted time . . . to get things clear between us."

"The trip to the beach?" Leaning forward, I put as much warmth into my words as possible. "Completely away from everything, just the two of us? Sounds perfect."

Nick's smile lit up his whole face. "Then what are we waiting for?" He let me go and started powering up his cell phone as he spoke. "As soon as I check that the Argannos are still okay, I'm free. We can be at the coast . . ." His voice trailed off as he listened to his messages.

I busied myself clearing up the remains of our picnic lunch, scattering a few random crumbs for the blue jays. Just then, I wanted everyone to be as happy as I was. I was sure Tyler would cover for me at Thornton's. Things were starting to shape up. It was only when I caught a glimpse of Nick's expression that I sensed trouble brewing.

"What's wrong?" I whispered.

He snapped the phone closed. "Those crooks. They're moving equipment into the woods right now, getting ready to cut the timber, in spite of the restraining order. Joe sounded frantic."

"Can't you call the law on them?"

He nodded grimly. "Can and will." He shook his head as he thought it through. "Handling something like this long-distance is a pain. The timber could be long gone by the time I get through to the right people." He looked at his watch and then ran a hand through his hair, frustration etched on his brow.

I jumped in. "Let's head home now. You can get back to Joe and Nellie tonight."

"I should've known those jokers would try an end run." Nick was deep into planning counter strategy already.

I handed him the pack. "Here, carry this. You need to get over there. If nothing else, your presence will reassure Joe and Nellie. How'd you like to be their age, in a fix like this and managing on their own? Remember how I said before how much I like it that you're a nice guy? So, go do your white knight thing. Impress me."

Nick smiled ruefully as we tumbled back into the Jeep. "Well, if it'll impress you, then I'm definitely going. Rain check on the trip?"

"You got it."

CHAPTER 14

Only after Nick dropped me at home and went rushing off to rescue his elderly clients did I think to check my own phone messages. I'd been planning to jump into the shower, but Alix's message changed all that.

"Jane, could you come to the Wedding Belle this afternoon?" A good ten seconds of silence followed before Alix spoke again. "We need to talk."

I listened twice. Unremarkable words, certainly, but the underlying tension in her voice struck like a hammer blow. I punched in her number, but it went straight to voicemail.

The message had arrived only an hour ago, at one o'clock, so I simply grabbed the car keys and ran back out the door. The same annoying door chimes announced my disheveled arrival at the Wedding Belle to . . . nothing unusual. I scanned the cozy room, seeking a clue to the reason for Alix's call, which had brought me flying over here. I hadn't imagined the distress underlying her words. Mozart provided background music; the scent of jasmine perfumed the air. Had I been planning a wedding, the ambiance would have been charming, but the tranquility of this room didn't square with that tension. No blood, no fire, no shrieks of pain.

Instead, I encountered Bianca coming from the hall. "Thank goodness, you're back." She tried to pull me toward Alix's bedroom without another word.

I balked. "Bianca, has something happened?"

120

"I don't know. It's Alix." She gestured toward the closed bedroom door. "She's been in there for an hour, ever since I got back. I'm really worried because that's not like her at all."

"Okay, take a deep breath."

"Maybe she's sick," Bianca whispered.

The bedroom door opened and Alix appeared, her face a mask. "It's okay, Bianca. I'm not sick, just resting. Have fun today, Jane?"

"Yes, great time. Beautiful day to be out." I made no mention of the voicemail.

"So, you're really all right?" Bianca's elation lighted her face. "I didn't know what to think." In her relief, Bianca waved her arms, dislodging a photo of cherry blossoms behind her and catching it just before it crashed to the floor. "Sorry, sorry," she said. She straightened it carefully.

"No problem," Alix said, her quiet words standing in marked contrast to Bianca's agitation. "Would you mind bringing some iced tea? You'll find sugar . . ."

"Sugar's not good for you." Relieved, Bianca's protest was automatic and playful.

"Please," Alix said.

Bianca raised her hands in mock surrender and gave a brilliant smile. "I'll bring the tea and the sugar." She whirled away toward the kitchen.

I stared at her retreating back. "How'd you do that? No argument."

"I'm not her mother."

"Yeah, well . . . want the job?"

"Not a chance. Being a friend is easier than being a mother."

"Depends on the friend," I responded.

"*Touché.*" My zinger had hit home. "I know you're my friend, but I hesitate to involve you in the mess I've made for myself. Please don't think I'm ungrateful, but it's just that I don't want

121

to bother anyone else."

"You aren't bothering me, Alix."

She looked uncertain.

I watched as she prowled the room like a caged tiger, looking at everything but me. At length, she pushed aside the curtains swathing the leaded glass front window and looked out. The ball was squarely in her court, but how long should I wait? Perhaps the fact that she kept her back turned to me was supposed to be a clue. I shifted my feet, uncertain what she wanted of me. Come here, go away, come here, go away.

"Don't go, please." Alix's words were low and choked.

At first, I wasn't sure I'd even heard them right, but when she turned, her face was slick with tears. Difficult to imagine the cool and cynical Alix in this state. As I moved to comfort her, Bianca reappeared.

"I put sprigs of fresh mint into our tea." Intent on balancing three tinkling glasses on a tray while simultaneously avoiding Wendell who was plastered to her side, no doubt hoping the tray also contained cookies, Bianca didn't look up as she entered the room.

Alix shot me one anguished glance before moving rapidly toward the bathroom, but she'd made her point. She didn't want Bianca to hear whatever it was she'd been about to say.

Bianca offered me a chilled glass. "I'm glad things are all right. Alix's hands were shaking something awful earlier. Then she disappeared into her room. What do you think happened?"

I shrugged my shoulders. "Guess she really needed that rest."

Bianca concentrated. "She probably hadn't slept much the night before. You know, I'd want to talk about it if I'd been pulled in and questioned by the sheriff. Wouldn't you? I mean, I'd feel a lot better to talk it all out. Alix is different about stuff like that."

"She's led a pretty solitary life. She's used to depending on herself." We sipped our tea in silence, but Alix didn't return. I wondered whether she was waiting for me to get rid of Bianca, so we could talk privately.

Bianca showed no signs of going anywhere as she settled back on the couch.

"She doesn't have to do that anymore. Now, she's got us."

"Right, but she might need some time to get used to the idea."

"Guess we'll just have to wait," Bianca said. "So, how long do you think it'll take?"

When I merely shrugged my shoulders, she switched topics. "So, your fishing trip went okay?"

"No fish, but fun, until Nick got a call and had to go back to Marion County."

"Nick broke a date with you? That's a switch. How'd you like that?" Bianca was a big fan of my relationship with Nick.

"I didn't, but then he didn't exactly break it. He just had to go to work." Bianca's intense scrutiny caused me to color slightly.

"That's too bad." Bianca finished her tea and plunked the glass onto the tray. "How long do you think Alix'll be in the bathroom?"

Inspiration struck. "I don't know, but maybe I can stay here while you help with something else. Tyler told you about Laurence, right?" At her nod, I improvised. "I told him I'd help him, but if Alix wants to talk . . ."

"I could go over to Thornton's, help Ty keep an eye on Laurence."

I pounced. "Great idea. Maybe you could even get Tyler out of there, give them some time apart."

"I haven't been over there yet today, with everything going on here." Bianca waved a hand in the direction of the bathroom, but the door remained closed. "Okay, I'll go. Ty's really worried, so I'll see what I can do there. Call if you need me. Come on, Wendell."

The minute the door closed behind Bianca and Wendell, Alix emerged. "Thanks."

Only a slight redness around the eyes gave away the recent tears. She was carrying a pack of cigarettes.

"Let's talk out back."

"I thought you were quitting."

"Not this week."

Alix led the way through French doors to the brick-walled courtyard beyond. The romantic décor of the interior was reflected out here in a ceramic Cupid fountain and wrought iron benches.

Alix lit a cigarette, drew deeply, and circled the fountain as though looking for an exit. The sight and sound of water cascading from Cupid's hand into the basin below should have been soothing, but it apparently wasn't having any such effect on Alix.

After watching her do silent laps for a while, I decided to open the conversation myself. "You're not exactly the chintz and lace type, so how'd you get into the wedding business?"

"You really want to talk about that?"

"Beats watching you pace and smoke."

She sank onto the bench across from me and looked at the cigarette as though she'd forgotten she was holding it. "Sorry. Just trying to think . . ."

"Yesterday you weren't worried. Today you're crying in the bathroom."

She nodded, but didn't look at me.

"I've been thinking about the money." She traced the pattern on the iron railing of her bench, talking in such a low voice that I couldn't tell whether she actually wanted me to hear the words. "I hope they won't find out about it, but . . . well, there's sort of a connection . . . to Hunter."

"What are you talking about?" I leaned forward. "What connection?"

She finally looked at me and grimaced. "A bank account. It'll look bad." Now that Alix had finally started talking, her words poured out. "I didn't say anything before, but the more I got to thinking about it, the more I'm afraid the police will find it and think . . . they'll wonder about my deposits."

"They're not the only ones." My astonishment was complete. "What on earth—"

"It was an old account. It belonged to his grandmother, Irene Cook, in Redmond. I didn't think he even remembered it."

Now it was my turn to stand and pace.

"I can explain."

I gripped the back of the bench. "I hope so. You scared Bianca by hiding out in your room, and all of a sudden you don't want to say a word in front of her. You say we have to talk and then you bring up people and bank accounts I know nothing about. None of this makes any sense. Please level with me . . . that is, if you want my help."

Alix bowed her head. Then she drew a breath. "I do. I need your help." She exhaled.

"I've paid Irene Cook's bills for years, but she doesn't know it. She thinks . . . thought . . . she never had any idea what her grandson was really like. At first, I didn't know that he was stealing from her, but I'd have a hard time proving that. He told me . . . well, it doesn't matter. Back then, I believed whatever he said. By the time I learned better, her cash was gone, and so was he. I've been putting money into her account ever since."

I had a flash of understanding. "You felt responsible. But you were just a kid. You were eighteen and he was . . . ?"

"Thirty. Took me two years to understand what he was like, and another to get him officially out of my life." Alix looked down at her hands. "I should have done better by her. She was a nice lady."

"You did better by her than her own grandson. Isn't that good enough? And why don't you want Bianca to know? She'd sympathize."

"I know Bianca means well, and I don't mean to insult her, but . . ."

"But she's a little excitable," I finished.

I had to strain to make out her next words. "And I like having her look up to me. But I was so foolish about Hunter."

"You were young, Alix!"

The ringing of the telephone interrupted her response. Alix jumped up to answer it, welcoming the opportunity to escape. How embarrassing she must find it to be caught having a human emotion.

Her beauty, intelligence, and skill as a businesswoman were undeniable, so it wasn't hard to see why Bianca had been drawn to her. We'd always passed off Alix's comments about the uselessness of men as lighthearted banter. But today, I'd pushed her to drop her self-reliant facade. She must be terrified, or she'd never have confided in me. Well, she should be scared, with the skeleton of Hunter Blackburn rattling around in her closet. I'd implied I could help. But what could I do?

I wandered back into the room through the French doors and marveled as Alix calmly discussed flower arrangements with the person who had called. What amazing self-control. It illuminated the determination she had shown in rebuilding her life after the disaster she'd faced at eighteen. I was proud to be her friend.

When the conversation ended, Alix turned to me and spoke in a completely different tone of voice. "You're not going to like this, but there's more, and it's not ancient history. The day he died, I just wanted him to leave Irene alone and get out of town. That's the reason I met him, argued with him that afternoon." She hesitated for a long time before finishing. "I also deposited three thousand dollars in Irene's checking account later. Arnie might somehow trace that. If he does, I'll look like Hunter's accomplice."

"So? You'd been doing that for years."

Alix hurried on, pleading with me to understand. "He tried to shake me down, as usual, but . . ."

"Oh, no. You didn't pay him this time, did you? The paper said they found a lot of money on him."

"No. Turns out he didn't need my money this time. When I said no, he laughed and told me it didn't matter. Then he bragged that he'd already used Irene's debit card to withdraw three thousand dollars, leaving her about five dollars so as not to trigger an overdraft. It didn't occur to me he still knew about that account, but I should have guessed. He didn't miss a trick. What a skunk. I was so mad, I told him that if he didn't get his worthless hide out of town pronto, I'd call the sheriff on him myself this time. He just smiled and told me to calm down. Said he was leaving anyway. Then he walked away and that's the last I saw of him. I wanted to shoot him myself."

She must have noticed my startled expression. "But I didn't, of course. Somebody else took care of that later. Want to hear the icing on the cake? Irene always used the same PIN, his birthday, 'cause she was so proud of him. I knew she'd need money to pay her bills, so I replaced the money later. I didn't think it was relevant to his murder—"

"Not relevant?" My frustration erupted in a torrent of words. "Even Arnie could make a connection out of that. What else don't I know? You asked me to help you. You certainly aren't making it easy. Did you write a check?"

"No. Always cash. I'm sorry I didn't tell you before. I'd hoped, perhaps foolishly, that no one would ever realize that

Irene's money came from me. But the longer this drags on without another suspect, the more I'm afraid they will. And if Arnie ever puts those deposits together with me, I'll look like Hunter's accomplice, which would give me a motive for his murder. You know, thieves fighting over money . . ." Alix collapsed onto the chair beside her desk. "Now you know absolutely everything."

I let out my breath with a whoosh. "And it's plenty. I'll say that much. I know this wasn't easy for you, Alix, and I appreciate your trust. But now what?"

"I was hoping to convince you to talk to Hunter's grandmother, see if she can shed any light."

"Why don't you talk to her yourself?"

"I can't. She thinks I was the one who stole her money years ago. I told you, she never really understood what Hunter was like."

"So, what could I say that would help?"

"Maybe . . . well, I don't know, but it's the only idea I have. You'll think of something." Alix twisted her slender fingers together while she waited for my response. She stood very straight, braced for the worst, but her eyes pleaded with me.

I doubted her confidence in my abilities, but didn't think I could resist the pleading in her eyes. "I asked you a while ago why you'd opened the Wedding Belle. I'd really like to know." Some instinct told me that Alix's answer to this particular question was important.

Alix came over and trailed her crimson nails along the arm of the chintz loveseat before sinking gracefully onto one of the cushions.

I sat on the other cushion and waited.

"Okay, but you won't believe it." Alix smoothed the flowered fabric beside her over and over as though trying to remove nonexistent wrinkles. About the time I was ready to grab her hand to make her stop, she spoke. "I used to play with dolls when I was little. That pretend world was easier than . . . well, anyway, when I was about eight or nine, I won a bride doll at a community Christmas party. The most gorgeous thing I'd ever seen. She came in her own box—you know the kind, with the clear plastic on the front—and her blue eyes opened and closed. She had a detachable veil, too. I loved that doll more than anything. So I dreamed of dressing up in a white gown someday and being a bride just like her. Beautiful, no problems, handsome prince." She waved her hand dismissively and cleared her throat. "The usual kid stuff. Never happened. I moved away . . . did this and that . . . and then the Wedding Belle came on the market. I bought it on a whim, and here I am."

"Can I see the doll?"

Alix seemed startled. "Why would I still have a kid's doll?"

"Because you loved her."

My understanding of Alix was growing by the minute. She did her best to keep herself hidden inside her protective shell, but the necessity of asking for my help had cracked that shell wide open. Alix did have a separate personality that I hadn't seen before, but it was exposed now, and it wasn't the personality of a killer.

"In that bench, under the window seat," she whispered, her face bright red.

The white satin dress had yellowed with age, and the box was scuffed, but the doll's bright blue eyes opened wide as I lifted her, and her smile never wavered. She was ready and waiting for the good things of the world to happen.

My eyes filled with tears. "She's beautiful. What's her name?"

"Mirabella. I thought it sounded romantic."

I nodded. After a moment, I settled Mirabella comfortably back in place and turned to face Alix. "I'd better get started for

Redmond. We still have things to clear up before we all live happily ever after."

CHAPTER 15

Armed with as much information about Irene Cook as Alix could provide, I intended to drive to Redmond to interview her before I could lose my nerve. Since I had no idea what I could possibly accomplish, the sooner I put this project behind me, the better. Alix wouldn't be able to think about anything else until I did.

I was halfway out the door when Bianca bounced in, followed by Tyler. "Look who I found."

Her cheerful tone didn't match the anxious look she sent my way, so I gave her a thumbs-up to indicate that my conversation had calmed Alix's earlier distress. No need to disclose that my own anxiety level had shot up to record levels with my new knowledge and assignment.

Clearly relieved, she smiled back before picking up the conversational ball. "I told him we needed his help to carry things." She looked expectantly at Alix, who didn't seem to be tracking. "You know, the Palmer wedding?"

Alix's blank look changed to a consternation she wasn't faking. "My god. It's . . . it's tomorrow."

"Don't worry about a thing. I'm just glad I remembered in time." Bianca's smile was luminescent, now that she had thought of something useful to do. "Ty and I have it all under control. You just stay here and . . . and take care of things at this end. We'll do the wedding prep, and Ty will help me tomorrow, too."

"Things okay at Thornton's?" I directed my question to Tyler, who looked particularly glum.

"Fine. Grandpa was happy to get rid of me. But this wedding stuff isn't my bag."

Normally Tyler was happy to be anywhere near Bianca, but he didn't seem to be in the mood for this outing.

"You think Wendell'd be more help?" Bianca gestured behind her at the ever-faithful dog.

Hearing his name, Wendell regarded Bianca intently with his one good eye, waiting for instructions or, better yet, food.

From my own dealings with Bianca's determined nature I suspected that Tyler would end up helping, regardless of his feelings about weddings.

Bianca made it easier for him by sweetening the pot. "It's a nice afternoon for a drive in the convertible."

Smothering a smile, I saw that Tyler was toast even before he spoke. The lure of riding in Alix's cream-colored Saab would be irresistible.

"What do you want me to carry?"

"Start with that box by the door. I'll take the programs."

Tyler hesitated. "This? You want a box of grass and vines?"

"I told you. Matrimonial vines, for the frontier theme. See? The programs are made of gingham squares tied in rolls with grass."

"That's stupid. The grass will break."

"Probably. But Melissa's an old-time movie buff and her all-time favorite movie is 'Seven Brides for Seven Brothers.' That's what she wanted. Simplicity. The guests sit on hay bales . . . harmonica and fiddle for the music."

"Does the groom get to wear bib overalls?" Tyler asked.

"Now you're getting it." Bianca beamed at him.

"That's probably what made him go for such a dumb theme." Tyler still didn't sound convinced.

"That's a cute movie," I said. "But I hope the wedding doesn't duplicate the barn-raising scene."

Bianca laughed before turning to explain the reference to Tyler. "She brought us the DVD to watch before we started planning. See, in the movie the guys get to fighting over the girls and the whole barn falls down. Total disaster."

Alix glanced at Wendell, soberly guarding the box of grass. "Speaking of disasters, what's Wendell's job tomorrow?"

"Wendell will be fine," Bianca assured her. "We'll keep the food trays up much higher this time. Besides, you know he brings in more business than he costs us. He'll escort the flower girl—carrying wildflowers, of course—and then he'll go back to escort the little boy with the rings. Other than that, he'll just be a frontier dog, sitting beside the preacher. At first, they wanted him to bark when the preacher asks, 'Who giveth this woman?' but the bride's parents didn't go for that idea, so they dropped it."

The ringing of the phone cut off any need for further comment. While Alix answered it, Bianca and Tyler each hoisted a box. Bianca lagged behind.

"So," she said in a low voice. "Alix is okay?"

"She's fine. Just a little jittery." I carried a third box out to the curb. "If you and Tyler can take care of the wedding, it'll be a big help." I wished I could banish my own jitters so easily, but she didn't need to know about that.

"Great." With a grin, Bianca returned to the office and struggled back under the weight of the last box. It contained a battered blue-speckled tin coffee pot and several cast iron skillets. At my questioning look, she enlightened me. "For the coffee and corn pone the womenfolk'll cook at the potluck reception."

Tyler and I stowed the boxes in the back seat and made room for Wendell to sit.

"How's your grandfather today? Think he'll be okay alone at the store?"

"Better than okay. He caught me snooping in his desk and got really mad, so he was happy to get me out of there for a while. He was trying to hide some sweepstakes entries by locking the desk drawer, but I found the key."

"Would you want someone poking around your private papers?"

"That's different. I have a good reason for snooping."

"Come on, Tyler. He doesn't know that."

"Well, still . . . have you come up with any ideas? I know this deal with Alix has probably . . ."

"Sorry. Not yet. Look, are you absolutely sure you shouldn't tell your mother about Laurence? I know you don't want to, but—"

"You haven't met her," Tyler said flatly. "She's not like a regular mother. I mean, she used to be, but not now. She called late the other night, asked if 'the old man' was around anywhere. When I told her he was already asleep, she made a joke about me staying up late to sneak his booze."

"Think she's drinking again?" Tyler had mentioned before that his mother often described her own habits, not her son's.

"I hope not. Her voice sounded pretty clear this time. Anyway, she talked again about how much easier it'd be for her if I came back. Said she could use some help."

No question about that. "What'd you tell her?"

"That Grandpa needs me a while longer. She took that to mean he's just found himself some cheap help. Said there was no need to let the old faker take advantage."

"She actually said that?" My words erupted before I could censor myself and issue an automatic reassurance.

"Guess she didn't want him to beat her to the punch."

His realistic assessment made my heart ache. "I'm sorry, Tyler. She's probably doing the best she can."

"Yeah, that's what they told me at the clinic." He gave a rueful laugh. "But what else can they say, right? Anyway, she's talking about coming to visit, see how things are going." He pressed his lips together and shook his head. "I told her, 'Good idea,' but I'm not too worried. She won't be able to get herself organized enough."

"You're sure?" I could barely squeeze the question past my suddenly constricted throat. Tyler would hate it if I cried at his matter-of-fact recitation. He wasn't asking for sympathy. He was simply giving me enough information to help him cope with his wreck of a family.

"Yeah. Been down that road a few times already." He held out his hand, palm up, in a "stop" gesture. "And you don't have to tell me again about resentment being bad for me. I got the message." He looked down and blinked rapidly a couple of times. "The thing is, she can't help the way she acts, but I can't help her. At least for now, I need to stay here."

This poor kid had already heard every bit of useful advice I had to offer, and he didn't need any platitudes, so I told him exactly what I thought. "I agree. You belong in Juniper—regardless of what's going on with your grandfather—and I'll do everything in my power to help you stay here. Okay?"

He took a deep breath. "Okay."

Tyler still had faith in at least one adult in his world. I wouldn't, couldn't let him down.

CHAPTER 16

Quilts formed a colorful kaleidoscope on every wall of the Prairie Home Retirement Living reception area. A crackling fire in the freestanding fireplace augmented the cozy atmosphere, though the warmth of the late afternoon didn't call for additional heat. A replica of a frontier cabin on an oak table drew my immediate attention.

"Welcome."

I whirled to face a receptionist seated at a vintage roll-top desk. "I didn't see you there. I was just admiring . . ."

"Incredible, isn't it?" The young woman rose to greet me, her fresh-scrubbed face lighting with pleasure at the chance to explain. "Made by a wonderful retired engineer who's one of our guests. He got everything exactly right. Look." She lifted the log roof. The interior décor continued the perfect simplicity of the outside. Miniature pine planks formed the floor. A plain table rested on a rag rug and sturdy bunk beds hugged one wall. In front of the tiny fireplace, complete with a miniscule cast iron kettle on an iron rod, sat an exquisitely carved rocking chair.

"It's like peeking into perfect tranquility." I straightened and glanced around me. "This room has the same feel."

She nodded with satisfaction. "That's exactly the message we want to convey. See? It's even on our business cards: 'Prairie Home Retirement Living . . . our home, your home.' We want our guests to feel like family."

On a sudden hunch, I checked her name tag and asked, "You're not just an employee, are you, Marcy?"

Marcy's wide brown eyes shone with amusement. "My family owns Prairie Home. How'd you guess?"

"I suppose because you seem so upbeat . . ."

"Well, I hope all our employees feel that way, but you're right that our family tries extra hard to make this a home people want to share. In fact, my own grandparents live here. That's how we got started."

"From what I've seen so far, you and your family should be proud."

"Thank you. Were you thinking of—"

"Actually, I'm here to see one of your residents. Irene Cook?"

As Marcy twisted to look through an archway, her straight hair cascaded across the collar of her plain shirtwaist. It was as though I'd stumbled onto the set of the *Little House on the Prairie* TV series.

Marcy turned back with a happy smile. "Oh, good. She's playing cards. That's an improvement." She hesitated. "I guess you've heard about her grandson. I mean, it's none of my business . . ."

In my preoccupation with helping Alix, I'd hardly given a thought to how Irene Cook must feel at the loss of her grandson. "It's . . . it's good of you to care, Marcy. I'll do my best not to upset her."

"She's been so sad, but today she's wearing that beautiful turquoise outfit again, so I hope she's feeling better. She usually wins at cards, too. That ought to help."

"Gin!" The triumphant word echoed from the next room.

"Told you." Marcy patted me on the arm and returned to her desk.

I smiled my thanks and made my way to the next room.

"You won again, Irene!" A huge woman swathed in a scarlet

muumuu glared across the card table.

I couldn't help noticing, with total irrelevance, that she bore an unfortunate resemblance to George Washington. Life couldn't have been easy for her, whether she won or lost at cards, but at least she fit nicely into the historic motif of Prairie Home.

"How do you do that?" A stick-thin lady spoke from her wheelchair at the table. A black sweat suit hung on her frame, and the chalky tones of her hands and face indicated an ongoing battle against serious illness. She was smiling though, perhaps in simple appreciation of being alive.

"That's two million you owe me."

Of medium height and weight, Irene Cook fit neatly between her larger and smaller opponents at the card table. I guessed her age at a well-preserved eighty.

"Tomorrow . . . double or nothing," demanded the scarlet muumuu.

"Fine with me." Irene shuffled the deck with practiced ease and slapped it down on the table.

I hovered nearby until she looked up.

Her eyes showed the telltale redness that followed the shedding of tears, but her voice betrayed no emotion. "Want to play?"

"Be careful if you do," muttered the George Washington clone. "She'll rob you blind and smile the whole time."

"She's a shark all right," the thin woman agreed in cheerful tones. "But she's fun. Join us?"

"Thanks, but I was hoping to talk to Mrs. Cook, if she's available."

Irene Cook's quick glance at her tablemates told me she anticipated the subject matter and didn't want to talk in front of an audience. "Let's go to my room."

She used a handsome ebony cane to lever herself to her feet.

With her back straight, she led the way past a group of arm chairs with crocheted afghans slung over their backs. Bouquets of fresh yellow and white daisies adorned nearby end tables. Noting the high quality of everything I saw, I surmised it wouldn't be cheap to live here. Had some of Hunter's schemes helped to pay for his grandmother's comfort, or did it all come from Alix?

When we reached Irene's room, she opened the door and turned to face me. "Are you from Sheriff Kraft's office?" As I'd feared, they'd already talked to her, making my difficult job just that much harder. "I hope you've come to tell me you've made an arrest."

After a tussle with my conscience, I stifled the impulse to lie. Posing as a deputy might net information, but would likely cause more trouble than I needed. "Sorry, I'm not, but I don't think there's been an arrest." At least I hoped Alix was still free. I'd be celebrating with Irene myself if Arnie had arrested anyone else.

She made an impatient gesture. "If you're a reporter, you're wasting your time. I told the others that I don't know anything about what happened." The old lady's words were abrupt, but her hands, so steady while shuffling the cards, now trembled as they rested on the cane.

I fumbled for the proper response. "My name is Jane Serrano. Mrs. Cook, if I might have just a minute of your time—"

"You *are* a reporter. Can't you leave my Marty alone?"

Hunter had started life as Martin Selway, and Marty he'd remained to his grieving grandmother. Her eyes, so bright while she played cards with her friends, now filled with tears. She entered her room and closed the door in my face.

I retraced my steps to the reception area. Marcy wasn't at the desk, but her replacement—I glanced at the name tag—Cyndi, was delighted to answer my questions about the facility. As I'd expected, even the lowest-priced units weren't cheap.

She echoed Marcy's hope that Irene was feeling better today. "Having company ought to do her good."

I nodded noncommittally and thanked her for her time, tucking a business card inside my bag as I turned to leave.

Cyndi's words stopped me. "Poor Irene was so proud of her grandson, introduced him to all of us."

My breath caught in my throat. "He was here?"

She nodded. "Monday afternoon. He was real friendly. Handsome, too. It was a real shame, him getting killed and all."

"Yes, a real shame." I answered automatically while my mind raced. So Hunter had seen his grandmother on the day he was murdered. Why? Feigning annoyance at a forgotten task, I said, "Oops. I meant to give Irene a . . . a letter I brought."

"I'll take it to her," Cyndi offered.

Marcy would be pleased that her employee was extra-helpful, but that didn't suit my purpose at all. "That's okay."

I escaped before she could renew her kindly offer. As I waited for Irene to answer my knock, I had plenty of time to admire the calligraphy spelling out her name on the door plaque. About the time I concluded that she wasn't going to come to the door, it opened a crack.

"You again." I couldn't see much of her face through the narrow opening, but her scowl was clear enough.

"I'm sorry about your loss."

"Huh." The single syllable was accompanied by the closing of the door.

"I can't imagine the pain of losing one of my grandchildren." I was speaking to the door plaque.

As I stood there, unsure what else I could do to reach her, whispered words floated through the closed door. "You got grandkids?"

"Yes, two. They're wonderful." I waited.

The door swung open, and Irene and I looked at each other, one grandmother to another. Whatever she saw on my face apparently tipped the balance in my favor. Wearily, she stood aside. I hurried past her into the room before she could change her mind.

She made her way to a recliner and moved a burgundy afghan aside so she could sit down. A framed studio portrait of a much younger Hunter Blackburn rested amid the clutter of pill bottles, a magnifying glass, and a box of tissues on a nearby table. The front section of yesterday's *Juniper Journal* lay on the floor. Irene probably had been reading—no doubt for the umpteenth time—the latest article about Hunter's death.

She saw the direction of my gaze. "They're saying such terrible things about Marty. Maybe he wasn't perfect, but he was the sweetest little boy."

"Of course you loved him." I sank onto a loveseat opposite Irene's chair.

"Yes." She looked up gratefully. "I did." Once released, her words flowed like water down a hillside. "Always quick with a smile or a joke. Just a little scamp, really." Her expression softened as she sorted through memories of her grandchild.

I felt an occasional pang of guilt at pumping her for information, but she obviously needed to talk to someone, and I couldn't see what harm I was doing. If anything, I was doing her a kindness by listening, regardless of my original purpose in coming here. Irene seemed to have lost all interest in asking why this stranger was sitting in her room. She simply accepted me as a grandmother who understood her loss.

"This was a gift." Irene caressed the cane by her side. "Ebony. Marty always sent interesting things from his travels." She smiled at the handsome picture that stood in the place of honor. I was glad the newspaper had featured a different photo with the article about his murder. "Why, I wouldn't even be able to live here if not for Marty."

Irene apparently had no suspicion of Alix's involvement in financing her stay at Prairie Home, but I saw no percentage in bringing that up at the moment. "Was Marty able to see what a wonderful place this is?"

"Just once. He had the bank transfer money directly into my account—he traveled so much, you know." Ah, now I understood. "But then he came to see me that last day, just before . . ." The animation faded from her face, and she struggled for control of her voice. "It was wonderful to see him again, introduce him to everyone. He was so handsome. The others just crowded around. You can't imagine the excitement. I wanted him to stay for dinner, but he couldn't. And then, he was gone."

At length, Irene returned to the present and recalled that she was talking to a stranger. Her nostalgic tone was gone when she next addressed me. "You want to know how he made a living, don't you? That's what everyone keeps asking. Marty earned lots of money because he was a fabulous salesman. I already told Sheriff Kraft everything I know."

I allowed myself a small measure of hope since Irene hadn't yet mentioned Alix.

"We're simply trying to cover all bases, to find out who might have held a grudge against him." I didn't define "we."

"You ask me, that Alix woman's the one you should be investigating. A thief and a liar she is, stole from me and blamed Marty. He told me all about it years ago. He divorced her, you know, but I wouldn't be surprised to find she'd had a hand in his murder. Nasty piece of work."

My fledgling relief was swept away by her vitriol. Alix had been right. This nice old lady had tunnel vision about her, courtesy of her dear grandson. Nothing I said was likely to shake her conviction. Still, I'd promised to try. "But Alix Boudreau has a thriving business in Juniper and seems to be—"

"Butter wouldn't melt in her mouth. Oh, she tried to apologize years ago, but I wasn't having any of it. Marty told me what happened. Good riddance to bad rubbish."

I opened my mouth to tell her just who had been her benefactor all these years, then swallowed my words as I saw Irene's lips pressed together in a tight line. I flipped open a small notebook to play for time, turning the pages with unnecessary force as I struggled to bottle my anger at the injustice of hearing Alix unfairly maligned. I had to be smart. If I defended Alix further, Irene would shut me out completely. My effort would also point a finger right at the bank deposits Alix had worked so hard to hide. Irene would be on the phone to Arnie before I could get out the door. I took a deep breath and shifted gears.

"Did you ever suspect she could be violent? That she might do Marty harm?"

"No, I never thought that," she said doubtfully, "but he's gone, isn't he? Who else would've wanted to harm him?"

Who, indeed? My heart sank. Her arguments sounded logical to me, even though I knew better. Unfortunately, Arnie did not. I was betting that more than one person around here was minus some money after running into the saintly Marty. Still, this poor woman hadn't done anything wrong, and she'd lost her grandson.

And Alix stood a good chance of losing her freedom. Perhaps forever. Even though I hadn't asked for or wanted the job, it looked like it was up to me, for better or worse, to ride to the rescue again. I fervently hoped I was up to the task. "That's what I intend to find out, Irene. Here's my telephone number. Please call me directly if you think of anything else that might help us in our investigation."

"You look hard at that woman before you bother looking someplace else."

Having no good response to that comment, I stood to leave. "Thank you for talking to me. I'm sorry for your loss. I don't mean to pry, but will you be all right? Other family?"

Her face brightened. "The people at Prairie Home are all the family I need. They take wonderful care of me, and I'll be able to stay here as long as I live, thanks to Marty. He set everything up in something called an annuity. I got a nice letter from the bank about it just yesterday. See?"

She fumbled underneath the newspaper and brought out a single typed page.

Apparently, she hadn't noticed the absence of letterhead stationery or considered the lack of a handwritten signature odd. I hoped she wouldn't take it into her head to call the bank to thank "Barbara Highman," who had ostensibly written the letter.

Would Irene believe me if I revealed the true identity of "Barbara Highland"? Probably not. To Irene, her grandson was a kindly prince who had been led astray by a wicked witch.

CHAPTER 17

I made my way back to the Volvo, newly energized by my resolve. I needed to tell Alix just how recently Hunter had been here. Maybe we could figure out together how this information could help her.

I also wanted to talk to Desmond McCutcheon again. Our SOS speaker elevated pomposity to an art, but he also knew a lot about scams, and I hoped to turn up useful information about the psychology of the confidence racket by quizzing him. While I deliberated about which task to do first, I watched as a couple of teens bounced out of a shiny Lincoln Continental. They corralled their youthful energy long enough to wait for an elderly man to extricate himself from the passenger seat. A summer drive for Gramps in a car he could no longer operate? The girl held the door while the boy placed a walker close at hand. They passed before me on their way into Prairie Home, chatting amiably. The teens slowed their pace to match that of the older man and his walker. He had visitors who loved him.

I smiled as my thoughts turned to Tyler's loving concern for his own grandfather. Plenty of nice people in this world. Too bad Hunter Blackburn, or Martin Selway, hadn't been one of them. He could have saved us all a lot of trouble.

I sighed as I picked up the cell phone. Alix would be waiting for my report. The screen showed one new voicemail.

My heart gave a sudden kick. Nick? No such luck. Alix's name glowed on the screen. Fair enough. One thing at a time. I

145

retrieved her message.

"Thought I should warn you. Minnie and Velda stopped by to tell me they had a plan. Yeah, scared me, too. Velda is even hotter to check out the idea than Minnie is. They're driving up to the Mystery River Casino tomorrow to check on Phil and Eileen Hedstrom."

So Minnie was still stuck on the Hedstroms. I didn't know how she'd convinced Velda to drop her pursuit of Alice Durand, but maybe they'd decided to join forces and harass everyone. Bad news for Phil and Eileen, but good news for me. Much easier to follow leads if those two were otherwise occupied and out of my hair.

Alix's message continued. "I'm turning my phone off now. Emergency meeting before tomorrow's wedding. Wendell ate the—" The message clicked off. Too long for the memory, or low battery, or something. I'd really have to make time to read the instructions sometime, but not today.

Alix's message settled the question of my next move. I drove to the nearest public phone, outside a rundown Koffee & Kook-ies. Only the cardboard cover of a phonebook chained to the counter remained, but the bored clerk inside surrendered his dog-eared copy after I bought coffee. Five minutes later, I was on my way back to Juniper.

"I was delighted that you found my presentation so useful, Jane."

Desmond McCutcheon and I inched our way forward in the line at Starbuck's.

"You caught me just as I was leaving the office, so I was able to gather more information for you. We all must do what we can to aid our elders, of course. Your charming daughter seemed very interested in helping them. Perhaps she'll take one of my classes soon."

I'd wondered how long it would take him to mention Bianca. This pretentious bore seemed more interested in being around youthful beauty than in crusading for "our elders." However, Dr. McCutcheon did know a thing or two about scams directed at senior citizens.

I fixed a pleasant expression on my face. "Perhaps. We were all honored to have such an expert address the group."

We shuffled a few feet closer, and I squinted at the plethora of coffee choices on the wall. Bianca preferred Juniper Joe's on the corner since it was locally owned and organic, but Desmond had suggested Starbuck's, so here we were.

"A grande soy mocha latte, my good man." Desmond rattled off his order with the confidence born of long experience.

"The same," I echoed as I paid for both our drinks. How did people remember all this stuff? "You come here often?" I followed him down the counter to wait for our order.

"Before teaching a class, I find it an admirable place to settle my thoughts."

And to be seen by your students, I thought as he smiled and waved to a couple of young women passing by. I remembered my adolescent reverence for professors during my own college years and figured Desmond would lap up that hero worship like extra cream in his soy mocha latte. He'd enjoy impressing coeds before they got out in the world and learned that some of his great insights were actually general knowledge to people a few years older.

After we made our way to a corner table, I sipped my drink. Smooth and sweet, definitely a treat I wouldn't be able to allow myself each day, even if I'd been willing to fork over that much money. It tasted a lot better than what passed for coffee at Koffee & Kookies though.

Ignoring me, Desmond surveyed the room for a younger audience. The fact that he hadn't protested my offer to pay for the coffee told me that I was off his social radar screen. No point in trying to impress a woman his own age. His hair was a little long and his cologne a bit strong in his bid to knock ten years off his age, but his crows' feet—salon-tanned though they were—gave him away.

Still, his personality wasn't the point of our meeting. Desmond might be full of himself, but he'd also brought along a sheaf of information on scams.

"It was kind of you to bring me this," I said, tapping the manila folder on the table between us, "and to speak to our group, too."

He frowned. "If you don't mind my saying so, some of the attendees seemed more concerned with the snacks than my information."

"Well, Minnie is a really good cook, but I'm sure everyone found your presentation enlightening. You're clearly an expert in the field."

"Yes, I am." His frown relaxed and he leaned back in his chair, mollified by my praise. "Seniors are often lonely, hungry for contact with people, even if it's only to buy something, so they're easy prey."

I nodded. "Especially if they don't have family to protect them."

"Sometimes that's even worse. Many family members prey on their own relatives. It's an old story, and not a pleasant one."

Irene Cook's fantasy picture of her grandson fit the pattern. "You're saying that to a lonely person, a visit from a family member would be so welcome that she—or he—wouldn't even be on guard."

"Exactly. It's common for a relative to poke around while visiting, make off with jewelry, money, whatever. Some elders even ask for help balancing a checkbook, for example, or assistance with financial forms. They never dream they're putting their money at risk since they're dealing with someone they trust."

"That's horrible."

"That's reality." Desmond's offhand tone told me this was all academic to him. He hadn't experienced firsthand the damage con men could cause vulnerable people, like Irene Cook. I hoped he never would.

Someone as cold-blooded as Hunter wouldn't hesitate to defraud anyone he could find, and another of his victims might not have been as blinded by his charm as his grandmother. More to the point, someone else might have had the power to retaliate.

"What about violence? Do con men use that as a tool to defraud people?"

"Not usually. They prefer to use their wits as a means of parting victims from their money. Sometimes they bluster and threaten, but violence doesn't normally come into the profile. It's all there in the documents."

"I see." I shuffled through his pages, pausing at the one giving the characteristics of con men. As Desmond had indicated, they tended to be nonviolent, as well as intelligent, personable, and amoral. Sounded like Hunter, but the nonviolent component also suggested that Hunter hadn't been killed by someone in the same line of work. The reasoning was weak, but plausible enough to lead me back to the tenuous hypothesis that Hunter had run afoul of one of his own victims. That made more sense than concluding that his murder had been a random act of violence, not in sleepy little Juniper.

I turned to another page.

"This FBI printout . . ." I stopped mid-sentence, aware that Desmond's gaze had wandered back to the young women watching us from their stools at the front window. When they saw Desmond smiling at them, they jumped down and headed our way.

"What? Oh, yes." He reeled off a list of reasons for targeting seniors. "Some have accumulated wealth, some are senile, others fear looking foolish if they admit they can't understand the 'too good to be true' offers coming their way. Feel free to copy it for your group." Obviously, Desmond was done with our conversation.

I excused myself, leaving just before the girls arrived at our table. Desmond's Starbuck's ritual must be the modern version of driving slowly down Main Street trolling for girls.

As I made my way back to the car, I wondered what Nick would think if he happened to spot me having coffee with Desmond at Starbuck's. Nick's idea of coffee came out of a battered percolator. To disguise the taste of the resulting brew, he added improbable amounts of cream and sugar. No matter what kind of coffee he drank, I'd give a lot right now to sit down and talk with him, but he apparently was still out of cell phone range.

The interior of the Volvo was baking in the afternoon heat, so I left the door open while I skimmed Desmond's pages. He might be a peacock, but his information had helped bring me up to speed about Hunter Blackburn's seamy career. Unfortunately, it hadn't provided me with a viable suspect in his murder. I'd have to be more creative, but controlling my racing thoughts was akin to stopping a runaway horse. Bianca swore by meditation. Okay. I'd try anything at this point.

I closed my eyes and let my thoughts drift. After they skittered around for a while, up floated a memory of a favorite college Shakespeare class. Professor Simpson had asserted that the motive for murder could always be traced to one of four elements: love, money, fear, or revenge. He'd also suggested that a contemplation of the Seven Deadly Sins would provide enough ideas to keep both playwrights and police busy for decades. Interesting ideas, but what could I do with them?

Since Hunter's murderer apparently hadn't been thoughtful enough to leave a calling card or fingerprints at the scene of the crime, I didn't have an idea in the world about how to find him . . . or her. The most obvious trail to follow seemed to be money, since money had been Hunter's special area of interest. If money had figured largely in his life, maybe it had played a similarly large role in his death.

An unwelcome thought started dancing around in my head: the Mystery River Casino had lots of money. Phil and Eileen Hedstrom were going there tomorrow, with Minnie and Velda hot on their trail. Could Minnie's hunch possibly be valid? No, of course not.

I sat there for a good twenty minutes, taking up and discarding various neighbors and friends as potential suspects. All ludicrous. At length, I admitted defeat. I knew who hadn't killed Hunter, but I had no better idea than Minnie about who had killed him. Now, that was a sobering thought.

I hoped Nick would return soon. Surely he could suggest a more brilliant approach than my idea of establishing a list of suspects based on a Shakespeare class twenty-some years ago?

Meanwhile, my next step was to see Alix. I drove to the Wedding Belle at well below the speed limit. She wasn't going to like my report any better than I did. Some detective I'd turned out to be. Unless she could make something more than I had from my conversations with Irene Cook and Desmond McCutcheon, we were at a dead end.

I chewed my lip in frustration. Her future now rested on the slender hope that Arnie wouldn't uncover the connection between her finances and Irene's. Arnie might be lazy in general, but this was one time he'd be a bulldog in searching for proof of Alix's guilt.

CHAPTER 18

Alix had waved away my apology for failing to come up with any new leads. I couldn't read her calmness when I described my trip to Redmond. Either her nerves had steadied considerably since that morning or she was trying to cheer me up.

"Hey, no news is good news. Let's wait for developments."

Easier said than done. Unable to think of where else to expend my restless energy, I decided to accompany Minnie and Velda to the casino the next morning. Alix had actually recommended the trip.

"It'll make a good diversion for you. Nothing about traveling with that pair will bear the slightest resemblance to reality."

"Want to come with us?"

"Can't leave town, remember? What a shame."

Tyler was ringing up an early sale when I arrived at Thornton's. The excited customers turned out to be Minnie and Velda. Their bright eyes and flushed cheeks signaled that they were in full battle mode and ready for our trip.

"No camouflage handbags?" I asked.

"Now you're being silly," Minnie said, "but we're glad you've decided to come. Still no word from Nick, I guess?"

"Not yet," I answered, "but soon, I hope."

I tried not to think about how much I'd rather be on my way to the beach with him than going to a casino with Minnie and Velda today.

"Look what we're bringing." Minnie held up two books: *Beat the System, Baby!* and *Everybody Wins!*

"These were on our shelves?" I was astonished that Laurence would allow them in his store.

"No way." Tyler was trying without much success to smother a smile. "Minnie put in a special order and caught the Ingram shipment from Roseburg just right."

"We were lucky they arrived in time for us to study on the drive today," Minnie said with satisfaction. "That is, if you're willing to take your car, Jane, so Velda and I can read. We don't want to look like novices. You know," she confided, "this is new territory for us. We haven't had much experience with . . . gambling." She lowered her voice as though even speaking the word would contaminate the air, but her sparkling eyes betrayed her willingness to explore this sinful activity as soon as possible.

"I'll be glad to drive," I said truthfully. I'd survived Minnie's haphazard driving before, and I wasn't anxious to tempt fate again. "However," I went on, in an attempt to make today's trip as painless as possible, "I have difficulty driving when people are talking, so could you read silently?"

Velda spoke for the first time. "Could Minnie and I sit in back and quietly share notes? We don't want to bother you, Jane, but if we whisper . . . ?" Her soft voice vibrated with an enthusiasm that matched Minnie's.

Hard to believe, but compared to Velda's usual daily routine, I had to admit that going to a casino would probably be a real thrill.

"Great idea," I agreed. Alix had been right.

As Minnie reclaimed center stage, I prepared mentally to enter Fantasyland. "I have it all figured out. After Velda followed Alice the other day and turned up significant clues, I did some detective work of my own." Minnie's face glowed with pride in her protégée's significant clues. Here we go, I thought, bracing myself for Minnie's unique brand of detective work.

"When I was picking up my Lipitor, I asked Sam Watson for counseling on its use. I've been taking it for years, but I asked for a consultation anyway. Once I had him trapped at the privacy window, I just winged it." Minnie turned to Tyler and tapped her forehead to indicate clever thinking. "Sam lives next door to Phil and Eileen so it was easy enough to slip Eileen's name into the same sentence as cholesterol." She returned her attention to me. "I know what you're thinking, but don't worry. I was subtle. The way Eileen went after my pound cake the other day, there's a good chance she takes Lipitor, so I'm sure Sam didn't suspect a thing. Anyway, we were talking about neighbors and garbage day and whatever . . . you know how conversations ramble . . ."

I nodded, fascinated. Having experienced Minnie's conversational leaps of logic firsthand, I was well aware of her mental agility, though how she could get a busy pharmacist to chat about everything from cholesterol to garbage day stretched my imagination. By the time I focused on her explanation again, Minnie was several topics down the road, but I tuned in just in time for the punch line.

"And all of a sudden, 'Bingo!' Phil had told Sam that he and Eileen were driving to Mystery River today. Now, what do you think of that?" Minnie stepped back from the counter, spreading her arms in triumph.

"And . . . ?" I felt like a particularly dull student.

Minnie eyed me over her glasses, reminding me of my sixth-grade teacher when I couldn't locate Peru on the map. I shrugged helplessly, unable to grasp Minnie's point. She and Velda exchanged looks before she took pity on me.

"So, we'll follow them." She lowered her voice to a whisper and leaned close. "If they spot us, we'll pretend we didn't know they were there. That way, they won't be on guard."

"Against what? What are we looking for?" I asked. I still didn't understand what valuable information they felt they'd unearthed when Velda shadowed Alice to the post office.

Minnie threw up her hands, stunned at my inability to grasp the big picture. "For heaven's sake, I don't know yet. That's why we're following them."

"We'll get clues, same as I did by following Alice." Velda seemed to have no trouble with Minnie's logic.

"Clues about . . ." I let my voice trail off, defeated.

Clearly, I wouldn't be able to divert these two from their mission. Minnie had discovered last year that solving a murder was more exciting than baking chicken pot pies for the New Community Church. And Velda, who apparently had nothing more exciting to look forward to than an occasional SOS meeting, had now discovered the thrill of the chase as well. Might as well get this over with.

"Tyler, you're sure Laurence will be okay covering the store while you help with the wedding?"

"He's fine with it. Seemed really good this morning. I'll check in with him and—"

"—call me if you hear anything from Alix or Nick," I finished.

"Yep." Tyler's grin told me what he thought of the wild goose chase I had before me.

I wanted to throw something at him, but contented myself with a shrug. "Okay, girls. Let's go get clues."

Minnie started for the door, with Velda trailing her.

Magnanimous in victory, Minnie paused to offer an alternative plan, though her tone told me she considered it an inferior one. "You know, Jane, we could always talk to the sheriff again, though he hasn't proved particularly receptive."

"You threatened to throw gooey pastry at him last year."

"He wasn't any more cooperative yesterday. Besides, my cinnamon pull-aparts are not gooey. That would suggest that they weren't properly cooked."

Velda looked at Minnie, enchanted. "You did that?"

Minnie pursed her lips. "Jane exaggerates. Throwing pastry at someone wouldn't be a Christian thing to do, but . . . I certainly wanted to. 'Beware that there be not a thought in thy wicked heart . . .' Deuteronomy 15:9. Hmm. Should I bake him some scones when we get back as a belated gesture of reconciliation?"

I couldn't resist. "Good idea. They're lighter, wouldn't hurt so much when they hit him."

"Scones do have sharp points." Velda looked worried. I couldn't believe that anyone in town was less sensible than Minnie, but apparently I was wrong.

"Jane is mocking us." Minnie's formal tone told me I'd teased her enough. She was looking at Velda as she finished her statement, but her words were for me. "She doesn't think we are very good detectives, so she has now resorted to sarcasm. I notice, however, that she does not suggest any better ideas."

"I'm sorry. You're absolutely right. Following Phil and Eileen might be just the thing that breaks this case wide open."

I certainly didn't want to hurt Minnie's or Velda's feelings. Besides, she was right. I didn't have any better ideas.

As I followed Velda's ancient Dodge past the scattered houses on the outskirts of Juniper, I was hard pressed to avoid tailgating. Our first stop would be at her home to drop off the car. Good thing Velda wasn't driving us to the casino, or we'd have been all day getting there. Though she was only about forty-three, exactly my age, she drove like the stereotypical senior citizen, signaling carefully long before a turn and keeping so far below the speed limit that our five-mile drive seemed like twenty. By the time we reached her house, I was starting to think about lunch.

We jounced over the long driveway at a snail's pace, with Velda weaving from side-to-side to find the least destructive route though the weeds and rocks. I doubted that the Mary Kay lady came out here often nowadays, though the three-story house on its overgrown lawn must once have been rather grand. Velda's aunt used to buy books from Thornton's before her stroke a year ago, but I hadn't seen her since then. Velda's uncle, a Circuit Court judge, had died several years earlier. His funeral had brought mourners from all over Oregon, and the *Journal* obituary had listed a full column of his civic accomplishments. Sad to see the neglect of this once-illustrious family's home, but Velda had intimated that her aunt's staggering medical bills made it impossible to take proper care of both the house and yard.

Velda pulled up in front of the graceful brick entry and motioned for me to park beside her. "I hope you didn't hit that bad spot. I should have warned you. I automatically swing wide there."

"No problem." I followed Velda up the steps and into the house.

"Maria, *dónde estás?*" Velda called.

No answer. Her effortless accent reminded me that she had moved here from Florida, where she'd likely been surrounded by people speaking Spanish.

"She's supposed to be here."

Velda's round face creased into a frown as she passed the central staircase and clattered down the hall to the telephone stand. Normally, she moved soundlessly in tennis shoes, but today she was wearing sling backs, no doubt in anticipation of her big outing.

"I don't ever leave Aunt Eleanor alone for more than a few minutes. Maria was due to arrive an hour ago." She punched the answering machine button and listened to a message.

"Maria's car broke down. She's not coming."

Velda threw the words over her shoulder as she hurried toward the back of the house and opened the last door on the left to look inside. We waited in the entryway until she pulled the bedroom door closed and returned.

"Aunt Eleanor's sleeping just fine, thank goodness. No harm done, but I'm afraid I won't be able to go." Her dejected posture described her disappointment.

"Isn't there someone else we can call?" Minnie wasn't ready to give up. "You told me Alice used to clean for you. Maybe she could come."

"Yes, Alice used to help out occasionally, but she wasn't a very cheerful person to have around, always complaining about something. Besides, now that she's a suspect, I really wouldn't feel right about leaving Aunt Eleanor with her. Maria has worked out much better, though she doesn't speak a word of English. At least she smiles as she cooks and cleans, but . . . we'll see. Some things can't be helped."

"Bless you for an angel," Minnie said, grasping both of Velda's hands. "It's a shame you have to miss our trip."

"Don't worry about me. Today's mission is the important thing." Velda spoke earnestly, but her lips trembled.

Releasing her hands from Minnie's grip, she turned away to fumble for a handkerchief in the pocket of her shapeless sweater.

"I could stay here with her," I said. After just the short ride from town, I'd already had enough of this project.

"Oh, no." Velda looked aghast. "That would be asking too much."

"I'd be happy to stay." The more I thought about a peaceful day here, the better it sounded.

"Really, Aunt Eleanor would be alarmed to find a stranger here. I couldn't have that."

"But she knows me from Thornton's. She used to shop there."

Velda shook her head vigorously. "No, no. That would be quite impossible. I insist that you and Minnie go on without me."

"If you're sure . . ." I said. I'd always thought of Velda as Ms. Milquetoast, but clearly there was no budging her on this matter.

"Can we do anything before we leave?" Minnie asked. "What if you have to lift her or something? Your back . . ."

"I can manage."

Velda rarely mentioned her chronic back pain, so I tended to forget about it, but I doubted that she'd be able to move her aunt. However, her firmly lifted chin indicated that she'd do whatever was necessary. As I looked through the pocket doors to the gleaming table surface and polished floor of the dining room, I realized just how well this quiet, self-effacing young woman coped with a bleak situation.

"Is Eleanor able to get around at all?" I asked as Velda opened the front door to see us on our way. "It'd be a shame if she couldn't enjoy such a beautiful home."

Velda gave a brave attempt at a smile. "Aunt Eleanor gets around well enough most of the time. She loves to knit, for example, though she can't manage the elaborate patterns she used to before her stroke."

"The Knit Wits are always on the lookout for new members," Minnie said. "Maybe you could bring her sometime. We meet Monday nights in the church basement."

"It's kind of you to suggest it, but she stays at home now," Velda said.

Left unspoken was the impact her aunt's preferences had on Velda's own activities. No wonder chasing off to a smoky, loud casino today would have afforded welcome relief from her daily routine. I resolved to see what I could do to help Velda find respite care so she could get out more, even if she didn't have money to pay for more help than was absolutely necessary to ensure Eleanor's comfort.

Judging from the way Minnie was patting Velda's arm, she

was having similar thoughts. "We'd better be going now, dear, but I'll bring you some corn chowder later this evening and give you a full report then. Would that be all right?"

Velda clutched Minnie's hand as though it were a lifeline. "If it wouldn't be too much trouble."

"Nonsense. I'll be here as soon as I can. Of course, we might have to chase Phil and Eileen to their hideout or something. That could delay us."

At Minnie's words, Velda perked up like Wendell at the sight of a dog bone. "That's right. They could be planning a getaway. Promise me you won't break off the chase just to bring me soup."

"I promise." Minnie gave Velda's arm a final pat. "Come on, Jane. Let's bag ourselves some crooks."

CHAPTER 19

As we sped past the fragrant mint fields near Madras, Minnie read me portions of the book that purported to reveal surefire secrets for beating any casino system. I only half-listened to her wide-eyed recitation, suggesting once that the Native Americans operating this casino probably didn't intend it to function as a charity for our financial benefit. Her shining eyes indicated she wasn't listening to me any more than I was listening to her.

I didn't suggest a stop at the gigantic teepee housing the Native American museum as we swept by it. The sooner we executed Minnie's "plan," the sooner I could send her home to cook soup for Velda. We turned onto the newly paved secondary road to Mystery River, which I hadn't driven since the kids were small.

Tony and I had brought them up here to swim at the hot springs, so much more inviting to those shivering little bodies than the icy Deschutes River. Back then, we had camped in tents at this little-known destination, but the four-lane swath now winding through the sagebrush told me things had changed in recent years. If this highway was any indication, the casino had jumped the region to a whole new marketing level, easier access making it possible for eager gamblers to sweep in, lighten their wallets, and be home in time for dinner.

The stark beauty of the surrounding dry hills hadn't changed over the years, nor had the condition of the occasional dilapidated house haphazardly located along the way. The wealth generated by the casino apparently hadn't filtered down to improve the living conditions of everyone on the reservation.

As we descended the final steep grade and turned into the area where the hot springs used to sit in dusty isolation, glossy signage assaulted us with information about where to find gambling, parking, swimming, golf, food, and lodging. This place had everything, in fact, except the solitude that used to draw us here. The enormous flashing arrow pointing to the casino sent today's message loud and clear: No need to waste a minute ridding yourself of your money.

Minnie traded her usual black hat for a plain brown scarf and dark glasses. The expression of disbelief on my face caused her to set her jaw.

"Disguise. No need to let the suspects spot us if we can help it. You can use the outfit I brought for Velda." Reaching into the back seat, she produced an orange plastic sun hat and outsized green glasses. "Velda and I had this all planned out. Don't you want to help Alix?"

"By being arrested for public lunacy?"

"I told Velda you wouldn't like the disguises. Honestly, you're almost as cynical as Alix."

"Sometimes Alix makes good sense."

"Huh! She's the one with an ex-husband who got himself murdered. I'm going with my instinct."

Minnie discarded the scarf and grabbed the orange sun hat. After arranging it to her satisfaction, she snapped open the car door, quivering with anticipation.

When I didn't move, she asked, "Are you coming?"

"Why don't you slip in there first, do a little recon?"

Minnie brightened at the suggestion and saluted with more enthusiasm than skill, knocking her hat askew in the process. "Yes, ma'am. I'll get the lay of the land without blowing our cover."

"Roger that." I settled low in the seat to emphasize the need for stealth in our covert operation.

Minnie took a couple of steps toward the casino before wheeling and scuttling around to my window. "What's the name of our op? Missions always have names."

"Guess 'Operation Phil and Eileen' doesn't have much of a ring to it," I said.

I was contemplating "Operation Wild Goose Chase" when Minnie clapped her hands together.

"I've got it: 'Operation Hollow Feather.' It says it all . . . the setting, the betrayal, the corruption. What do you think?"

What did I think? For starters, I thought that all feathers were hollow. More to the point, I wondered how Phil and Eileen had fallen so far so fast. A week ago they were esteemed members of the Save Our Seniors group and now they had become evil incarnate. Still, if it made Minnie happy, who was I to quibble?

"Perfect."

My half-doze in the sunshine was interrupted by a timid knock on the car window a few minutes later. Startled, I turned to find a young woman holding up a piece of paper. Her flyaway red hair was bound by a multicolored headband, and she wore a glossy turquoise Mystery River Casino blouse with "Betsy" stitched in red over the pocket. I fumbled with the window and finally opened the door when I realized I couldn't roll it down without turning on the engine.

"For you." She smiled impishly. "From the lady in the orange hat."

"Thank you."

Minnie had used the back of a discarded Keno slip to write a cryptic message.

The young woman was already making her way back inside by the time I deciphered the clues and called out to her. "Excuse me. Which entrance is closest to the salmon waterfall?"

"That one." She pointed toward the far end of the long, low building. "It's awesome, worth seeing."

"I'm sure it is." I reread the scrawled words. "Come see birds in the trees near pool where something often served with lemon-dill sauce might try to climb while homeward bound."

I glanced at the brown scarf. No way. If my unwillingness to dress like a Russian peasant compromised Operation Hollow Feather, so be it.

As my eyes adjusted to the casino's lighting, I blinked at the fog of cigarette smoke that obscured the waterfall before me. Oregon's smoke-free regulations for public places didn't extend to Native American casinos. Too bad.

The cascade was indeed stunning as it picked its way through basalt columns to the pool below. In a mountain setting it would have induced feelings of awe and tranquility; here, its grandeur was overwhelmed by the plethora of orange and purple lights flashing nearby. Mist bathed my face as I moved close to the pool for a better view, but the music pouring from speakers in the ceiling assaulted my ears with such force that I quickly moved on to find Minnie. Even a five-minute stay in this room would leave my ears ringing, and my clothes in need of a good airing to rid them of the stench of cigarette smoke.

What sounded like a New Year's Eve celebration broke out somewhere in the room as I considered my options. Apparently at least one happy customer had beaten the odds, but sounds bounced around the cavern in such a way that I had no idea where the lucky machine was located. Brightly lit alleys stretched before me in all directions. How could Minnie hope to sneak up on Phil and Eileen, much less figure out what they were doing? The mirrored ceilings might provide some help, but we'd look pretty silly gawking upward at every corner. What I really needed was Tyler's homemade periscope.

Skulking along between double rows of slot machines, I found no need to pretend I knew what I was doing because the people seated at the machines took no notice of me. They punched buttons and waited, punched and waited, as the bright colors of the slots whizzed by and clunked into place. Try again. Clunk. Try again. How often did the machines pay off? In front of me a skinny woman with long arms encircled her slot machine like a vine. I wondered whether they pruned customers occasionally to keep them from taking root.

I reached the end of one row and surveyed the green felt-covered tables in the open room ahead. Since I didn't know enough about craps or blackjack or whatever to hide among the players, I melted back into the slot machine jungle.

Just then my old friend Betsy glided by carrying a tray of soft drinks. As our eyes met, she altered course to intersect my path. "Something to drink?"

I backed away. "No thanks."

"Are you sure?" Betsy turned the tray so the one glass resting on a napkin was closest to me. Again came that mischievous smile. "It's especially for you."

"Thank you."

I pulled the frosty glass and its accompanying napkin off the tray. The underside of the napkin contained a picture, which I turned this way and that. A diseased pine tree? A shedding dog? An arrow pointed to a stick figure next to a rectangle. Minnie and I would make terrible partners at Pictionary.

Apparently Betsy had anticipated my difficulty. A moment later, carrying a now-empty tray toward the kitchen, she paused by my side. "She wants you to go out the side door."

"Ahh." So I was the stick figure that the arrow was pushing toward the rectangle representing a door. Easy enough now to see it, though the mangy dog remained a mystery. "Did she go out that way?" Probably cheating to ask, but I didn't care.

"No. She's collecting her winnings."

I didn't bother asking for more information. With most activities involving Minnie, I'd found it best not to probe. Nodding my thanks, I found my way to the newly identified rectangle and exited into bright sunshine. While enjoying gulps of fresh air, I took my bearings.

Uh oh. Thirty feet before me Phil and Eileen Hedstrom supported a ragged young man as he moved unsteadily along the sidewalk. I whirled to re-enter the casino, but the door was locked from this side, so I dived behind a nearby potentilla. The young man was much taller than either Phil or Eileen, so they looked like two sturdy tugs maneuvering a freighter through a narrow channel. From their gestures and stiff posture, I guessed there was an argument raging, and at one point the stranger half-fell to the ground. Phil glanced around him before he hauled the young man upright again, and I pulled further into the protection of the bush. When I peered out again, the three of them had rounded the corner of the building. Follow them, or find Minnie?

My question was answered when Minnie popped out of the door behind me, stuffing wads of money into her tote bag. "Which way?"

"Toward the parking lot. They had—"

"Quick! They'll get away." Minnie scuttled down the sidewalk, trailing stray dollar bills as she went.

Scooping them up, I followed her. When we reached the car, I thrust the money at her so I could retrieve my car keys. We were hardly settled in our seats before I gunned the engine. An instant later, I stamped on the brakes as a family ambled into the crosswalk directly in our path, making their leisurely way to the casino. The young mother was juggling a stroller and diaper bag, while the dad held the hands of two toddlers in swimsuits and flip-flops. Grandma and Grandpa brought up the rear at a speed just slightly faster than the setting of cement. I stifled an urge to jump out and tell them they should be going to the hot springs for some outdoor exercise.

Minnie pounded on the dashboard. "Do something. We're going to lose them."

"Should I just run these people down?"

"Of course not." But she practically quivered in her seat.

Minnie's excitement infected me. Swept up into the mood of Operation Hollow Feather, I shot onto the main road as soon as the crosswalk cleared, slamming Minnie against the back of the seat. She pulled her hat down over her ears and braced for a rough ride. No cars visible either way ahead of us at the T-intersection, but Minnie gestured left, so I spun the wheel and pushed the car up the looping grade that wound from the river to the plateau above. Minnie's muffled squeal as we slid around the first bend reminded me that I was no NASCAR driver, so I slowed to a more reasonable speed.

Once on top, I hit the accelerator again and swept by a lumbering camper at the first straight stretch. Minnie had described Phil and Eileen's enormous RV, right down to the USC pennant on top, but there was no sign of it ahead. I pulled off onto the shoulder, checked for traffic, and swung in a U-turn.

"There's no way they could have gotten this far ahead of us. We must have lost them at the T. When we headed for Juniper, they went the other way."

"But why? They live in Juniper." Minnie, still deep in Operation Hollow Feather mode, narrowed her eyes to consider the problem. "Trying to shake the tail. Must have spotted us somehow."

"Never mind Phil and Eileen. You just about lost me in all that smoke in there."

"Wasn't that awful? My eyes are still stinging. Sorry. I detoured to pick up my winnings. Surprisingly easy to beat the system when you know how."

"Really. How'd you do it?"

"Strategy."

"Could you be a bit more specific?"

"When I spied Phil and Eileen heading for the door, I took cover behind the slot machines and sent you that note. While I was waiting for you to show up, I put a dollar in the machine in front of me and hit the jackpot. It was great!"

"Strategy."

"It provided good cover," Minnie replied modestly, "and we've more than made back our expenses for the day."

"Even including the cost of the disguises," I added soberly. "You gave such a good clue that I practically ran into them outside. They were with someone."

"Did he look like an accomplice?"

"You mean, was he wearing a ski mask?"

"Don't be silly. People don't walk around like that, not in June anyway. I mean, well, did he look shifty?"

"Couldn't tell. They were holding him up, one on each side, and they seemed to be arguing."

She nodded. "Probably an accomplice, mask or not. You know how thieves always get to wrangling over the loot."

We rounded a curve, and I identified the USC pennant on top of an RV barreling toward us.

"Duck!" I hunched over the wheel and pulled as far to the right as I could go.

The RV roared past without a sign that the driver recognized us, but I had swerved too far and the passenger side wheels bounced along gravel until I wrestled the poor old Volvo to a stop.

Minnie's voice came from under the cockeyed sun hat. "Do you think they saw us?"

I didn't answer. Instead, I rested my head on the steering

wheel and closed my eyes as I listened to my furiously beating heart. My hands didn't quit shaking for several minutes. What was I doing, driving like a maniac all over Oregon? Minnie might have a raging desire to swap her rolling pin for a tour with Delta Force, but this was nuts. I had let myself get sucked into silly excursions with her for the last time. No more chasing down phantom leads.

At least today's excursion had provided one unexpected benefit. Revisiting the hot springs where Tony and I used to bring our children for a simple swim had brought back wonderful memories of our early family life, but it had also jolted me to confront the sweeping changes at Mystery River in the intervening years. I didn't like seeing the commercialism encroaching on the formerly peaceful countryside, but I couldn't alter today's reality, just as I couldn't alter the fact that Tony had died two years ago. All three of our girls were now grown, and Tony wasn't coming back. Tony and I had promised to remain true to each other " 'til death do us part." We'd kept that bargain. It was time for me to look to the future, and the future was Nick.

"Jane, are you all right?" Minnie's anxious voice penetrated my thoughts. "You're crying. Are you hurt?"

How could I break the news to her that the chase was done? "Just nerves. I'm fine. How about you?"

"Terrific! That was some fancy driving you did."

"Thanks." I restarted the car and attempted to pull back onto the asphalt, but movement was sluggish, so I pulled back to the side and got out for a look. The right front tire was flat.

Minnie joined me beside the car. "We'll never catch them now."

"Nope."

We stood together for a moment, listening to the fading growl of the RV's big engine. When the high desert stillness again surrounded us, I popped the trunk and hauled out the jack and the spare in preparation for the dusty process of changing the tire.

"But your hands . . ."

Minnie's tearful distress seemed way out of proportion to the prospect of me getting my hands dirty. She must be mourning the ignominious finish of Operation Hollow Feather.

I searched for something to say that might cheer her up. "You can debrief Velda on our op when you deliver the soup."

Her wan smile told me she appreciated my effort. "Roger that."

CHAPTER 20

Bianca was slumped on the staircase with her head in her hands when I arrived at Thornton's. Heart suddenly thumping, I asked the obvious question. "Alix?"

Tyler gave me a playful smile and shook his head. Whew. Just the usual Bianca drama. That, I could handle.

As he offered Bianca a tissue, he spoke in soothing tones. "Not your fault. Nobody could've guessed a porcupine would come so close to a wedding reception, especially in broad daylight."

"Wendell spotted it fast enough." Bianca's words came from under a silken curtain of hair.

From her forlorn tone, I could imagine the scene, though I'd forgotten all about this afternoon's frontier wedding.

Tyler's face contorted in an unsuccessful attempt to stifle a laugh.

Bianca scowled as she snatched the tissue from him. "Not funny."

He turned to fill me in. "You should've seen him. Man, he's fast! That's one wedding no one will ever forget." As another laugh threatened to overtake him, he deliberately changed the subject. "How'd you do at Mystery River? Learn anything?"

"Are you kidding? This was Minnie's idea, and I'm sure she'll tell you all about our glorious detective adventure in due time. Anything from Alix or Nick?"

"Nope. Everything was quiet in town. I'm glad I went to the

171

wedding instead. Never laughed so hard in my life."

I pulled the cell phone from my bag. "Go ahead, finish your conversation. I'll report in to Alix, though there isn't anything to say." I started to punch in her number.

"If only the fight hadn't spooked the horses." Bianca stared into space, mentally rewriting the debacle. "A couple more minutes and the bride and groom would've been long gone."

Tyler gave me a "what now?" look as I passed him. I snapped the phone shut and tried to think of something that would cheer her up. "Look at it this way . . . er . . ."

Tyler's agile young mind sprinted in a new direction. "Yeah, look at it this way. The bride and groom wanted a taste of the Old West, right? They sure got it. Once they hauled the buckboard back out of the creek bed, everybody looked real happy." Tyler's lips twitched again, but this time he maintained control. "And don't worry about that porcupine. He had plenty of quills to spare."

At last Bianca rose from the stairs. "The bride and groom liked the 'jest hitched' sign on the buckboard. And they did ask me to save them some quills. What do you think, Mom?"

I lowered the cell phone and considered the big picture. "It's hard to beat porcupine quills as unique mementos of a wedding. They wanted an unforgettable day, and you gave them one. Maybe Wendell should raise his rates."

It was Bianca's turn to consider the big picture. "I don't think so. I kept him on his leash most of the time, but he still snagged a whole plate of grits."

Tyler shuddered. "The guests were probably begging him to take that stuff. Did you try them?"

"Yes," Bianca said. "The bride wanted grits, and they're nutritious."

"Weird. I thought she was kidding."

"That reminds me, Ty. Did you eat the carrot soup I brought back?"

Tyler's struggle between pleasing Bianca and telling the truth was written on his face. He glanced at me for assistance, but I could only shrug in sympathy. We'd all battled Bianca and her passion for organic food.

"I tried it, but Wendell seemed hungry after we got back from the vet, and I thought maybe it would be easy for him to eat."

Bianca's tender heart kicked in. "He did seem rather forlorn after our trip to the vet. I think he was sorry for what he'd done. His poor mouth must have been sore, so the soup was probably just the thing. What did you have instead?"

"Three corn dogs."

"And?"

"And a Pepsi and chips."

"And?"

"And a couple of Twinkies and a piece of that chocolate cake Minnie brought. I didn't want to hurt her feelings." As Bianca frowned at him, Tyler caved in. "Look, I'll have some of this leftover corn pone or whatever. See? I'm eating it."

I busied myself again with the cell phone so I wouldn't get roped into sharing Tyler's sacrificial act. Having been tied up all day with Operation Hollow Feather, I certainly wasn't in any mood for corn pone.

"Her line's busy. I think I'll just run over there, see how she's doing. You'll be okay to close on your own, Tyler?"

"No problem."

Bianca jumped in. "Before you leave, what do you think about us doing an intervention on his grandpa?" Bianca waved away Tyler's protests. "Just tell us what you think. You know, we could all confront him and make him tell us what he's been doing, meeting that man and all."

"The problem is, I'm not sure he even knows what he's been doing." Tyler was glum as he spoke. "I've caught him in outright lies, so he's either hiding something or he's losing his memory. I don't know which is worse."

"If we bring it out in the open though, Laurence might get mad and send Tyler back to Nevada. What do you think, Mom?"

"Are you worried about that, Tyler? You're not going back there, no matter what. If Laurence is just getting a little forgetful, no one's going to yank you away from here. It's not like you need him to fix your lunch or anything. If anything, it's the other way around."

"But what if she shows up here when he's acting weird?"

"She won't. You told me that yourself the other day." I didn't see any need to pussyfoot around. Tyler knew his mother and her grand schemes that somehow never worked out. "It's not going to happen. Just keep your head down for now, and you'll be fine. We're with you, but I need to get this deal with Alix sorted out before I can concentrate on Laurence's behavior."

Distress remained evident on Tyler's face. When he finally blurted out what he'd been thinking, I could see why. "That's part of what I'm talking about. I've been afraid that . . . I know this sounds really dumb . . . but suppose Grandpa somehow got mixed up with the dead guy."

"You don't think your grandfather killed him!" If Tyler hadn't been so pale as he forced himself to voice his fear, I'd have laughed at the very idea.

"No, but what if there's some connection? That weird guy he met the other day wasn't the one who got killed. I know that because the murder happened before they met, but something's going on with Grandpa." He shook his head as if to clear it. "Two strange guys come to town, and one of them ends up dead. That talk about scams the other day got me to wondering."

I was finally catching Tyler's train of thought. I clenched my hands at my sides to keep from rushing over to hug this poor kid who had been carrying such a heavy burden. He didn't need motherly coddling so much as he needed someone to keep a clear head and figure things out. "So you think the man Laurence met might be another con man, maybe even the murderer."

"Yeah." Tyler's face cleared as he explained. "But I don't know his name or anything. If I tell the sheriff about him, he'll go to Grandpa, and then all the stuff about Grandpa might come out."

"We can't leave Laurence on his own to deal with someone who might be a murderer, that's for sure," Bianca's voice was rising, her worry more evident with every word. "We ought to have an intervention right now."

"Hold on," I said. "We don't know whether this man had anything to do with the murder."

"Yeah, but we don't know he didn't either. Far as I know, there aren't any other suspects in the picture, except Alix, of course." Bianca pleaded her case for action well.

Especially since it concerned me that Arnie hadn't turned up any other leads.

"Wouldn't it help if we gave him someone else to think about?"

"It might. Let me think about it."

Of course, I was the only one here who knew that Arnie was aware of Irene Cook's existence and thus had every reason to concentrate his attention on Alix. It had been just a pipe dream of mine that another suspect would somehow walk in and confess. I felt an increased urgency to take action.

"What should I do, Jane?" Tyler looked at me with such trust that I gave him the only possible answer, wishing I could think of something more tangible.

"For the moment, nothing. Just keep a close watch on your grandpa while I think out our next step. And try not to worry, okay?" It was my job to shoulder the worry for all of us. "I promise we'll sort everything out soon."

Both Bianca and Tyler gave me that look of confidence I had come to dread. They now believed that the Bookstore Heroine was fully engaged in all aspects of the case—clearing Alix of suspicion, solving the murder, and figuring out what was causing Laurence to act strangely—so they could relax and wait for further instructions. I gave them a reassuring smile that stayed firmly in place just long enough to get me out the door and on my way to see Alix. I wish I was as certain as I'd sounded that I could fulfill my promise.

CHAPTER 21

While waiting for Alix to finish a phone call, I sank into her deep floral couch and rolled my head in a vain attempt to ease sore neck muscles. Sleep sounded better than just about anything I could think of, up to and including chocolate cake with chocolate frosting. Was it only a week ago that Nick and I were enjoying an evening over pepper-crusted rib-eye steaks and a smooth Argyle 2004 pinot? Probably best not to think of Nick at the moment. Much as I wanted his support, I couldn't get it until he returned to Juniper, or at least came back into cell phone range. Maybe I'd shelve everything and sleep for about a week.

"Your choice, Mrs. Querion. It all depends on how much you want to pay for flowers."

With my eyes still closed, I took in the rustle of pages being turned. It would be wonderful if Alix and her client would discuss the merits of flowers for hours, but Alix was wrapping things up.

"Tomorrow morning at ten o'clock? Fine. Roses are always a lovely choice. Yes, I'll check Wendell's schedule."

She clicked off and I opened my eyes, rest period over.

"You look like you could use some wine, Jane. I'll get it." Alix threw the words over her shoulder as she disappeared into the kitchen.

I called after her. "I'm too tired for wine."

Too late. Alix emerged a moment later with two stemmed

goblets and handed me one, as though I hadn't even spoken. "You just spent the day with Minnie. You need wine." She sank onto the loveseat across the glass coffee table from me and raised her glass. "Here's to logic."

I tilted my goblet at her and sipped. "For someone under investigation, you're sure relaxed. Minnie, Velda, and I have been shredding our nerves trying to come up with ideas, and Bianca and Tyler have taken over your business commitments, while you calmly discuss flower arrangements. Even Wendell's more on edge than you are. That could be from his porcupine encounter though."

Alix pulled flowered cocktail napkins from a drawer and slid one toward me. "Poor Wendell. Three weddings this week, and I haven't given him so much as an extra kibble for overtime."

"Tough employer. Are you as tough at your bank job?" I watched as Alix's creamy complexion turned a soft pink. "Irene showed me the 'official' letter."

"See? You're a great detective. Anyway, you got more out of Irene than I expected. She wouldn't have let me in the door."

"For a while there, I didn't think she'd see me either. Too bad I didn't learn much of use. I felt sorry for her. She'd been thrilled at her grandson's visit, completely blind to his reason for being there. Nice for her to have one last happy memory of him, I guess."

Alix smiled at me. "Thanks for trying, really. Now, tell me about your casino adventure."

"Useless, as expected. Typical trip with Minnie." I was still puzzled at Alix's calmness. "How come all of a sudden you're so relaxed? Yesterday, you begged me to investigate, and today you're all smiles and 'Have a glass of wine.' And you don't even seem upset that the police might discover the bank account connection. What happened?"

Alix set her goblet on the napkin and leaned forward. "You

know that kids' story about Chicken Little? I always expected the sky to fall if people in Juniper learned I'd been married to Hunter, built the fear in my head for years. When he turned up dead, I expected Arnie to arrive on my doorstep and, sure enough, here he came. Everybody in town now knows about my marriage to Hunter. That's the thing. It was my worst nightmare, but now," she spread her arms wide, "it's a couple of days later, and the sky's still up there. Mrs. Querion is only worried about the cost of roses for her daughter's wedding. If anything, business has picked up. Some people are actually excited by my connection to a guy who got himself 'whacked.' I think that's the popular term."

"That's sick."

"How else do you explain the fact that business is booming? Think it's the growing community awareness of Wendell's splendor in a tuxedo?"

"I don't know, but murder isn't funny."

"Come on. I make jokes about everything. Keeps me from worrying so much, the way you do. I'll probably live longer."

"I'll wear myself out worrying about you. You're still the best suspect they've got. And what if they trace those deposits?"

"I've got my fingers crossed that they won't, but it's still nothing more than circumstantial evidence."

I thought of how many people had been convicted on circumstantial evidence.

"So, cheer us both up and tell me about spending a whole day with Minnie and Velda, ace detectives."

I didn't feel cheerful, but I tried. "Just Minnie. Velda had to cancel at the last minute."

"Too bad. Hanging out with Minnie has spiced up her life."

"Minnie and I were on our own. She insisted we have a code name for our operation."

"Oh, I can believe it. Do I have a high enough security clearance . . . ?"

"Operation Hollow Feather."

"Excellent. Did you have a secret handshake in a smoky room?"

"No secret handshake, but the smoky room was sure there. You'd have loved it." I couldn't resist a dig at Alix's two-pack-a-day habit. "Smoke so thick you couldn't breathe. Part of the top floor was supposed to be smoke-free, but we didn't get up there."

"And did you find Phil and Eileen parked under a flashing red sign that said, 'We killed Hunter Blackburn'?"

"How'd you know?"

"Actually, we did see them, and something odd was going on. They were hauling a young guy out of the casino against his will. He was having trouble walking."

"Tall, thin kid with dark hair?"

Alix shrugged. "Simon. They work with him. Alcohol and gambling problems."

"How do you know anything about Simon and his problems? Working with troubled kids doesn't happen to be another of your secret charitable causes, does it? You never mentioned—"

"Why would I? Besides, Phil and Eileen as killers? Come on. That whole idea was a figment of Minnie's overheated imagination. At least you kept her out of trouble for a few hours. Can't beat that."

"Too bad I wasn't smart enough to deflect Velda when she followed poor Alice Durand to the post office the other day," I said glumly.

"She did that?"

"And she'll probably do it again, next chance she gets. Since you know something about Phil and Eileen, do you have any idea why they might have tried to ditch us on the way home?"

"You sure that's what they were doing?"

I sat back and sipped at the wine, mulling over what I'd seen. "Now that I think about it, probably not. I got so caught up in the chase that I practically drove off the road. Being around Minnie has an adverse effect on rational thought."

"If I'd spent a day in the car with Minnie, I'd probably have driven off the road between here and the casino on purpose. At least it was just Minnie, not both of them."

"Easy for you to say. You weren't part of the Hollow Feather op. That's spy shorthand."

"I read le Carré, too, you know. Makes a nice change of pace from *Gowns and Veils Weekly*." At my incredulous look, she nodded. "Honest. There's really such a magazine. Want to see?"

"I'll take your word. Anyway, Minnie was really in her element. She was disappointed when we had to break off the chase, but she's probably perked up by now. She planned to take Velda some homemade soup."

Alix laughed. "I'm sure Velda will be thrilled to the tips of her sturdy brown oxfords to hear about your near-death experience."

At Alix's reference to Velda's shoes, I flashed back to the sight of Velda in her sling-backs this morning. "She doesn't have much to look forward to. We shouldn't begrudge her a little excitement."

"Okay, okay. Lesson delivered, Preacher. But anyone who chooses Minnie as a role model needs to get out more." Alix picked up her cigarettes. "Now, let's go outside. I've been good long enough."

"Not if you hope to live to a ripe old age." I followed her out the French doors to the courtyard. "I thought you were giving up cigarettes."

"Seemed like a bad week for it." Alix fired up a Virginia Slim, considering. "Tell you what. You find Hunter's killer, and I'll quit."

"You mean it?" Alix's likelihood of having to pay off was next to zero, but I'd take the offer.

"Sure." She held out her hand, and I took it. Then we both laughed.

"Now that we have that settled, I'll get back to detecting. With an incentive like this, it shouldn't take me more than another day or two to wrap things up."

"If you really want to perform a public service, think of some way to keep Minnie and Velda from stirring things up."

I groaned. "And how do you propose I do that?"

"Logic?"

"Yeah, that'll work."

"You can tell them to offer their help directly to Arnie."

"I'm not that mean. Arnie has enough problems."

"Let's go finish that wine." Alix stubbed out her cigarette in a sand bucket hidden behind a blooming ornamental cherry tree and led the way. "How about the way Bianca and Tyler managed that wedding today? And Wendell, bless his furry little heart. When we steer him clear of porcupines and appetizer trays, he's all right."

"You've got yourself a unique set of wedding assistants, that's for sure. Heard about Tyler's problem yet?"

"His mother again?"

"Her, too, but right now it's Laurence. Tyler's afraid his memory's going."

"What are you talking about? That old man's mind is sharper than most."

"That's what I think, but he's been doing some odd things, getting secret calls. He even met a man on the street who appeared to threaten him, and lied to Tyler about it, so Tyler wonders whether he's somehow mixed up with a con man."

"That poor kid. Could it have been Hunter?"

"No, this happened after the murder. We were trying to

decide whether to tell Arnie, give him somebody else to chase besides you. What do you think?"

"I like that idea. Hunter always worked alone, but it's certainly possible there's someone else running a con here. Maybe they somehow crossed paths and argued. Hunter wasn't into violence though."

"Maybe the other guy was. Tyler doesn't want to stir up his grandfather unless necessary, afraid that'll bring his mother to Juniper."

"What does Nick think? I called him earlier looking for you, but he never called back."

"He's somewhere on the west side of the Cascades working on a timber theft case, but he ought to be back soon. Maybe he'll have fresh ideas."

"Maybe everything will be settled by the time he gets here."

We raised our glasses in a toast.

"Do you like the wine? It came from the Perkins' wedding. They loved the 'Moonlight in the Mountains' theme so much they presented me with a whole case of it."

"You've changed your door chimes. Isn't 'I Love You Truly' a bit hokey?"

"You bet. Eighty-five percent of wedding planning involves massive amounts of hokiness."

"Eighty-five percent, eh? And Bianca and Tyler handle the other fifteen percent. How would you describe that category?"

Alix laughed, shaking her head. "Central Oregon Cuckoo?"

I saluted Alix with my wine glass. "This is nice. I should take your advice and relax more often."

"I agree."

As if on cue, the strains of "I Love You Truly" began, and the door to the Wedding Belle opened. We laughed until we saw who had entered.

Alix jumped up as if on springs. Apparently, she hadn't been as relaxed as she'd pretended. "Hello, Arnie. How's the investigation?"

"Lookin' good." Arnie craned his neck in my direction. "Hello, Jane. Glad to see you here."

My muscles tensed. Arnie sounded much too pleased with himself. Did he know about my visit to Irene Cook? "Were you looking for me?"

Alix waved him into the room with an outstretched arm.

"Not particularly. Always a pleasure though." His attempt at a smile didn't quite work.

This was definitely not good news. How did Alix manage to look so unconcerned?

"Have you made an arrest?" I was sure they both could hear my heart pounding.

"Not yet, but we're close. I thought Alix might have something to tell me." He turned toward her. "Some little thing you forgot to mention last time we talked?"

"Nothing comes to mind." Alix's voice remained level. She leaned casually against the arm of the loveseat, but I could see the trembling of her slender arm.

"Me and the guys'd like to take a quick look-see around your place. You don't mind, do you?"

"What are you looking for?"

"Look, we can do this the easy way or the hard way." He waved a paper in the air. "Here's a search warrant that Judge Taylor signed not fifteen minutes ago."

I had no doubt that Alix was about to make everything worse. She did. Advancing toward him, she said, "Actually, the hard way sounds like more fun."

I pushed between them. "What could you possibly hope to find here, Arnie?"

He handed me the paper while focusing on Alix. "You know what we're after."

I scanned the warrant before looking back at Arnie, incredulous. "A thirty-eight caliber revolver? Alix doesn't own a gun."

"Didn't I tell you?" Alix said. "I have a complete shooting range in my basement. Oh, wait. I don't have a basement . . . or a gun. Sorry to disappoint."

"That's not all we're after."

"In that case . . . I sent my bloody hatchet out for sharpening last week. Go ahead and look." Alix waved vaguely around the room. "Don't forget to check the garage for rat poison, and there's my portable bomb-making kit under the bathroom sink, of course."

I half-listened to Alix's remarks as I slogged through the rest of the legalese on the warrant. Where was Nick when I needed him? Surely no one but an attorney could make sense of this stuff.

Unfortunately, one line was clear enough to freeze my blood. I put my hand on Alix's tense shoulder and spoke quietly. "Financial records."

"You won't think this is so funny by the time we're done." Arnie stepped back outside and waved.

Deputies Brady Newman and Jim Cozinski appeared at the front door and stood there hesitantly. When our eyes met, Brady spread his arms in a gesture of resignation.

"Come on in," Alix said. "Sorry I can't offer you wine when you're on duty. Jane, have some more?"

In a daze, I followed Alix back to the loveseat and held up my glass.

She sat beside me to pour. "We can sit on the revolver stashed under the loveseat."

"Stop playing games! They have a search warrant."

Apparently startled at my anger, Alix spoke seriously. "Sorry, habit. I don't know anything about the gun."

I sat, stunned, at the sudden turn of events. Maybe I hadn't really accepted that it could come to this. Alix was much better at putting up a brave front than I was. She'd had years of practice.

Arnie lumbered back into the room, carrying Alix's sleek leather bag. "Hope I'm not interrupting." He looked back and forth between us.

Alix leaned back and drank more wine. "I must say, Sheriff Kraft, that bag looks stunning against your uniform. You really ought to get one."

Arnie flushed, but he didn't rise to the bait. He was too delighted at having the upper hand, for once. "Little upset, are you, Alix?"

I looked at Alix. Her grip had gone slack; wine dripped from her tilted goblet onto her beige linen slacks. Seeing it, she started. Then, like someone emerging from a dream, she set her glass on the table and smiled peacefully at Arnie. "What amazing powers of observation you have. You really should consider a career in law enforcement."

Arnie rocked back on his heels. "Brady, Jim, come on out here." As soon as he had the audience arranged to his satisfaction, he continued. "Alix Boudreau, I'm arresting you on suspicion of the murder of Hunter Blackburn."

I clutched at the arm of the loveseat to steady myself. This couldn't be happening.

Alix frowned. "Gee, Arnie, I don't know whether you've quite got it yet . . . your technique, I mean. You've got the strut, but the official voice needs work." She rose and sauntered past him toward the door. "Don't worry. You might still get a chance to arrest Hunter's real killer someday, once Jane locates him for you."

She looked back at me and shrugged. "You wanted me to quit smoking, didn't you? Here's your chance to win that bet."

She stepped through the door, leaving Arnie and his deputies to scramble after her like puppies following their mother.

CHAPTER 22

The luminous clock radio dial read five-forty-two A.M. as I gave up on sleep and kicked free of my tangled sheets the next morning. Rolling onto my back, I tried again to formulate a plan. Alix's predicament had been floating around in my head all night without resolution. Even in the clear morning light, the situation remained a nightmare. Alix had been arrested for murder. That was the reality, though the idea of her killing a human being, even her detested ex-husband, was beyond ridiculous.

I flipped onto my stomach and buried my head under the pillow as I attempted to produce a picture of Alix at her most violent. I could see her stabbing someone with a cutting remark, or looking daggers at a rude person, but that was about it. Some hours removed from the shock of the arrest yesterday afternoon, I couldn't help smiling at the way she'd dared to mouth off to Arnie, causing him to puff up like an outraged turkey. Her tart sense of humor must be rubbing off on me.

By the time he'd led the late-night news on Z21, he'd calmed down enough to give a reasonably noncommittal statement, though a self-satisfied smile had threatened to break out from time to time. He'd apparently watched enough *Law & Order* segments to avoid saying too much at this stage of the investigation. Too bad someone hadn't reminded him to take off his hat before the interview. He'd glanced at the monitor shortly after it began and suddenly yanked the hat off his head to keep it from

188

shading his face. His subsequent attempts to smooth his thinning hair into place were both unsuccessful and distracting.

"Enough!"

Critiquing Arnie's TV presence wasn't getting me anywhere. Unearthing myself from the bedding, I sat up and fumbled for the cell phone I had placed by the bed in the vain hope that Nick might call. I carried it with me as I padded to the kitchen. Coffee first. I filled the carafe with fresh water and arranged a filter in place before measuring the shiny Ethiopian beans into the stainless steel grinder nearby. The unearthly racket was a small price to pay for a good cup of coffee, and I needed every bit of help I could muster to figure out what to do next.

Two cups of coffee and a shower later, I still felt like crawling back into bed and pulling the covers over my head. I went back to the kitchen table and stared at my empty coffee cup. I should call Minnie, tell her why Phil and Eileen had been in the casino. Nope. Talking to Minnie first thing in the morning was more than I could manage. The phone rang at my elbow, startling me.

"Aren't you coming?" The call was from Tyler. The background sounds of conversation at Thornton's made it hard to hear him. "The SOS meeting?"

No need to tell him I'd forgotten all about it. "Be right there."

Twenty minutes later, Bianca intercepted me at the door to the crowded bookstore. "You're just in time. Leave everything to us."

If she'd heard about the arrest, Bianca's cheerful demeanor made no sense. "You've heard about Alix?"

"No problem. We're hot on the trail."

I grasped her elbow as she turned away. "Who's 'we'? And whose trail are you on?" I was afraid to hear the answer, but better to know before things got out of hand.

"The suspects, of course." Bianca nodded at Phil and Eileen

Hedstrom, ensconced in the middle of the front row. "Minnie and Velda made a plan."

Oh, Lord. Things were already out of control. Too bad we'd wasted our time—not to mention gasoline—chasing them all the way to the casino yesterday when they were right here in our clutches today. "Do we have a new code name for this op?" I asked faintly.

Bianca looked puzzled. Apparently, Minnie hadn't educated her on the finer points of espionage. I waved my hand in a "never mind" gesture and dropped helplessly into a folding chair to watch the disaster that was about to unfold. I closed my eyes, longing to rewind the morning and revisit the excellent idea of crawling back into bed.

Bianca herded everyone into their chairs. Minnie and Velda made the rounds with cookies and juice.

Once everyone was seated, Bianca addressed the group. "I'm sorry that I don't have the information I intended to get on Oregon senior services. Next meeting for sure. I got sidetracked by a veterinary emergency, but you'll be glad to know that in spite of having thirty-three porcupine quills removed from his tongue, Wendell is going to be just fine." She smiled at Wendell, lying beside her and staring fixedly at the plate of cookies. Apparently the quills no longer concerned him. "Instead, I thought we could use today's meeting to compare notes on what brought each of us—"

Alice Durand's harsh voice cut across Bianca's comments. "Seems your fool dog's always getting himself in one kind of trouble or another."

Minnie jumped to Wendell's defense. "He saved Jane's life a year ago!"

"Maybe so, but what about the time he swallowed that rock?"

"Poor Wendell has only one eye. Maybe he couldn't tell it was a rock," Velda said.

"He's got a nose, doesn't he? Even with one eye, seems he could recognize a rock." Alice was not about to back down. "Pets are a lot of bother and money, if you ask me."

"But they give you so much love," Bianca swept aside Alice's objections. "Have you ever had a kitten or puppy?"

"Had a cat once. Not likely I'd get another. By the time I finish what I got to do each day, I'm not lookin' for more work."

"Wasn't it nice to have your cat waiting for you at home?" Bianca persisted.

"It was just a cat." Alice fell silent and then abruptly stood up, causing her empty paper plate to slide to the floor. "Now look what I did." She swept crumbs onto the plate with her crumpled napkin before looking up, red-faced. "We just gonna sit around talking about fool animals?" she asked, apparently forgetting she'd introduced the topic.

"I'm sorry, Alice," Bianca said, flustered. "Minnie?"

Minnie stood up and smiled at the group, but it wasn't her usual friendly smile. In fact, she looked more like a shark than anything else. I listened, fascinated, as she circled her prey.

"Wouldn't it be interesting to find out how each of us came to join the group?"

"No," said Alice. "We already did that. We all got ripped off by someone, or we're related to someone who did."

Minnie frowned. "Yes, of course, but how have our experiences continued to affect us? For example, Phil, how did you spend yesterday?"

Eileen nudged her husband with an elbow. "Honey, she wants to know what you did yesterday."

Phil merely looked back at Eileen, who finally answered for him. "Why'd you want to know, Minnie?"

"Just wondering if those crooked roofers have continued to affect your lives."

Phil found his voice at last. "You want to know about those

crooks, I can tell you plenty."

"We're just talking about yesterday."

The shark was closing in for the kill. I sank lower into my chair. Where was a shark cage when you needed it? Just one phone call and I could have averted this. Too late. I closed my eyes.

"We haven't seen hide nor hair of them since they took our down payment three months ago and left town," Eileen answered. "Leaving no forwarding address, I might add."

"But you haven't told me what you did yesterday," Minnie repeated.

"What are you driving at?" Eileen's voice rose in annoyance.

"I'm driving at what you did yesterday." Arms crossed, Minnie stood directly in front of the Hedstroms. "Where were you?"

"None of your business," Phil said flatly.

"I'm making it my business. I want—"

Eileen lumbered to her feet. "Let's go, Phil."

They made a nice little procession as they swept out the door, with Minnie in hot pursuit and Velda scurrying behind. Minnie's voice grew fainter with distance, but the silence inside the store seemed to expand.

I cleared my throat. "Anyone else like to speak? More cookies?"

Chapter 23

After the meeting disintegrated, we didn't find much to say. Tyler and I packed up the folding chairs, Bianca gathered discarded cups and plates, and Wendell snuffled around in search of stray cookie crumbs. I stowed extra chairs in the office, and then leaned against the desk, discouraged.

Laurence poked his head inside the back door. "They gone?"

"Oh, yes. They certainly are."

For once I was glad he hadn't been here. This SOS meeting would have put him off the group forever.

Tyler carried in a double armload of chairs. "Grandpa! You're here."

His grandfather looked at him sharply. "Where else would I be?"

"I thought maybe you'd . . . slept in or something." Tyler's lame attempt to hide his relief apparently agitated his grandfather further.

"I don't need a morning nap, sonny. Waited out back 'til that bunch of old fools stopped milling around."

"How 'bout I find us some lunch? Tuna melt from Gifford's, with pickles and chips? Won't take ten minutes to get it here." Tyler picked up the phone without waiting for an answer.

From the anticipatory expression on Laurence's face, I could see that Tyler had diverted him, though the old man spoke gruffly. "I'll be out front, working. Somebody's got to keep an eye on things around here."

Was it my imagination, or was Laurence limping more than usual? I watched from the office as he made his slow way to the front counter. Laurence had a real sweet tooth, so I was surprised when he shook his head at Bianca's offer of Minnie's giant oatmeal cookies.

Tyler still had his hand on the phone after placing the order when the phone rang, so he picked it up. His shoulders slumped as he listened. At my questioning look, he mouthed "Mom" before trudging to the front of the store to where his grandfather stood. Tyler started to hand him the phone, but, at the last minute, he jerked it back against his chest, covering the mouthpiece.

"I can't go live with her again. Please, Grandpa. I don't care about your problem. I'll take care of you."

"What are you talking about? Give me that thing!" Laurence tore the phone from Tyler's hand and glared at him. "What's the matter with you these days?"

Obviously stunned by the heat in his grandfather's voice, Tyler retreated several steps, backing into me where I hovered near the doorway. Laurence continued to stare at his grandson.

Tyler finally smacked the doorjamb with the flat of his hand and brushed by me into the office. "Might as well start packing."

I followed him and let the door swing shut behind us. Avoiding even a stray glance at Tyler, I sat at the desk and shuffled through a stack of year-old invoices.

Tyler crept back to the closed door, muttering to himself. "Sound normal, Grandpa. Please, just for a few minutes, sound normal."

We didn't bother to pretend we weren't eavesdropping, but we could make out only an occasional word. When quiet finally descended on the front room, Tyler glided away from the door and picked up a book at random from the shelf behind the desk.

The door crashed open, and Laurence limped in. "What's this business about wanting to go live with your mother? First I've heard of it."

Tyler whirled to face him. "I never said I wanted to go there."

Laurence fixed Tyler with a long look. "You didn't, eh? She can be convincing. Fooled me more than once along the way. Still, maybe you'd be better off there, since you—"

Tyler produced barely a whisper. "What?"

Laurence closed the two steps between them. "Since you've been following me, hounding me—"

"I have not . . . maybe, but only because I care about you. You're meeting someone and acting all mysterious about it."

"Who I see is none of your business." Laurence's voice had risen with each word and his face was turning a dangerous shade of red.

"Laurence, you're not supposed to get excited," I said. If nothing was wrong, why would Laurence be reacting so strongly?

Tyler swallowed, but stood his ground. "I'm afraid he's dangerous."

"Why would you think that?" Laurence gripped Tyler's arm. "You haven't been talking to him?"

Tyler wrenched away from Laurence's grasp.

"Suppose he's involved in . . . in that murder?"

The hurt in Tyler's eyes made me jump to my feet. If I could see it, why couldn't Laurence?

Laurence stepped back, as though slapped. "If you think, if you could entertain the notion that I'm mixed up in something like that, you'd better go live with your mother."

"Not mixed up in that . . . just mixed up."

Tyler's words hung in the air.

Finally, Laurence shook his head in disgust. "Even you. You

think I'm losing my marbles, don't you? Everyone says, 'Come to the SOS meetings.' Those meetings are for silly old fools who can't think straight. I had a heart attack last year, not a brain meltdown. You're treating me like a baby."

"Can't you see he's trying to protect you?" I'd stayed out of it as long as I could. They were talking right past each other. "From yourself, Laurence. From sleazy people who might want to take advantage of you."

Tyler softened his tone. "I don't think you're a baby, Grandpa. Look, I found the key to your desk . . . the sweepstakes entries and stuff."

Laurence made a strangled sound in his throat.

Tyler swept on. "Yeah, I snooped through everything. I followed you. I listened in on your phone calls—"

"You did what?" Laurence's question was a howl of outrage.

"To help!" Tyler's voice rose in frustration. "That's all I was trying to do. Everybody needs help sometimes, Grandpa."

"Do you?" Laurence fired back.

Tyler blinked in surprise.

"Yes. I need your help. I want to stay with you, but they won't let me if you keep sneaking around like this, acting crazy."

I held my breath waiting for Laurence's response, knowing Tyler had just risked the one thing he wanted more than anything: to stay right here with his grandfather. They stood toe-to-toe, the two of them glaring like roosters about to fly at each other.

"Crazy? Is that what you think?"

Like magic, the tension drained out of Laurence's face and he dropped into the chair I'd just vacated. I was relieved to see that his complexion was starting to return to its normal color. He sat looking at his knotted hands for a few minutes, thinking. Finally, a smile pulled at the corners of his mouth.

He looked up at me. "Feisty, isn't he? Chip off the old block.

Tyler, my boy, we need to talk."

I tried to slip out of the room, to give them some privacy.

Laurence stopped me. "Stay put. Seems you already know more than I do. Might as well hear the rest." He paused and shifted in the chair, then sighed. "There's no good way to say this. All that stuff . . . the plain truth is that I thought I could show you all a thing or two. Hate to admit it, but I'm an arrogant old fool."

Tyler got it before I did. "You've been using yourself as bait!"

"Trying to, anyway. Responding to bogus roofing ads, that kind of thing. Started a few months ago when you were hounding me about joining that old folks' group. Then, when Alix's ex-husband got himself murdered, I thought maybe I could really do something. The man you saw me with downtown? I even thought he might be the killer, or maybe an accomplice."

"Laurence, what were you thinking?" I was outraged.

"You put yourself in danger, Grandpa." Tyler sounded half-shocked, half-thrilled.

"That was the idea," he said with a grin. "But I didn't. That two-bit chiseler was a big waste of my time. He wouldn't know a murderer if he saw one."

"Thank goodness, you weren't hurt," I said. "A man your age, running around like some undercover cop. You should've stayed out of it."

"The same way you do, Jane?" Laurence's smile widened as he observed my consternation. "You might be right. But so what? Most fun I've had in a long time. Last year, I didn't get to help at all when you solved that murder."

"You were in the ICU at the time," I reminded him. "Or had you forgotten?"

He waved this away as a minor point.

"We've asked you a million times to join us at the Murder of the Month meetings. You've never shown the slightest interest."

"Don't want to sit in a damn rocking chair reading about crimes, unless maybe it's Dostoevsky doing the writing."

"Would being a guest speaker for the SOS group count as fieldwork?" I asked the question half in jest, but I immediately started to see some possibilities. "You could tell them what you learned while you were undercover. They'd be fascinated."

"Didn't learn much."

"You did great, Grandpa." Tyler's smile was back full force. "Remember, I saw your act. You sure fooled that chiseler."

"Bah! He was all bark and no bite."

"How can you be sure? Tyler told me he seemed to threaten you."

"He did. Tried to scare me into paying him money I didn't owe him." Laurence looked positively exhilarated as he recounted the experience. "I've done enough blustering of my own to recognize a blowhard when I see one. He's no problem."

"Maybe not to you, but he is a con man, right? What if he'd threatened one of those old ladies from the group?" Tyler continued. "Might've scared her to death. You can give a firsthand account about what to watch out for."

"I'll think about it." Laurence levered his bony frame to a standing position, looking about ten years younger than he had only a few minutes ago. "But this afternoon, I'm busy. Right after that sandwich you promised me, I'm going over to describe my oily friend to the police. Didn't plan to originally, but since that knuckleheaded sheriff of ours has gone and arrested Alix, it's about time to widen his view of the possibilities."

I breathed a sigh of relief. "My sentiments exactly."

"Thought you'd approve." Laurence turned and put a hand on Tyler's shoulder. "Now, about your mother."

"What'd you tell her?"

"The truth. Told her I couldn't run Thornton's without you, that I still needed your help."

"And she was okay with that?" Tyler sounded dubious.

"She'll have to be." Laurence hunched his shoulders in an exaggerated way. "I'm just a frail old man, you know. Need a lot of help. Now, suppose you could stop jawing long enough to get out front and sell some books? About time you earned your keep."

CHAPTER 24

Sounds of the banter between Tyler and Laurence floated down the stairs as Bianca and I gathered bestsellers to restock the display windows. Their emotional conversation had certainly cleared the air. My thoughts returned to Alix. Too bad her situation couldn't be resolved with a few words. When would Nick get back to Juniper? I needed him here, and not just because of our escalating relationship.

Apparently, my expression reflected these concerns. Bianca turned from placing an oversized travel book about Sicily on a stand. "What's wrong? Aren't you happy about Ty and his grandpa?"

I continued to place crisp new hardbacks on their stands. "Of course. I'm just thinking . . ."

"About Wendell? Don't worry. I've been feeding him scrambled eggs and cottage cheese in case his mouth is still sore, and he eats everything just fine."

"Actually, I wasn't thinking about Wendell either."

"About Nick then."

"That's right. As Alix's attorney, he'll have much better access to her, and he can advise her on strategy."

"He'll be back soon." Bianca's voice oozed confidence. "He won't stay away from you any longer than he has to. Everybody knows he's hooked."

"I see. And you're some kind of an expert on men?"

The pitying look she gave me spoke volumes. My beautiful

daughter had been the subject of men's attention for some years now. It was only by luck that no one had yet captured her heart.

I burst out laughing and hugged her. "Yes, I guess you are. For Alix's sake, I hope you're right about Nick getting back soon."

"And for a lot more than that, Mom." Bianca raised her eyebrows significantly, making me feel about ten years old, but she didn't wait for a response before finishing her airy dismissal of Alix's very real jeopardy. "He'll help Alix when he gets here, if you haven't already snagged the killer by then." She checked her watch. "I'd better scoot if I'm going to get to that appointment. I'd love to skulk around with you, watch you solve the murder." She looked wistful at the idea. "But I have to take care of business until Alix is free. You have your job and I have mine. Would you like to take Wendell with you?"

I'd forgotten about Alix's appointment to talk to some woman today about wedding flowers, but Bianca hadn't. In fact, Bianca's general calmness about Alix's arrest had puzzled me, but now I got it. While Bianca discussed the merits of red or white roses at the Wedding Belle, I was supposed to catch a murderer and clear Alix's name. Simple, right? Bianca seemed to think so.

"That's okay. You take Wendell. He's probably very good at choosing flowers."

Under normal circumstances, I'd have found it entertaining to deal with the indignation of Thelma Garstrom who couldn't believe that Thornton's didn't have a picture book featuring the marble-toed woodpecker of Argentina. Under normal circumstances, I'd be looking forward to getting off work and telling Nick about my day as we relaxed over an Australian Shiraz and a plate of garlicky Greek olives. But nothing was normal at the moment. Bianca might assume that the Bookstore Heroine could just walk out the door and nab a killer on the sidewalk, but when I looked out the window, I didn't see any likely candidates.

True to his word, Laurence had gone to the Sheriff's Department to report the incident with the strange man he'd encountered, but he'd been informed that Sheriff Kraft was busy and would get back to him later. To me, that sounded ominous, but I came up empty when I tried to think of anything else I could be doing now to help Alix.

I continued to shelve books while willing Nick to call. Even supposing he did, I could imagine his incredulity at my recitation of recent events. From the ridiculous casino trip to Alix's arrest, things had certainly spun out of control since he left. I didn't even want to think about the disastrous SOS meeting. As far as I knew, Minnie and Velda were still out harassing Phil and Eileen Hedstrom over absolutely nothing. Nick might well decide to turn around and head right back over the mountains to deal with the relatively sane activity of pursuing timber thieves.

The door burst open and banged against the wall. Minnie and Velda, red-cheeked and out of breath, raced inside, mouths open and ready to tell me about their latest adventure. They skidded to a halt at the sight of a customer at the counter.

Making a fast recovery, Minnie advanced on the startled Thelma and enveloped her in a bear hug. "Welcome home. How was the cruise?"

Thelma disentangled herself from Minnie's grasp. "Everything I could have hoped for. Lectures on native birds every morning and evening, jungle hikes midday, tapes of bird calls to put us to sleep at night. It was magical."

"But the buffet." Minnie moved right to her favorite topic. "How was the buffet?"

"Truth be told, I hardly noticed."

"Really?" Surprise arched Minnie's eyebrows. "I'd heard . . . the warm crullers for breakfast, the savory crab bisque for lunch, the won tons stuffed with tiny shrimp."

"Yes, yes, I know people rave about dining on cruises, but when I have a chance to see a red-fronted coot or a two-banded plover, all thoughts of food just go right out of my head."

"You don't say." Minnie's astonishment matched her ample waistline. Nothing drove food from her thoughts.

"People tell me I have the appetite of a bird. Isn't that appropriate?" Thelma looked expectantly at us until we laughed politely at the well-worn joke.

I followed up. "Should I order that book for you? Be here in a couple of days." I fiddled with the order blank to avoid staring at the woman's sharp nose and tiny round eyes. Maybe Thelma was actually related to those marble-toed woodpeckers.

"I guess I can wait that long. Go ahead. So nice to see you, Minnie, and—"

"Where are my manners? Thelma Garstrom, this is my good friend Velda Kubek."

"Do you like birds, Velda? We have a group you might enjoy—"

"That would be wonderful." Velda's soft voice made a nice change from Minnie's booming contralto. "I'd love to join you sometime if . . . if I can get away."

"Velda cares for her aunt—you know, Eleanor McKay," Minnie explained. "Maybe I can watch Eleanor for you sometime, Velda, so you can go."

"Oh, would you? That would be such a treat."

"Can't think why it didn't occur to me before. Of course you need a break now and then." Minnie turned back to Thelma. "Give me a call before the next meeting."

"I'll do that. Nice to meet you, Velda."

Grasping the startled woman by the elbow, Minnie ushered

Thelma toward the door.

"You must have a million things to do after your trip, so we won't keep you." She waved a cheery goodbye and closed the door firmly behind Thelma before striding back to the counter, her company manners erased as though by magic. "Arnie showed up at Phil and Eileen's house. Pulled in right behind us, made a lot of noise about a possible complaint for harassment. They must've called him on a cell phone when they saw we were following them. Talk about rude."

"You can't exactly blame them, the way you attacked them at the meeting," I said.

"Minnie merely asked for a simple answer," Velda said. "No need for them to take such offense."

Could Velda seriously support Minnie's position? One look at her earnest face told me she did, but I couldn't help making one last stab at normalcy. "Minnie demanded an answer. Doesn't that strike you as offensive?"

"And why shouldn't they have given one, if they were innocent?" Minnie and Velda exchanged virtuous nods. "Could've saved everybody a lot of trouble."

"And saved Arnie a trip out to their house. Terrible waste of taxpayers' money," Velda added. "Their trip to the casino shouldn't have been any big secret."

"Right," Minnie said.

"Maybe it wasn't a secret. Maybe they just didn't feel it was any of your business." I knew I was talking to myself, with no hope of convincing them. I was looking at two stone walls. "So, after all this fuss and furor, did you ever discover what they were doing at the casino?"

After a pause, Minnie replied sullenly. "Outreach for their church-sponsored AA group. Helping some young man."

I couldn't help needling her. "So Operation Hollow Feather caught them doing a good deed?"

"When they wouldn't answer my questions, naturally that made me suspect—"

"—that they were murderers," I said. "How could they have possibly found that offensive?" Minnie didn't seem to have anything more to say on the subject, so I prompted her. "Unless they happened to confess to murdering Hunter Blackburn."

"No." Minnie sounded bitter.

Velda cast a sidelong glance at her friend. "They were the keynote speakers at a revival in Woodburn the day the murder took place."

"With three hundred witnesses," Minnie added glumly.

Hiding a smile, I turned away to answer the telephone.

"Can you talk?" The strain in Alix's voice caused me to hesitate for an instant before replying.

Both Minnie and Velda had pricked up their ears. "Alix?" They asked in unison.

I placed my hand over the receiver and grabbed an order form. I didn't want to lie to them, but I certainly didn't want them in the conversation.

Apparently, I was successful in deflecting their interest.

Velda mouthed, "Sorry."

Minnie contented herself with a stage whisper. "You need to keep the line open in case Alix calls."

I nodded and pretended to search the computer for an account before speaking into the receiver again. "No, they haven't been mailed. That last book hasn't arrived yet."

"Nick's not back? And Minnie's there, right? This is my lawyer call. Have you talked to Nick at all?"

"Still waiting. Are you okay with that?"

"I'll have to be. Arnie's never going to look for anyone else now." Alix's voice was low, defeated. "I'm such a fool. Between the money connection and my argument with Hunter, even Arnie can see a perfect case shaping up."

I gripped the phone harder as Alix's voice broke on the next words.

"But I didn't do it."

Minnie waved her arms in the air and hissed at me. "How can you worry about books at a time like this?"

Ignoring her, I turned to the wall. "Of course. There's absolutely no question of that! I'll . . . I'll take care of it, Mirabella."

I replaced the receiver and took a deep breath before turning back to the room.

"Who has a name like Mirabella?" Minnie asked. "What a pushy customer. Last thing you need is her hysterics. I tell you, Jane, sometimes people make me tired. We have an investigation to run."

Velda attempted to soothe Minnie. "On the other hand, that customer doesn't have any way of knowing what we're going through. I thought Jane handled her problem with great sensitivity."

Minnie was not to be appeased. "But we're wasting valuable time. We have to do something else, find another suspect. You can't let your work here distract you from our primary mission. Laurence will just have to take care of his own store while we . . . ah, there you are, Laurence."

Laurence and Tyler were coming slowly down the stairs together. Laurence held tightly to the polished oak banister while Tyler effortlessly managed a heavy box of books to add to the sale table.

Once they reached the main floor, Minnie continued. "I was just telling Jane that she can't waste time working here right now. She needs to head up our investigation because Arnold Kraft most certainly will not be able to find the real killer."

"Good of you to manage my store and the police investigation, too."

Instead of erupting as I'd expected, Laurence was smiling. He hadn't looked this happy in weeks.

"Don't think I can't recognize sarcasm when I hear it, Laurence," Minnie said. "We can't let Alix rot in jail. I'm serious about this."

"I'm sure you are. Would you like to rearrange my window display while you're here?"

While the two of them jousted verbally, I pulled Tyler aside. "Can you manage without me?"

"Okay," Tyler said, "but I'd rather go with you."

"Believe me, I'd love to have your company, but if I can just sneak away before Minnie and Velda . . . you know how they are. Keep them occupied. That's the best way to help. Besides, honestly, I don't know what I'm going to do next."

He grinned at me. "You'll figure it out. I'm not worried."

"Thanks. Neither is Bianca. Nice that you both have such faith in me. I'm going to make a break for it. Cover me."

CHAPTER 25

If I went home, Minnie and Velda were likely to track me down. Instead, I drove to Nick's house as the daylight faded, aware I was merely putting in time because I had no plan. Nick would call as soon as he was back in range, and maybe we could come up with something.

Several newspapers littered the porch and the driveway was empty. I retrieved the yellowed papers and dumped them on the passenger side of my car. There. I'd done something. Big deal. Even if Nick drove up the street right this minute, what could he—or anyone—do for Alix?

I returned to the driver's seat. Slumped behind the wheel, I started to shake as I acknowledged for the first time that I was totally at a loss. It had been pleasant to allow myself to be momentarily buoyed at the faith Bianca and Tyler had shown in my ability to clear Alix, but now I was face-to-face with the reality that I didn't know what to do.

As I reviewed the day's events, I was stung by the realization that Laurence certainly hadn't been plagued by a similar lack of initiative when he launched his preposterous plan. What had that cantankerous old man been thinking, putting himself in that kind of danger? I could guess at his likely answer: "Somebody had to do something."

"Right," I whispered.

A wave of sadness swept over me as I pictured Alix as a hopeful little girl with her beloved doll. That innocent little girl had become a lovestruck teen duped by a persuasive older man. It didn't take much imagination to understand how Alix had ultimately become a determined, aloof woman. Alix had made her solitary way in the world for a long time, hiding her generosity toward Hunter's grandmother and others, guarding her emotions, not daring to get close to anyone . . . until last year.

For the emotionally scarred Alix, joining our book club had been a gigantic leap of courage, though her offhand manner had made me wonder why she bothered to come so regularly to our meetings. Without ever betraying that belonging to the book club mattered to her, in the course of the past year she'd helped us solve a murder, managed Thornton's temporarily after Laurence's heart attack, and created an opportunity for Bianca to work and develop her creative capabilities. Alix had also become my close friend. I'd never realized before this week what a daring act it had been for her to risk forming relationships, something so simple that the rest of us took it for granted.

Now, Alix was in real trouble. She had turned to her friend for help, and what had I accomplished? Exactly nothing. I slapped the steering wheel in frustration. The brutal reality was that since I'd actually solved a murder last year, it had been tempting to flirt with the fantasy that I could do it again, all the while assuming the real killer would be found in a couple of days. Bianca and Tyler had been so confident of my abilities that they'd left me to play at being a detective as they took care of real responsibilities at the Wedding Belle and Thornton's. I knew Minnie and Velda were likely to be more stumbling block than help to any investigation, but I'd done little to head them off. At least, they'd been doing the best they could, while I hadn't treated this seriously enough.

But now . . . the evidence against Alix was piling up. She was right that Arnie wasn't likely to look further for a suspect. At the best of times, Arnie wasn't much of a sheriff, and in this case Alix's ingrained habits of secrecy had particularly worked against her. She couldn't have made herself look much guiltier if she'd tried.

The muffled tones of my cell phone sounded from my bag. I didn't recognize the number that came up, but I crossed my fingers and answered.

"What the hell is going on? I'm calling from a gas station."

In spite of the words, my heart leaped at the sound of Nick's voice.

"I called the store, and Bianca told me about Alix."

I could hardly hear him. "Oh, Nick." The tears fell thick and fast as I tried to squeeze out words between sobs. "I'm sitting in front of your house right now. You're on your way back?"

"Can't hear you. Yes, I'm coming back. What about Alix?"

"It looks bad, and I don't know what to do." I was crying so hard now that my words came out in gasps.

"We'll sort everything out together." Nick spoke in his lawyer voice, all calmness and reason.

I loved that voice. My shakiness began to subside.

"Alix is innocent. All we have to do is prove it, okay?"

I nodded vigorously and wiped my cheeks. I wanted to jump out of the car and shout with joy.

"Damn it. I was planning to be down on one knee at the beach right now, talking about something else entirely, but for once I agree with you that Alix comes first. Okay?"

It wasn't until he asked again that I realized he couldn't see me nodding. "Okay," I breathed.

"I'm seventy miles away, but I'll get there as fast as I can. Will you have stopped blubbering by then?"

The beep in my ear indicated that my phone's battery was about to give out. "Yes, I promise. Nick, my phone's about to quit on me."

"Bianca said Alix had been arrested, but what else? Quick."

"It's complicated. Alix just wanted to get rid of him."

"So did somebody else. Tell her to keep her mouth shut until I get there."

Once more my low-battery indicator sounded. "She knows that. Nick, please—"

The phone went dead. Probably just as well. He'd be here soon. I tossed the phone onto the passenger seat and started the car. Just knowing that reinforcements were on the way, I pulled away from the curb with a flourish.

My thoughts drifted back to Laurence's gallant attempt to link other fraudulent activity to Hunter's murder. Maybe the concept wasn't so far-fetched, after all. If the newspaper would run a story asking for community assistance, possibly someone who'd been a victim two years ago would connect old information to the current crime, link it in some way that hadn't happened before. Arnie himself said that he hadn't investigated that line of thought. It was a long shot, but worth a try.

Velda's bitter comments at various SOS meetings had made it clear that her aunt had been one of those victims, but I hadn't ever talked to Eleanor herself about what had happened. It wasn't likely that she could shed any light, wasn't even likely that Hunter Blackburn had been the one who'd defrauded her, but it wouldn't hurt to ask. Had Eleanor even looked at his picture this week in the paper? Possibly not, since she'd been sick.

I reached for the cell phone to call Velda, but remembered the dead battery. I had at least an hour until Nick's arrival. Taking positive action would make the time pass more quickly. It wouldn't take more than a few minutes to drive the five miles out to Eleanor's house. I hesitated at the junction stop sign. Right toward town or left to Eleanor's? No contest. Excited about following the only lead I had, I swung left onto the country road. Velda was protective of her aunt's need to rest, but I wouldn't stay long. In fact, Velda might not even be home from Thornton's yet.

As I wound through the curves so popular with local daredevils, I resisted the impulse to speed. It would be just my luck to find Arnie lurking under his favorite ponderosa pine. Sure enough, I spotted the hood of his patrol car poking out from his usual hiding place. This was one time I actually wanted to talk to him though, so I signaled carefully before pulling off the road. No use giving him an excuse to ticket me when he was already bent out of shape by my meddling.

He didn't bother getting out when I approached the driver's window.

"See you've learned to be a mite more careful with your driving. Heard about your flat tire yesterday. Shouldn't drive too fast, even when you're chasing 'suspects.' " He almost managed to keep the smirk off his face.

"You do keep a close eye on things, don't you? Surprising, really, when you have so many important tasks."

I watched his eyes go blank as he turned that idea over, trying to determine whether he'd been insulted.

Before his sluggish mind could work through the problem, I switched topics. "Have you ever thought about backtracking to see whether any of those unsolved fraud cases from two years ago involved Hunter Blackburn? He might have been here then."

"Why don't you just ask your friend Alix about that? She was married to him."

I didn't bother to answer. "So, did you check the other cases against this one?"

"Didn't need to. I already know who killed him."

"Did you talk to Laurence this afternoon?"

"I'll get to it. Didn't seem like much of a lead to me."

"I have another one. How about coming with me right now—"

He shook his head. "I'm busy. Besides, I've got the killer locked up. You and your friends, always thinking you're so smart—"

I suddenly discovered the accuracy of that old saying about "seeing red." Before saying something I'd regret later, I clamped my lips shut and retreated. As I jerked the seat belt across my body, my hands shook so badly that it took me several tries to engage the latch. Pompous jerk! As soon as Alix was cleared, I'd make it my mission to get Arnie recalled from office for incompetence, or gross stupidity, or something.

Ostentatiously signaling once more, I pulled onto the road again, traveling well under the speed limit. Just as ostentatiously, Arnie signaled and pulled out behind me. He followed for about a mile before tiring of the game. The tires on his patrol car squealed at his Hollywood-style turn back toward town. Probably eager to get back to his heavy schedule of harassing innocent people.

CHAPTER 26

Velda's Dodge in the drive signaled that she was home. Good. I glanced at the back seat as I passed her car and noticed a sun hat resting atop a gaily-striped beach bag. Hope springs eternal. Our June weather had been pleasant, but as a long-time resident of central Oregon, I knew that frost could strike on any night of the year. Velda apparently was making the common newcomer's mistake of thinking that the arrival of June meant summer had arrived to stay. Her Florida upbringing no doubt accounted for her false optimism.

I mounted the brick steps of the graceful old house, thinking how sad it was that the once-prosperous McKay family had now dwindled to just Velda and her Aunt Eleanor. Eleanor's only brother had died suddenly in Key West, Florida, a year ago, scarcely a week after Eleanor had broken her hip in Oregon. Since Velda had previously kept house for her ailing father, she was unexpectedly available to help her aunt during her rehabilitation. She rushed to Oregon and poured her energy into Eleanor's care. According to Minnie, Velda had originally envisioned this stay as temporary, but it had become permanent as Eleanor's health deteriorated. Velda never complained, but I knew it must be lonely for her out here, so far from home.

It was good she was making an effort to get out and about more often, though joining a bird-watching group could hardly compare with the excitement generated by Minnie's improbable detective schemes. Still, Minnie's offer to provide respite care

214

for Eleanor should soon pay dividends. Whenever Minnie took on a cause, a flurry of activity soon followed, but I couldn't help wondering how Velda would react to Minnie's offers. Velda always stood ready to help others, but such helpful people often felt uncomfortable on the receiving side of the equation. Still, my money was on Minnie, whose efforts had the force of a tidal wave. It would be an interesting match-up.

I twisted the brass lion's head in the center of the solid wood door and heard chimes. No light showed through the etched glass panels framing the entrance, but I heard shuffling sounds, followed by the closing of an inside door. Eventually, the door swung open, and Velda stepped out onto the covered porch.

"Jane. Is everything all right? You just disappeared from the store, and we didn't know where you'd gone."

"Yes, I had to run an errand. Everything's fine—as fine as it can be until we clear Alix—but maybe I should ask you the same question. Are you all right? You're flushed."

"Really?" Velda put her hands to her reddened cheeks. "How odd. I was just lying on my bed upstairs, reading."

"I guess I'm seeing things." And hearing things, too. The earlier sounds had come from the hallway, not from upstairs.

"Has there been a break in the case?" Velda asked.

"Not yet, but I have an idea to try, if you'll help me."

"Of course. Whatever I can do."

"I'd like to talk to your aunt."

Velda abruptly stepped back and shook her head.

I hurried on. "I just want her to look at a picture, tell me whether Hunter Blackburn was the man who cheated her two years ago. She probably hasn't followed the news this week, being sick and all, so she might not have made the connection . . ."

"Sorry to disappoint you, but she and I talked about this earlier today. Not the same man. She was positive."

"She actually saw his picture?"

"Oh, yes, in the newspaper. She told me the swindler from before was much younger, with light hair and a slender build. I'm sure the sheriff has the description in his records of the investigation."

I wasn't so sure about Arnie's records, but, unfortunately, the description didn't fit either Hunter Blackburn or the man Laurence had met on the street. "I knew it was a long shot, but Arnie won't think of anyone but Alix, so I thought—"

"Sorry she can't help." Velda retreated further into the darkened hall. "We'll have to think of something else."

I was grasping at straws, unwilling to leave without at least talking to Eleanor. "Several of them could have been working together. Your aunt might know some detail—"

"No, I'm sure she doesn't." Velda shook her head more vigorously, causing her owlish glasses to slide down her nose. An oily sheen of perspiration glistened on her skin as she pushed the glasses back into place. "Maybe you could ask some of the other victims from the SOS group."

"I will, but I'm here now and—"

Again, Velda's glasses began to slide. What was the matter with her? Sweat was now streaming down the sides of her plump face. "You know I'd love to help you, but Aunt Eleanor's asleep."

"Would you mind checking? I don't mean to be rude, but this could be important. If she's asleep, I'll come back tomorrow. How's that?"

"All right. I'll go see."

Could she be having a stroke? I'd never seen her like this before.

"May I come in?" I held the door open to keep it from closing in my face.

After a slight hesitation, Velda gave a little giggle and inched the door wider. "I'm sorry. It must be hunger. I was about to sit down to dinner."

"I didn't mean to interrupt." Why had Velda told me she was upstairs reading? Maybe afraid I'd want to stay for dinner. "This won't take a minute. I'll be out of your hair in a jiffy."

"That's okay. Wait here, and I'll just go see—"

As though coming to some decision, Velda broke off. Motioning me to stay where I was, she strode to the back of the house and entered her aunt's bedroom. While I waited, I peered into the unlighted dining room. No place setting. No aroma of cooking from the kitchen either, but maybe Velda was planning a cold meal in front of the television, wherever it was. Something was off-kilter. That was for sure.

The hall closet immediately to my left reminded me of the earlier shuffling sound I'd heard, followed by the closing of a door. Was someone hiding in that closet? That would explain Velda's nervousness better than a sudden need for dinner.

I stared at that closed closet door, my heart racing. I could leave, call Arnie from my car. No, I couldn't. That stupid battery. Besides, how likely was he to believe that some sinister person just happened to come all the way out here to threaten Velda and her aunt?

This was ridiculous. I was spinning a fantasy out of tiredness and worry, nothing more. The most logical explanation was that the inoffensive Velda was embarrassed about having told a white lie to get me to leave. What was stashed in the closet was probably nothing more threatening than a dozen glazed doughnuts she didn't want to share.

With a mental apology to Velda, I took a deep breath and opened the closet door a couple of inches. No assassin jumped out. The expected collection of coats lined the closet rail. I had just enough time to register the presence of two hunter green suitcases topped by a set of keys held together with a smiley-face logo before Velda tiptoed out of her aunt's bedroom. I quietly pushed the closet door closed and stepped into the middle of the hallway before she turned toward me.

"Just as I thought. She's asleep."

Embarrassed at almost being caught snooping, I banged my elbow on the doorjamb as I scrambled to leave. "That's fine. Thanks for checking. You'll be here tomorrow morning?"

"Where else? But not too early. Breakfast and physical therapy first, and then Aunt Eleanor's morning nap. Tell you what. I'll call when I figure out the best time."

She didn't do more than open the door for me, but I felt she was pushing me out. I'd barely cleared the threshold when the door closed behind me. I nodded agreement and fled to my car, questions buzzing in my head. Was I being paranoid? I'd recognized Velda's distinctive key ring, but why had she put the suitcases and key ring into the closet before opening the door? As I bumped from the driveway onto the road, I glanced back and caught movement at an upstairs window. Was Velda making sure I'd actually left, or was someone else watching me?

CHAPTER 27

Once away from the property, I pulled into the first dirt track I encountered and hid the car among a stand of poplars which had long ago framed a settler's cabin. On a sudden hunch, I unsnapped the seat belt and delved in the glove compartment for the cell phone charger cord. Stale soda crackers, a tattered Oregon map, and a packet of Altoids, but no cord. Likely home on the kitchen counter. Great.

I slapped the glove compartment shut in frustration. Should I speed into town for help? But I had no idea what was going on. Surely Velda could have signaled me that something was wrong if she'd needed to . . . unless she didn't dare.

Once more I visualized her agitated state. Something was dreadfully wrong in that house. I needed to find out what. After a brief hesitation, I left the keys in the ignition, in case I needed to make a fast getaway. Then I scribbled a note and climbed out of the car, leaving the driver's side door open and the note on the front seat. Someone might come by. I was hoping for a friendly neighbor, rather than a car thief, but the chances of either were slim on this back road. Retracing my route from the house, I followed the road at first. I forced myself not to think how idiotic I would sound in describing my suspicion that Velda was being held prisoner. "She was sweating a lot and the dining room table wasn't set for dinner." Hardly enough to merit a nine-one-one call, but I was going with my instincts.

Once the roof of the house became visible through swaying

green branches, I abandoned the road and made a wide circle around the neglected sweep of lawn behind the house itself. An enormous hedge of purple lilacs shielded me from view. I crouched behind the fragrant bushes to watch. The only sounds came from invisible birds calling to each other from somewhere nearby. What should have been a peaceful country moment was spoiled by the atavistic thundering of my heart as it pumped adrenaline to my muscles in preparation for battle. Nothing stirred. It was nearing dusk, and I wouldn't be able to see much longer. On the other hand, no one would be able to see me. My nerves tightened another notch.

An old-fashioned brick root cellar jutted from the back of the house, providing my nearest cover. The window of Eleanor's bedroom lay just to its right. I flicked a glance at the curtained upstairs windows, hoping no one was keeping watch from that vantage point, because I couldn't avoid crossing open ground to the cellar. Once there, I'd make my way around the side to her bedroom window. If nothing seemed amiss, I'd creep back around the cellar and peer in the larger kitchen windows. Drawing in another deep breath of the surrounding lilacs, I thought what a shame it was that I couldn't just remain in this peaceful bower until dusk fell. But, as Minnie would say, "There's no rest for the wicked." No reason to think things would improve while I lingered here, either. I broke from my shelter.

Running in a half crouch, I sprinted across the grass and flattened myself against the bricks of the cellar, which still held some warmth from the afternoon sun. So far, so good. I eased around the side, rehearsing what to say if I looked in the bedroom window and found Velda holding a slab of pepperoni pizza in her pudgy hand.

An old-fashioned roller shade covered the window from most of the sun's waning rays, but there was a slight gap at the bottom. I slowly raised my gaze above the peeling paint of the window sill to look inside. It took a moment for my eyes to adjust from the outside brightness, but at last I made out a figure lying on the bed. Eleanor was alone in the room, and she was staring right at me. My heart jumped as I realized what a fright I must be giving that poor old lady, but she didn't move or cry out. Had my sudden appearance scared her into immobility? No. A strip of duct tape covered her mouth, while cords secured her outstretched arms to the bedposts.

I gasped. What was going on? Velda! Velda must be tied up inside, too. This was no time for amateur heroics. I needed to get help. Eleanor's eyes blinked at me. I gave her a thumb's-up, turned to run, and stumbled right into Velda.

"Hello, Jane." Velda blocked my path. "You'd be a very bad poker player. I knew you'd be back."

My mouth dropped open at the sight of a revolver in her steady hand. The Velda I knew—the one who served cookies and washed dishes and liked birds—had disappeared. In her stead was a woman with steely eyes and a gun. Confused, I looked over her shoulder, half expecting to see someone forcing her into this bizarre role. We were alone. "Velda?"

"Come off it, Jane. You wouldn't be sneaking around here if you didn't have some idea."

"Your aunt . . . she's tied up." I struggled to assimilate the situation.

"Yes, dear Aunt Eleanor is all tied up. If you'd given me a little warning before you came, I wouldn't have had to do that. My wonderful pills need time to take effect. Don't you know it's rude to drop by without calling first?"

"My cell phone wasn't working." My apology for bad manners was automatic.

"What a shame. Could've avoided a lot of problems. Once I saw you on the porch, I figured you suspected."

"Suspected what?"

My brain had turned to gelatin at the sight of that revolver pointed at me. I could hardly breathe, let alone determine what alien universe I had entered.

"Don't be tiresome. You see Aunt Eleanor tied up, and you don't put two and two together?"

"I thought someone was hiding in the house, that you and Eleanor were in danger."

Velda snorted. "Guess you're not as smart as I thought. Water over the dam. Can't play it that way now. Like you haven't guessed . . ."

"I . . . I . . . you told me you'd never touched a gun in your life."

I ducked as she waved the revolver carelessly. "Told you lots of things. Here's a tip: Guns come in handy. You think Hunter was just going to stand there while I hit him on the head? Now keep quiet while I work this out."

She didn't need to tell me twice. The shock of her casual confession to murder was enough to rob me of speech. She'd killed Hunter. I had no idea why, but so what? Alix was home free. A huge weight dropped from my shoulders.

My elation swung to terror in an instant as my stunned brain finally kicked to life. Velda's willingness to talk indicated that I wouldn't live long enough to tell Alix anything.

Her next words sent ice water through my veins. "As for you . . . you've messed up everything."

I swallowed a couple of times before speaking. "Look, you don't have to—"

"It's your own damned fault. I can't just let you waltz out of here." Velda's annoyance seemed to be escalating. She regarded me with a new and unpleasant glint in her blue eyes.

"Leave me with Eleanor. You're going anyway. I saw the suitcases."

Velda remained silent. Maybe she was even listening.

I hurried on. "No one will look here. You'll be long gone. Please, just . . . you don't want to complicate things."

"You already did that, snooping around." Velda gave a mirthless laugh. "Not as much fun when you can't order everybody else around, is it? This time it's your turn to serve the tea and cookies, Jane."

Sweat trickled down my back as I tensed for action. "Velda, I never meant—"

"Friends, family, money . . . even a gorgeous guy. If Hunter'd been like Nick, maybe he wouldn't have got himself shot." Velda's voice grew more strident. "You've never given a single thought to what I've had to—"

"That's not true, or . . . or if it seemed that way, I'm sorry. Let me help you."

"Oh, sure! You and your fancy friends." I backed away from the fury building behind her words. My attempt to soothe had agitated her more than ever. "Where were all of you when I . . . ? Never mind. Won't matter in a few hours anyway."

I risked a question. "What happens then?"

Velda's tone abruptly turned conversational once more. Somehow, the lowered tone chilled me more than her outburst. "Why, the mail arrives with my passport. Never needed one before this, especially for a vacation, but now . . . I even paid extra for expedited service, so it damned well better arrive. On my way out, I'll also collect a significant amount of cash from dear Aunt Eleanor. If that prissy Joe Framington at the bank hadn't insisted on talking directly to her yesterday, I'd already have taken care of that little detail." She pointed the revolver directly at my face. "This convinced her to tell Mr. Nosy exactly what I wanted. The old buzzard can live to be a hundred now, for all I care. Her standard of living's about to go way down, but that's not my problem. Should have given me money when I asked nicely. My father had the same lousy attitude."

So this was all Aunt Eleanor's fault for wanting to spend her own money. And Velda's tightwad father hadn't given her as much money as she wanted, either, and he'd died suddenly. Adrenaline flooded my system. Velda had already killed at least two people. Eleanor was still alive on the off chance the bank manager needed more information, so she might last until tomorrow. I would live just long enough for Velda to sift through her options.

At length, she smiled, but her eyes remained cold. "Guess if you don't cause me more trouble, you can live to be a hundred, too. That cellar there should do just fine."

She gestured impatiently with the gun.

I turned toward the outbuilding, my mind working furiously while I dragged out my steps as slowly as I dared. Velda tugged on a rusty padlock until the stout wooden door creaked open on ancient hinges.

The air from inside cooled my hot cheeks, but I was in no hurry to disappear into that dark vault. What could I do from there? I continued the pretense that I'd be allowed to live. "Please, Velda, no one will think to look for me here."

"Sure they will. Once they find Eleanor, they'll comb every inch of this property. Could take a couple of days, but maybe you can find some home-canned beets."

"Please, let me stay with your aunt. She's an old lady."

"That tough old gal climbed out of bed and tried to call the cops yesterday, but I got to her in time. Think I'd let the two of you put your heads together? Besides, I want you someplace where you can't rig up a signal. Don't get any ideas about yelling either. These brick walls are plenty thick."

Torn between a desire to stay out of that dark cave and a fear that too many questions would goad Velda to lethal action, I braced my hands on each side of the doorway and looked back at her. "Velda, you don't want to—"

"Shut up!" Velda cocked her head at the sound of an approaching car. Her breath came faster as she turned back to me. "Get in there now . . . or I'll shoot you where you stand. And if you make a racket, I'll shoot whoever's in that car, too!"

She punctuated her last word with a shove between my shoulder blades that propelled me into the gloom.

The door slammed behind me. Instinctively, I whirled and put my shoulder to the old wood. It didn't budge. I ran my hands over the rough surface in a frantic search for an inside latch, but succeeded only in driving a splinter deep into my left palm.

Knowing my situation would only worsen if I annoyed Velda further, I bit back a cry of pain and worked to dislodge that painful splinter. Each attempt merely drove it deeper. It didn't help that I couldn't see a thing, but my nerve endings screamed out the exact location of the sliver each time I touched it. Since I was left-handed, my right-handed efforts were particularly clumsy so I tried using my teeth instead. That was better, but I still couldn't quite grab it. Beads of sweat broke out on my forehead. Nuts. I took a few deep breaths to steady myself. Maybe if I sat down I could do better.

The dusty air held a faint odor of rot. I hoped the smell came from a moldy sack of potatoes and not from some long-dead squirrel sprawled nearby. My thoughts turned to spiders— particularly the black widows and brown recluses common to old buildings in central Oregon. Nope. Couldn't go there. Nothing to be gained by letting that mental picture take hold. Still, I tapped one foot methodically over the packed earth floor to give fair warning to any nearby living thing before I sat down to attack the splinter.

"Anybody got tweezers?" I whispered.

Listening to my own quavery voice was better than bracing for the furtive sounds of rats scrabbling around, but I reminded myself that rodents and spiders were the least of my worries.

My initial excitement at stumbling upon Hunter Blackburn's killer seemed far in the past. Velda had urged me to be patient, to wait for the rescue party that was sure to come. If only she weren't a pathological killer and liar, I'd love to take her advice. No matter how fast a rescue party showed up, it would come too late for me. My only solace was that eventually Alix would be freed.

If I hadn't seen it with my own eyes, I'd never have believed the helpful, submissive Velda capable of violence. She should have been an actress. No wonder she'd been so eager to help Minnie chase phony suspects around the countryside. Staying close to Alix's friends had given her all the information she needed about the murder investigation, such as it was. She must have had some good laughs over that. With Alix in jail and Arnie congratulating himself on having caught the killer, Velda had been able to risk waiting for that passport.

No wonder she'd started sweating when I'd shown up unexpectedly and asked to speak to her aunt. With a hefty withdrawal from her aunt's bank account, Velda would be sipping margaritas in a tropical climate long before anyone caught on to her.

But she was right. I had definitely messed things up for her. How rational was she? I knew what she was planning to do before she left. I had no intention of waiting around to find out how and when.

I returned my attention to the splinter, working at it until a stab of pain signaled that at last my teeth were gripping it securely. I pulled again and the sliver came free. Instant relief. Step one, completed. Now what?

CHAPTER 28

Hoping for a miracle, I pressed my back against the door and opened my eyes wide, searching in all directions for a telltale light pointing the way to a convenient hole in the wall or roof. Unfortunately, the old cellar was well built. The phrase "dark as a tomb" came into my mind, and I tossed it right back out. I needed a plan of action, not a prescription for panic.

Turning to face the wooden door, I moved clockwise along the wall. At first, I encountered only bricks, but as I approached an adjoining wall, I touched wooden shelves. An unfortunate sweep of my searching hands dislodged a glass jar, which crashed to the floor. The sharp odor of sauerkraut filled the room. I froze. Would the noise bring Velda? No sound from outside. Good. Shuffling carefully through shards of glass, I inched further along the side wall, feeling my way past more glass jars, pruning shears, and a layer of dirt that likely contained rat droppings among other disgusting things. I gave a nervous giggle, which sounded out of place. An infection was the least of my worries. Still, I'd drown the wound with Bactine at the first opportunity. And some triple-antibiotic ointment. Maybe get a tetanus shot, too.

The back wall had no shelves, just a forest of cobwebs. I brushed them aside, flinging my arms wide and shuddering as some caught in my hair. If there were any current residents of the webs, they were going to be very unhappy with me as I groped my way through them, hoping to locate another exit. Nothing.

I made my way to the next corner, turned, and moved along the last remaining wall. More shelves. How long before Velda returned? No way to tell, but I was running out of walls to explore. I couldn't glimpse even a crack of light that might indicate an escape route.

Midway along the fourth side, I felt a slight breeze on my face. I stopped, heart beating faster. Was it my imagination? I moved back and forth until I could pinpoint its location. Reaching across the shelf, my exploring fingers traced the rough outline of a window-sized recess in the wall. Eureka!

Holding my breath, hoping against hope, I explored the area with my fingers. Yes. A window lay behind the shelves. I collected the pruning shears from the opposite wall, stumbled back, and pried at the shelves. I wanted to tear into them, but was afraid to make any noise. Once I had the shelves down, though, I scrabbled to pull the shutters apart. They wouldn't budge.

Sucking at my bleeding fingers, I almost burst into tears. But tears wouldn't do me much good. Stay positive. It was my best hope.

But it was hard. What would happen if I couldn't find a way out? I debated whether this question was a positive one, and decided it was. If I couldn't break out, I had to think of another plan.

I knew I couldn't depend on Velda having a change of heart. She was already in too deep. I pictured again the coldness in her eyes as she'd debated whether to shoot me immediately or stash me in the cellar for a few minutes. I'd already had one close call. The very notion of another such encounter chilled my blood. I needed a weapon. The pruning shears might do, but this was a matter of life or death. I couldn't afford to overlook anything. I checked every inch of the shelves, front to back, the second time around. Way at the back, my hand closed over the handle of a hammer. With scarcely a pause, I stuck it in a loop of my jeans and searched further. I had never before hit anyone with a weapon, but if I got near Velda and her gun again, well, there was a first time for everything. I continued my grim search and stuffed a screwdriver into my pocket. Unfortunately, nothing else that might prove useful came to hand.

Still no sound from outside, but I probably wouldn't be able to hear a car leaving anyway. Maybe Velda had actually decided to leave me locked in here, after all. A great wash of hope flooded me at the thought before reality broke through.

Time for another dose of positive thinking. I reconsidered my options. I could hide by the door and hope to hit Velda if she opened it. What else? Maybe I could dig my way out, but that would take weeks. I could pry at the shutters again; the tools would likely be more effective than my fingers. Or . . . could I go through the cellar's roof?

I tested a shelf. Rock solid. Closing my eyes to protect them, I clambered onto the lowest, knocking another couple of glass jars to the floor in the process. Once more I froze, heard no movement above me or outside, and resumed my work. At this point, what difference did a little more noise make? Time was running out. Stretching, I jabbed the screwdriver upward. No give to the wood. I tried another spot, this time striking the end of the screwdriver with the hammer. The blows jarred my hands and accomplished nothing.

I stumbled blindly to the other wall and repeated the exercise, climbing up and probing the roof in a frenzy until I'd convinced myself that it was as solid as the shelves. Spent at last, I sank to the floor. The door was the only way out.

A muffled crack from somewhere outside broke the silence. I jumped to my feet in terror. Was that a shot? It had to be. Velda must have shot whoever had come to the house. This was it. My blood pounded through my body. I was next. I was as ready as I was ever going to be.

With the hammer clutched in my hand, I took up a post behind the door. A moment later, the door screeched open. I squinted in the sudden light as a bulky shape, much larger than Velda, darkened the entry and stumbled inside. Uncertain, I dropped the hammer and charged. We tumbled to the floor, arms and legs entangled. The door slammed, leaving the cellar once again in utter blackness. I knew only one person who baked every day and smelled perpetually of cinnamon.

I sat up. "Minnie? What are you doing here?"

"I might ask you the same question," came the panting reply, "but first, please get your elbow out of my ribs."

Minnie maneuvered until we were shoulder to shoulder. I could have kissed her. Good old bulldog Minnie. Not exactly the U.S. Cavalry, but always there to help. I should have known she wouldn't let me down.

"That's much better," she said. "I'm here because Velda shoved me in here at gunpoint. How about you?"

"The same."

"Just as I suspected," Minnie said. "That woman is crazy. We need to get out of here before she comes back. Things will go very badly for us when she does, you know."

"Yes. What's the plan?" When Minnie didn't reply immediately, I prompted her. "You did bring help?"

"No." The disappointment was plain in her voice. "I was just bringing her a chicken pot pie for dinner. I didn't know I needed someone to ride shotgun for that. When I saw your car down the road and read your note, I came to provide backup."

While I silently applauded Minnie's courage in trying to come to my rescue, I fervently wished she'd chosen to use her new cell phone instead, or to call the police from a neighbor's house.

She read my mind.

"I know what you're thinking, Jane. I forgot the darned cell phone at home. I thought of calling from the Janssens' house, too, but I figured bringing dinner was the perfect cover. I planned to hand Velda the pot pie and get the lay of the land, so to speak. When she opened the door, she seemed relaxed and happy to see me, thanked me for the food, and even asked me to join her. She didn't mention seeing you, so of course I had no idea you were in the root cellar. Really, by that time, I thought the coast was clear, and you'd been all wrong about any threat to her and Eleanor, although I did wonder what had happened to you. That's when I told her I'd seen your car on the road and said we should call the sheriff.

"Imagine my shock when instead of offering help—as I quite reasonably expected—she pulled out some kind of a pistol and threatened me. Can you believe it? After I'd brought her my special chicken pot pie?"

"That does seem a low blow, Minnie."

"Really though, Jane, we'd better chat about this another time. She's gone to hide your car—"

"And I conveniently left the keys in it, so I could leave in a hurry. Do you have any ideas about how to get us out of here?"

Minnie's disembodied voice, now laced with bitterness, came out of the darkness. "I found you. That was all I set out to do, that and deliver dinner. The rest of it is your department. You never like my plans anyway . . . like Operation Hollow Feather. Your heart wasn't really in it. I could tell."

Dear Minnie. Even in these dire circumstances, she was still hurt about my lack of enthusiasm about her prowess as a detective. She was definitely one of a kind. I chose my words carefully. "That idea didn't work out particularly well—"

"No it didn't, so now it's your turn to think up a plan. It's not as easy as it sounds."

"So no one is outside except Velda? No one else knows you were coming here?"

"Exactly. Now, what are we going to do?"

"What just happened out there? I heard a shot."

"I heard it even closer. The gun went off when I grabbed for it. Didn't get it, but you probably figured that out already. Once Velda started waving that thing around, I knew I wasn't going to get to the phone. So here I am. You didn't have to tackle me."

"Sorry. I thought you were Velda coming back. At least I didn't hit you with the hammer." Unwilling to hurt her feelings again, I didn't mention that she was spared that blow only because she was twice Velda's size. "Do you know about—?"

"Hunter Blackburn? Yes, I still don't quite understand why she killed him, but once we got the gun thing settled, she told me that she had. I think she knew that hearing about it would keep me from arguing with her. She was right about that." Minnie fell silent, no doubt thinking the same thing I was. Velda didn't plan to give Minnie the opportunity to tell anyone else what she had learned.

I reached out in the darkness and gathered the older woman to me in as much of a hug as I could manage, given Minnie's stout frame. "Don't worry. I'll think of something."

No response.

"Minnie, are you okay?" I gave the plump shoulders a little shake.

"Of course I'm okay. Stop rattling my teeth. I was thinking of something else—"

"What else is there to think about right now?"

"You just work on your little escape plan and leave me to think whatever I want since my ideas aren't useful anyway."

I stifled the urge to tell her to give it a rest. Instead, I took a deep breath and apologized once more. "I'm sorry I hurt your feelings about Operation Hollow Feather. You have some excellent ideas and I'd be very interested to hear any suggestions you have." Being kind to a friend seemed more important than a strict adherence to the truth at the moment. After all, Minnie had tried to grab a loaded gun in her effort to help me. I threw reason to the wind and expanded. "That business with Phil and Eileen could have . . . could have . . . happened to anyone."

"You're not just saying that?" The lilt in Minnie's voice told me I'd struck the right note.

"Look, Minnie. I really need help." That much was true enough. "I've looked all over and I can't find a way out of this cellar. It's going to be bad for us when Velda gets back."

"Bless your heart! Let's get to work," Minnie exclaimed. "What's your plan so far?"

"Hide behind the door and bash her when she comes in. You just about got a hammer planted right on your head."

"It was bad enough to be wrestled to this dirty floor like a prize steer. Worse. Now Velda will expect that move the next time she opens the door." Minnie as military strategist was an entirely new concept, but she was obviously thinking furiously. "Probably won't come that close, likely start shooting from outside."

"Minnie!"

"Well, that's what I'd do. 'Needs must when the devil drives,' as the Bible says. You know, I've never exactly understood what that meant."

"Neither have I. But it's Shakespeare, not the Bible."

"Are you sure? Sounds like it should come from the Bible. Anyway, if I were Velda, I'd come in blazing away. No sense letting the prisoners get a chance to hack away at you."

I couldn't help laughing. "Minnie, you are something else. I'd definitely vote you The Most Entertaining Person To Be Locked In A Root Cellar With. And if you know a way to get us out of here, that would be a nice bonus. You don't happen to have a stick of dynamite on you?"

"No, but remember when I said I was thinking of something else? It was my grandparents' farm up in Milton Freewater. The swish of sprinklers in the apple orchard at sunset, the smell of ripening fruit. It was wonderful."

"Must have been." I tried to keep the impatience out of my voice.

"But that's not the point. One summer they were building a root cellar, and I used to balance on the brick walls, you know, like a ballerina."

"That should've been easy. These walls must be eighteen inches thick, and solid."

"That's just it. Maybe they aren't solid."

"What are you talking about? Brick on the outside and wood on the inside—"

"And in between my grandparents dumped whatever was handy, like hay bales and rubble and—"

"You mean . . . ?"

"Exactly!"

I was already feeling along the wall, mindful of splinters this time. "Help me look for a gap where we can pry these boards apart. Never mind. Got it!" I inserted the blade of the screwdriver in the space, braced myself, and pulled. The plank didn't budge.

"I can't move it. Not enough leverage."

"Maybe the hammer?" Minnie suggested from over my shoulder.

"See? You have good ideas." I pulled the forgotten hammer from my belt and lined it up against the wall. "Maybe if we both pull." I stood to one side so Minnie could slip in beside me.

" 'My strength is as the strength of ten because my heart is pure,' " Minnie recited. "Now that quote must be from the Bible."

"Sorry. Tennyson writing about Sir Galahad," I answered. "Anyway, let's hope our hearts are pure. One, two, three!"

We pulled in unison. The nails holding the board in place gave way with a shriek, the wood so dry that the board split as we tugged it from the wall. Removing the boards above and below it took only seconds.

I reached into the dark hole, my hand at first encountering nothing but air. "You were right. The wall's not solid." As I wiggled through the enlarged opening, the odor of moldy hay told me what I would find before my searching fingers confirmed it. "In fact, it's better than we'd hoped. Some hay bales have come apart over the years." I sneezed violently several times at the dust my movements had stirred up.

"God bless you."

Minnie's muffled words floating from the cellar made me smile. Even in this situation, automatic habits of reassurance remained strong. Automatic or not, I'd take whatever blessings I could get.

How much time had passed since Minnie's arrival? Probably not more than fifteen minutes, more than enough time to move a car. Of course, Velda had to hide Minnie's car, too. That would give us a little longer.

I dug my way through the prickly hay with a swimming motion, muttering, "Any minute, any minute . . ." to myself. At last my outstretched fingers encountered brick. Twisting around in the cramped space, I called out, "Get me that hammer. I've reached the outside wall."

The bricks were at least as old as the hay bales, but, unfortunately, they hadn't disintegrated. I smashed at the wall without success.

"Minnie, could you find me that screwdriver again? Maybe I

can use it as a chisel."

"Here you go." Minnie leaned into the hole to touch my arm with the cold metal of the screwdriver. "This would be a lot easier if we could see."

"It sure would." I positioned the blade of the screwdriver against the wall and lined up the hammer behind it. Several preliminary taps gave me the right angle before I reached back and swung the hammer with the force of desperation, knowing that freedom was on the other side of that wall. A shower of caulking material erupted.

"It's working!"

I swung three more times. Each time, the pile of debris increased. I attacked the other side of the brick with the same result. Elated, I changed the angle and aimed for the top of the brick, but this time the hammer head glanced off the handle and smashed my right thumb. I smothered an exclamation as I rocked back and forth in pain, literally seeing bright lights before me in the darkness. It was several minutes before Minnie's frantic voice penetrated my misery.

"Are you all right?"

"I'm fine, Minnie. I just . . . banged my thumb." An understatement if there ever was one. Cradling my hand close, I waited for the pain to subside, but it didn't.

"Oh, you poor thing. Can I . . . uh . . ."

"—bring me chicken soup?" I gritted my teeth as I tried to joke. "Isn't that what you do when someone is sick?"

"Actually, yes . . . and I do have those pot pies."

"Then, let's go get them."

Minnie's voice dropped to a near whisper. "Oh, Jane, are you close yet? She's had plenty of time."

I rested my cheek against the scratchy bricks for a moment before attempting to grip the screwdriver again. No way. Pain knifed through my thumb. Something must be broken in there.

No point in trying to keep the truth from Minnie. "I know, but we have a problem. My hand is . . . well, I can't use it. Maybe I can tie something—"

"You'll do no such thing. Come right out of there, and let me have a turn." Minnie emphasized her order by pulling on the back of my now crumpled and sweaty blouse.

I hesitated. Minnie was twenty years older, and easily fifty pounds heavier. What could she do in this cramped space?

"How about if you come in here with me? We can each—"

"There's not enough room for both of us, and you know it. Now, come out of there right this minute. Snap it up."

"Yes, ma'am." I crawled back out of the wall, protecting my injured hand as well as I could. "Maybe if I rest—"

"That's a good idea. Just let me do my fair share, for once."

For the first time I was glad it was dark. If Minnie saw the condition of my thumb, she'd realize how far my usefulness had plummeted. Come to think of it, I was probably better off not being able to witness her struggle to get through the hole in the wall, either. Her grunts and groans provided enough of a picture.

"Ouch. This straw is poking me all over," Minnie reported once she had made it through. "I'm getting us out of here sooner rather than later." The sound of the hammer striking the screwdriver soon punctuated her words as she continued. "You know, I should have realized right away you'd really hurt your hand. You know how? It was that business about having a pure heart."

I rested my head against a shelf. "The Tennyson quote? What about it?"

"I always thought you had a very pure heart, but the words you uttered a few minutes ago . . . I've never heard you use such language."

"I wasn't really aware of it," I answered, embarrassed. "And I don't usually—"

"Oh, don't worry. You didn't shock me. The books I read use all those words. I just brought it up because of that pure heart thing."

"I'm sure we both have pure enough hearts, Minnie."

"Good enough. And guess what? My pure heart must have given me the strength of ten. I can see daylight."

"Hallelujah!"

"Don't worry, Jane. I'll have us out of here in a jiffy."

My spirits rose as the hole in the outside wall grew larger. Minnie was really slinging those bricks around with a vengeance.

"Can you climb out yet?" I asked.

"Just about," came the reply. The twilight from outside was abruptly cut off as Minnie forced herself through the hole, huffing and puffing with the effort. Once outside, she turned to urge me on in a stage whisper. "Your turn. Hurry!"

"I'm moving as fast as—"

"Stay put!" Minnie's harsh command froze me in place. "She's coming. Velda's crossing the lawn."

CHAPTER 29

No way could I get out through the hole in the wall and away before Velda crossed the lawn, but Minnie might make it to safety. "Get out of here, Minnie! Quick, before Velda spots you."

"Too late. She's running this way, and . . . I can't believe it. She's not limping at all. What happened to her sore back? She was lying about that, too?"

Minnie's aggrieved tone suggested that in her book, lying ranked right next to murder as an unpardonable sin. I could tell she was itching to give Velda a good talking to.

"Probably, but for heaven's sake, get to your car and go. She has a gun!"

"I can't leave you." Minnie's voice wobbled.

"You have to. I can't get out fast enough. It's all up to you. Remember, 'God helps them who help themselves.' "

"The Bible?" Minnie sounded uncertain.

"Ben Franklin." I didn't know how much weight Ben's words would carry with her; she liked inspirational quotes, and that was all I could come up with. No use for both of us to get caught.

"Bible or not, it makes sense." All of a sudden, her voice came back strong, crackling with energy. "I have a plan."

Of all the things I didn't want to hear in this terror-filled moment, that sentence was at the top of the list. A gallery of Minnie's previous so-called plans flashed through my mind.

What had she come up with this time? "Please, just run for help."

"Follow my lead," Minnie whispered. In the next instant, she shrieked, "Jane, get out of the house now! Velda's coming!" It took me about half a beat to realize she was shouting for Velda's benefit, not mine. "Meet me at the car."

Her voice diminished as she moved away from the cellar, presumably on her way around the house to the car. I allowed myself a moment to marvel at the ingenuity of her plan, which stood head and shoulders above Operation Hollow Feather, before listening for approaching footsteps. If Velda didn't go for Minnie's decoy, I was trapped.

The immediate sound of labored breathing told me she had arrived. Good thing I hadn't tried to exit. I had no desire to come face-to-face with her ever again, especially when she was holding a gun. The light coming through the hole in the wall was suddenly blotted out. Drawing back into the deeper darkness, I held my breath as Velda hesitated in the opening. Sweat tickled my back, but I didn't move a muscle. She was panting too hard to listen effectively, but my heart was thumping so wildly that I was sure she'd hear it.

She poked at the opening from the outside, dislodging a fresh cloud of dust and hay that tickled my nose. I willed myself not to sneeze, but I couldn't hold it back. I pinched the bridge of my nose to stifle the sound. Had she heard it?

No. After an eternity, Velda moved off toward the house. I dared to breathe again when I heard her pound up the back porch steps. The screen door screeched open and slammed shut. Why hadn't she run around the house, following Minnie? Maybe she was trying to trick me into coming out. No percentage in waiting. I'd have to chance it.

I scrambled over the hay and through the rough brick opening, protecting my injured thumb as best I could, but the need for speed trumped everything else. After stumbling outside at last, I looked toward the back porch. No Velda. It hadn't been a trick.

I ran to the house, wedging myself with difficulty behind an overgrown clump of Oregon grape. There I paused, drinking in the fresh air like a tonic and hugging the wall while I considered my options. Running directly away from the house sounded best, but I couldn't chance leaving Eleanor with Velda. The telephone was located in the central hall, but the vision of Velda standing beside it, gun at the ready, squelched that idea. Where was Minnie? I hoped her "plan" had included going for help, but I couldn't be sure.

The crack of three shots fired in rapid succession flattened me to the ground, even though they hadn't sounded close. They'd seemed to come from the front of the house, where Minnie presumably had headed on her way to the car. No, wait. Minnie had told me that Velda intended to move both her car and mine. Had Minnie remembered? Those shots suggested that she hadn't. Oh, God. Please, not Minnie. The image of her sprawled on the driveway, covered in blood, caused my stomach to heave. I bent at the waist, sweating, until I got control of myself. No fantasy nightmares allowed. Reality was bad enough. And there was still Eleanor. I shook my head to clear it. Think, Jane.

If Velda was outside, this was my best chance to reach the telephone. I jumped up and scraped my way past the prickly leaves that had formed my hiding place, then sprinted up the back steps and pulled open the old-fashioned wooden screen door. It gave another unearthly shriek that probably could be heard in the next county, but the bright yellow kitchen was empty, peaceful. The green oilcloth on the sturdy table showcased an oil lamp and a jaunty set of ceramic cows holding salt and pepper. Nothing overtly threatening. It could have been any country kitchen in the state, if not for my knowledge that a murderer lurked nearby.

The blood roared in my ears as I tiptoed through the room, expecting Velda to jump out at me with every step. I peeked around the door into the dimness of the central hall. Stepping into that hallway took all the courage I could muster. I thought of Hunter. Of Velda's father. Of Eleanor, Minnie, and me. Logic was not in control here. A single look at the overturned table and smashed phone on the floor told me I could scrap the idea of dialing nine-one-one. That was the reason Velda had come through the house. The front door gaped wide at the other end of the hall, reinforcing the likelihood that Velda was outside. What now?

Minnie might have a plan, but I certainly didn't. Eleanor's room was directly across the hall from the kitchen, but I didn't dare take the time to go back and free her. Instead, I crept to the open front door and poked my head around it. Prepared for the sight of blood and bodies, I nearly fainted with relief at the absence of either one. Minnie's Buick wasn't out front. Only Velda's old Dodge remained.

Distant movement drew my eye to the far end of the long driveway, where I spotted Minnie's plump form making her unsteady way toward the road. The much younger and more agile Velda pounded along behind her. Those first shots had apparently been fired from too far away, but Velda wasn't limping, and she would catch Minnie before long.

I jumped to my feet and wrenched open the closet door. Perfect! I snatched up the smiley-face key ring. Bolting out the front door and down the steps, I dived into the driver's seat as another two shots rang out.

Minnie was still on her feet, running faster than before. "Hang on," I muttered.

I maneuvered awkwardly to insert the key without using my

injured hand. The engine finally roared to life. Heedless of the rutted driveway, I stomped the accelerator and raced toward the running women. The car bounced crazily over the uneven surface as I steered one-handed. Velda was gaining ground steadily, and she still clutched the revolver.

Wild to distract her, with my good hand holding the wheel, I slammed the other on the horn. Waves of pain shot up my arm, but I kept at it. Finally, Velda broke stride and focused on me. Good. The car afforded me partial protection, while Minnie was out in the open, vulnerable.

I knew what I had to do.

Velda showed no squeamishness. She grasped the gun in both hands and leveled the barrel.

I ducked. She fired twice. The windshield exploded. One hole bloomed where Velda had last seen my head. My heart was in my throat.

Driving blind and crouching low, I aimed the car straight at her. Blood pounded at my temples. "Run away, Velda!" I screamed. "Don't make me do this!"

She didn't move.

At the last second, I muscled the car right. I wasn't Velda. I couldn't kill another human being. A glancing blow should stop her, had to stop her. No impact. I'd swerved too far. One look out the window, and my fear doubled. Velda ran alongside me, then stopped, gun pointed directly at my face.

I gunned the Dodge and shot off in a cloud of dust. Face twisted with malice, she fired. I steeled myself for the pain, but it didn't come. The Dodge roared on toward Minnie, now stopped at the end of the drive, bent over, hands on knees. I glanced in the rearview mirror. Velda stood once more in shooting stance. I again braced myself, felt my blood thump through my veins as Velda aimed and fired again. But nothing happened. She must be out of bullets.

With frequent looks behind me to make sure Velda wasn't following through the swirling dust, I approached Minnie at last. From the look of hatred I had glimpsed on Velda's face, I half-expected her to attack us with her bare hands, but she wheeled and sprinted the other way, toward a stand of cotton-woods that bordered the field.

I pulled to a stop beside Minnie and shook. She could haul herself into the car. I didn't think my legs would hold me if I tried to stand.

Minnie moved slowly, too. She looked a long time to determine which way Velda had gone before she wearily crawled into the front seat. Even then, she rested her head on the back of the seat and closed her eyes before speaking. "She must be heading for a car. I like being a detective, but I think I'm too old for the fieldwork."

"Me, too," I said. "Time for Bianca and Tyler to take over."

"But we'll stay on as the brains of the outfit, right?" She gave me a shaky smile.

"That goes without saying." Minnie had earned full honors today.

"Good."

"Velda smashed the phone, but her cell must be there somewhere. We'll see to Eleanor first."

"Now, isn't that poetic justice, using her own phone? I like it. You don't think . . . I mean, she won't come back?"

"Not the way she was sprinting. Besides, she's too smart. I don't think she wants to explain things to the police." I swung the car around and we bumped our way back up the rutted drive.

"We'll call for backup, of course, but we don't really need it." Minnie's voice carried the satisfaction of a job well done. " 'God helps them who help themselves,' no matter who said it."

"I really have to hand it to you, Minnie. Your plan was brilliant." I wanted Minnie to bask in her well-deserved moment of glory. "Velda's probably putting as much space as possible between herself and us, but she won't get far."

"You know, Jane, this is one time I'll be positively delighted to see dear Sheriff Kraft." Minnie's voice turned wistful as she continued. "I suppose he'll take all the credit though."

"Not if I have anything to say about it. Arnie will just mop up your case. I'll tell all the reporters that your bravery got us out of there alive. You're a heroine."

"All the reporters? Do you think . . . ?"

"Better get ready for a media blitz."

When Minnie didn't answer, I glanced over to see her rummaging in the glove compartment. "What are you doing?"

"Looking for something to write on. I'll need brown sugar, cinnamon, butter. Let's see, what else?"

"Right, for the press conference."

No use fighting it. The Murder of the Month Book Club would soon take center stage again.

"Guns and knives. We'll need lots more cookies. I expect there'll be quite a crowd."

"Maybe I should add a little car shape in honor of today. It'll take more dough, but I have just the cookie cutter, though, unfortunately, it won't show the bullet holes in the windshield."

After we'd called the police from Velda's cell phone, I stood guard with a battered shotgun, while Minnie soothed Eleanor by alternating kindness and chicken pot pie. From the moment we'd released Eleanor from her bonds, she had talked nonstop, surprisingly alert and not at all the pallid invalid Velda had described to us. As Velda had assured me, she was a tough old bird, and she was mad through and through. She'd not only directed me to her husband's shotgun in the attic, but she'd loaded it expertly before ordering me to stand guard on the porch until the sheriff arrived. It wasn't likely that Velda would circle back, but we weren't taking any chances.

By the time I took up my post, the wail of sirens filled the air, and a moment later two Russell County Sheriff's Department cruisers careened into the driveway, lights blazing, while three others screamed past on the highway, heading in the direction Velda had fled.

Arnie climbed out of the first patrol car and approached me warily.

Probably thought I intended to make some kind of crack, so I obliged him. "I hope you left someone at the jail to keep Alix from escaping."

"Don't you worry about her. That'll be taken care of in due course." He gave me a sour look. "Right now I got work to do. Any sign of Velda?"

"Oh, you mean the real murderer? Nope, haven't seen her since she tried to shoot me."

Arnie retreated without another word. He conferred briefly with someone in the second car before returning to his cruiser. He slammed the door and tore off, siren wailing.

A crisp young deputy I didn't recognize made his way toward the porch through the cloud of dust Arnie had stirred up with his flamboyant exit. He looked glum at missing the big manhunt—or woman hunt, in this case—but he was prepared to do his duty.

"Deputy Tallis, ma'am. Don't worry about a thing. The ambulance is on its way for the elderly lady. Oh, wow!" His professional manner slipped a bit at the sight of my puffy hand. "That must smart! Can I rig a sling or something?"

I felt sorry for the kid, missing all the excitement. "That would be a big help, but first could you take a look out back, where we were held prisoner? I'd feel a lot safer if you—"

"—secured the premises? Right. I can do that." He bounded

up the steps, apparently cheered by the prospect of professional action.

The ambulance lumbered up the driveway, shadowed by a familiar Jeep. "Back bedroom on the left," I told the EMTs before running down the porch steps as the doors to the Jeep flew open.

Bianca was the first to reach me, hugging and scolding me at the same time. "Mom! What were you thinking? You could have been killed!"

Nick hovered behind her, his eyes searching my face as though he would memorize it. What he saw there seemed to reassure him, and his face relaxed when I spoke over Bianca's shoulder.

"I'm fine. Everyone's fine."

"What happened to your hand? Your thumb's huge!" Tyler yelled. He was still beside the Jeep, assisting Laurence to alight from the front passenger seat. "Were you shot?"

"Sorry to disappoint you. I did it myself, banged it with a hammer."

"Bummer." Tyler gave Laurence his arm and they made their halting way up to the porch. "That must hurt."

Laurence hurriedly ascended two steps before pausing for breath. Then he looked at me directly for the first time, studying me without speaking, much as Nick had. I felt like some sort of exotic fern. Once again, I passed muster.

His words, when they finally came, were delivered with his trademark sarcasm. "I think Tyler was hoping you'd produce something more exciting for his blog. Maybe let that woman have another go at you."

"C'mon. I didn't mean anything like that." Tyler blushed and shot me a worried look. When he saw that I was laughing, he smiled and amended his comment. "But it sure would make a better story."

"This one's good enough for me," I said. "But be sure to interview Minnie. She saved the day with her plan."

"Minnie's plan?" They said in unison.

"Wait 'til you hear. Believe me, it'll provide plenty of thrills for the blog."

"And I missed the big chase for the second time," Laurence grumbled. "Can't you arrange these things better?"

"Maybe next time."

Minnie scurried out of the house, leading the way for the gurney carrying a reluctant Eleanor. "I don't need this fool thing. Minnie, make them put me down."

Minnie was in her element. Someone needed her help. "You just stay put, young lady. I'll go along and make sure they treat you right. You have your glasses?"

"Yes, they're right here."

The rest of us stood aside as the EMTs maneuvered the gurney down the steps.

Eleanor protested all the way. "Have they caught her yet? I want to stay 'til they do."

"Won't be long," Minnie assured her. "We've got everything under control."

CHAPTER 30

The special evening SOS gathering at Thornton's three days later was a far cry from our last, disastrous meeting. For starters, Minnie had insisted on personally escorting Phil and Eileen Hedstrom to front-row seats. Nick and Tyler set up every chair we had before driving to the New Community Church to borrow more for the overflow crowd. Minnie assured them no one would mind.

Laurence and Eleanor McKay were the featured speakers for the meeting itself, each of them giving a spirited account about their own experiences with elder fraud and abuse. Laurence's salty recounting of his bold efforts to trap a confidence man made a real hit. The old curmudgeon surprised me by being a charming and gifted speaker. Eleanor's fiery account of Velda's treachery was a fitting companion piece. I was certain the two of them would soon be making similar presentations at other groups. From the admiring glances they occasionally stole at each other, it appeared they wouldn't mind spending extra time together.

After the presentations, Alix and Minnie gave back-to-back interviews for a KATU reporter from Portland. Minnie was in her element, even buying a set of bright new scarves for the occasion. Alix, reluctant at first to speak of her past, had been persuaded by the outpouring of sympathy she'd received—both in the community and over the Internet—after her story became public.

Tyler rang up book purchases, and Bianca passed trays of Minnie's giant gingersnaps. I was relegated to telephone duty since the splint on my thumb rendered me unfit for anything requiring manual dexterity. I now understood why possessing opposable thumbs was such a big deal in the animal kingdom.

Little by little, the crowd thinned out. As we cleared things up, Wendell policed the floor with his usual diligence, searching for forgotten crumbs. After a while, Tyler drove Eleanor home, accompanied by Alice Durand, who was picking up extra money by staying with Eleanor for a few nights. Laurence went home to bed, or perhaps to contemplate his budding career as a crusader against elder abuse.

Nick gently relieved me of a folding chair as I clumsily attempted to collapse it. "How about letting me do that?" he suggested. "You look beat."

I nodded my thanks and collapsed into one of the armchairs in the bay window. "I had no idea we'd get such a crowd."

"Or that they'd get so into it." Bianca pulled a chair over to join me. "Laurence and Eleanor were cute together, weren't they?"

"And effective." Tyler, returning from his errand, snagged a handful of cookies before hooking another chair with his foot and pulling it into what was becoming a circle. "No con man will dare to show up in Juniper now."

"I hope you're right." Minnie passed the tray again before settling into the other overstuffed chair. "But I still hate to think there are people like that out there anywhere. Velda . . . was she all bad?"

"Close enough," Nick said. "We'll never know for sure how her father happened to die so conveniently, since he was cremated, but I wouldn't be surprised if—"

"Or maybe," Bianca offered, "her father just died." My daughter, the eternal optimist. "Velda must have had a horrible life to have tried . . . to do what she did."

I'd seen the look on Velda's face as she aimed that gun at me—would probably see it for years when I closed my eyes—but I liked it that Bianca continued to look for the good in people. Why not? Usually that attitude brought out the best in others.

Minnie—dear, kind soul that she was—encouraged Bianca's hopeful line of thought. "Yes, that's right. Maybe her father just got sick and died. Maybe Velda really wanted to help Eleanor at first, or thought coming to Oregon would be an adventure, a chance to meet a nice young man. It could have happened that way."

"She met someone, all right," Tyler said. "Too bad it was Hunter."

"I've told you how persuasive he could be." Alix stood just outside the circle. "When he made a run at Eleanor's money, sweet-talking her niece into helping him would be child's play."

Even the ever-cynical Alix was trying to present Velda's actions in the best possible light. She, of all people, had reason to hate Velda, the person who had tried to frame her for murder, but she, too, had been fooled by Hunter. So Alix just couldn't stop herself from being kind, from reassuring Minnie and Bianca. In spite of her own disappointments in life, or perhaps because of them, she wanted her friends to continue to look on the bright side. "He was a slick customer. Then, when he tried to run off without her, humiliated her. . . . We all know how it ended."

Minnie remained thoughtful. "So after she fell in love with Hunter, she just went off the tracks? That's so sad. I wish I could have helped her."

"You did all you could." I placed my hand on her arm. "You tried to bring her into the book club and to help her with Eleanor's care. I'm afraid she'd already gone too far down the wrong road."

"I suppose you're right." Minnie sighed and patted my hand. "Or maybe I'm just naive."

I couldn't interpret the emotions playing across Alix's face as Minnie spoke, but suddenly she burst out, "Better to look at the world your way than to . . . miss out on the best things life has to offer." She turned away from the group.

I tried to say something, but no words made it past the lump in my throat. I looked through brimming eyes at Tyler, willing him to help.

"Like gingersnaps," he said, reaching for another handful of cookies. "Lots of them."

"And good dogs like Wendell." I wasn't surprised to hear Bianca's first thought.

"And a day fishing the Metolius," Nick added.

"Why, bless you all, how about good friends?" Minnie asked. She clapped her hands in delight. "Sounds like we've got everything . . . except our next book club selection. Alix, you'd better get over here. We're a week late in making a decision."

Alix hesitated just a beat before pulling another chair into the circle. Minnie continued as though nothing momentous had just happened. "Neglecting our readers is a mistake. That's no way to build a fan base. Even though we've been busy this week—"

As though we'd rehearsed it, the rest of us completed her thought in unison, "There's no rest for the wicked."

Minnie's startled look turned to a smile. "I couldn't have said it better myself. Alix, do you have a recommendation?"

For the first time since we'd formed our book club a year ago, Alix made a suggestion without an accompanying sarcastic remark. "I was thinking maybe Sue Grafton's *T is for Trespass.*

It's about elder abuse. Nice tie-in to the new links on Tyler's blog."

"Good idea," I said. "Alix, there's something else I—we—need to know."

"Yeah, yeah. I'm way ahead of you." Alix retrieved a brown paper shopping bag she'd parked by the front door. Without further comment she dumped the contents in my lap. Three cartons of Virginia Slims tumbled out and slid onto the floor. "That's the last time I'm making a bet with you."

"That'll teach you." I smiled at her. "This is great, Alix, really. And if you need any help, there's the Quit Line—"

"Don't worry. This time it'll stick. I just needed a push."

"Some push. Now that we have that settled, there's something else I—we—wanted to talk to you about."

"What? You want my blood, too?"

"Just your time. Would you be willing to organize an additional wedding?"

The smile started in Alix's eyes and spread across her entire face, but her voice remained calm and professional. "I'll check the schedule, but I believe I can handle one more. I have an excellent staff."

"We'll want Wendell in it, too," Nick said, "even if it costs extra."

"Will you require the services of the porcupine?" Bianca asked.

"Probably not," I said. "I suspect we'll have enough excitement as it is."

ABOUT THE AUTHOR

A Northwest author who taught high school and reared a family before turning to writing, **Elizabeth C. Main** found inspiration for her first Jane Serrano mystery, *Murder of the Month,* while selling books at an independent central Oregon bookstore for ten years. Though, alas, no murders occurred in the real store to provide drama, her experience working there, coupled with a hefty dose of whimsy, provided ample material for her bookstore mystery, which won the 1998 Pacific Northwest Writers Association contest for Best Adult Mystery Novel. She has also published two novels in the romance and young adult genres, as well as short stories and essays. She lives in idyllic Bend, Oregon, with her husband and dog.